GRAIN OF SAND

BRENT LADD

A Cable Janson Adventure Thriller

Published by: AR PRESS
Roger L. Brooks, Publisher
roger@americanrealpublishing.com
americanrealpublishing.com

Dedicated to Thomas, a bright young man with a
zeal for life and an adventurous spirit.
A grandson who is always wanting to know more and why. Not
sure who's teaching whom—can't wait to see what's next!

Love ya,
Top, Top

WEST COAST OF AFRICA, JUNE 570 BCE

BOAZ'S FINGERS BLANCHED AS HE gripped the wicker fence railing that skirted the perimeter of the Phoenician warship. It had a round-bottomed, cedarwood hull and a single-masted, large, square-rigged sail. The red-and-white-striped cloth slowly filled with air. He glanced at the large clay amphorae tied to the tall horsehead bowsprit, picturing the last few cups of fresh drinking water it contained. His orders to go ashore and restock their dwindling supplies weighed heavily on his mind. Could just one anxious decision doom the entire expedition? He would know in the next few minutes.

Rope-like muscles strained and his dark eyes turned to slits as he processed his options. Risking his ship or crew was not an option. They needed to cut their losses and put some distance between them and this place.

He called out desperately to the other ships, hoping he wasn't too late. "Get clear. Cut the lines. Row for your lives."

The incredibly tall Alkebulan natives continued their attack from the shoreline with spears and arrows, some flaming.

One ship burned uncontrollably while another struggled to gain distance from the onslaught. Wearing only weathered tunics around their waists, sailors pulled their oars for all they were worth. Others returned fire from the deck, arrows crossing in the air without regard for one another.

A flaming arrow impaled the hull just to the right of Boaz, and he plucked it out and tossed it overboard like an unwanted stowaway. One of the sailors quickly extinguished the remaining flames with a bucket of seawater.

The flotilla had stopped to gather supplies and fresh water in a small bay. After an hour of foraging and hunting, a local tribe of warriors appeared as if by sleight of hand through the jungle. They attacked without warning. It had been a monumental task to fight them off and return to the ships, leaving a trail of bodies and supplies as they ran.

Three weeks back, they had lost a ship to an invisible reef that had taken the bottom out on a moonless night. Luckily, no lives were sacrificed to Yamm, the Sea God, but today would be an unmitigated disaster. Boaz's heart ached for his murdered men like a burning arrow to the solar plexus. There would be time to mourn, but that time was not now.

The next flaming arrow dropped into the ocean short of its target. Boaz allowed his shoulders to relax slightly. They were out of range. Now, it was up to the other ships to get free of the melee. He willed them to move faster—a useless pleading born of frustration and desperation.

Horror filled him once again as some of his Phoenician brothers, trying to escape the burning ship, were picked off one by one. His face filled with impotent rage as he watched the smallest ship in his fleet suddenly turn back toward shore when the tillerman slumped over. Before the men could recover, they were cut down, and flames slowly engulfed everything above the waterline.

Two ships were all that escaped, carrying forty-two sailors. In less than an hour, Boaz had lost more than half of his remaining crew and fleet. The world was a dangerous yet curious place. Why the extremely tall natives, dark as a moonless night, had taken offense to their layover would remain a mystery to Boaz, but their prowess with fighting weapons was on par with the best fighter he had ever encountered.

Boaz had seen the pillars of Hercules and sailed beyond the gates of the Mediterranean Sea. He had shaken hands with kings and killed off entire villages. Losing men and ships was not uncommon, both in conquest and to Mother Nature, but so many deaths over a few baskets of fruit, meat, and jugs of fresh water—that was a first. He considered returning in the night and teaching the savages a lesson, but his orders were clear, and they did not include revenge. This was strictly a fact-finding mission, but who would be the wiser if he did? Anger bubbled just below the surface like a waiting volcano. Only time would ease the fire.

He slammed his hand against the railing in frustration and turned to Tanith, one of only two females left on this voyage. Her long, dark, curly hair mirrored her eye color and accented an angled face that most men found attractive, but her determination and professionalism were too much for them to handle. Sailors said she could give and take as well as any of them, and they had made her a sort of mascot aboard the ship. Boaz treated her like a sister and counted on her skills with her parchment and ink to tell their story and to mark the way for those who would follow.

"Mark this cove as hostile. I don't want those sailors' sacrifice to be for naught."

A single tear was all that showed on Tanith's face as she nodded. "Of course." She collected her supplies and went to work, adding more details to her growing parchment map and lengthening journal.

Boaz watched from the stern as Adad, his number one, leaned into the rudder, pointing them south once again. The two remaining sister ships had almost identical features. That included the clay amphoras with nearly empty drinking water and their limited food stores. They would need to stop at the next river that flowed into the ocean.

Boaz's parched lips pressed together as he remembered the day he left Carthage. The jewel of the southern Mediterranean. Queen Dido herself was present and had presented him with a Tyrian purple cloak worth almost a year's pay. The send-off had been a grand affair. A limestone monument of the voyage was erected, and a representative of the Egyptian Pharaoh Necho personally blessed their ships. There was more at stake here than on any other voyage he had ever taken. Two dynasties were counting on their success to open trade around the Mother of Mankind, also known as the continent of Alkebulan, *Africa*.

After five weeks of mostly uneventful sailing, they encountered many friendly and receptive villages along the coast. Some had access to gold and others, unique items that would make this trade route very profitable to the Phoenicians and the Egyptians. Boaz had been impressed with the people who lived here—their dark skin and eyes held a genuine kindness and intelligence. They lived off the land, in harmony with it, rather than by consuming it like so many civilizations he had encountered in the Mediterranean, including his own.

One aggressive and deadly tribe could easily be avoided in the future. Boaz set his eyes on the upcoming horizon and let his anger toward them slowly fade with the tide and distance.

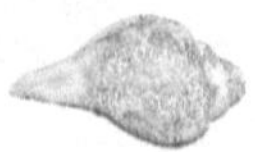

After two more days skirting the coastline, the weather and seas changed, as did their heading. From south to southeast, and finally, they were traveling due east. They had come to the bottom of Africa. The end of the known world. Unprepared for cold weather, the faded white tunics worn by the men only covered them from their waists to their knees. The women had it slightly better as their garments wrapped from neck to ankles. The few horse-hair blankets onboard were all they had to stave off the increasingly low temperatures.

The real problem was the sea. Here, two oceans collided. It tossed and turned like two raging rivers smashing together. This wasn't a storm—in fact, there wasn't a cloud in sight. It was a tempest born of nature and physics. The ship creaked out her protest as she bucked and heaved with each swell. Waves came from the side while others blasted them bow and stern. Even the most hardened sailor found his legs weak and his stomach churning.

"We can't last much longer," a soggy and shivering Adad cried out to no one in particular. Even his usually perfectly groomed beard had lost its form.

"We are just passengers now, my friend," Boaz called back.

"The edge of the world is no place for us."

After nearly two days of hard sailing, the waters slowly mellowed, and their course changed once again. Northerly. They had come through the worst of it and were heading into the unknown. Every sailor had a weary and concerned look on his face. Boaz knew it wouldn't take much to spook his men into a mutiny. But where they could go from here was perhaps worse than the weathered decks of his fleet.

Boaz lifted his bearded face to the sun and let it warm him. He was beginning to believe that the cold in his bones would never leave. At five foot ten, he was taller than most men he had met. His years at sea had hardened his muscles and weathered his skin, making it bronze and lined. The salt-crusted hair on his head was dark and curly. Initially, he was a man of action, not words, but action without words only got you so far in this world. Boaz had forced himself to engage learned men whenever he was in port, making his weakness a strength. It had caught the eyes of several noblemen and ultimately reached the queen's ears. That alone was enough to put him on the shortlist to lead this expedition. After bringing home three ships laden with Tyrian purple silks, worth ten times their weight in gold, through the storm of the season—a tempest that had been the doom of so many other sailors—his nomination for this mission was guaranteed.

The next week pushed them farther north with fair seas and a brisk wind. The oars had been stored for the last few days as the sail did all the work. The morale had improved, and thoughts of returning home were heavy in the air, like a draping wet blanket. Their course angled slightly more east, and the temperature continued to rise.

Boaz stepped next to Adad where he stood with his arms locked on the tiller. The man's beard was once again trimmed and pointed. A fashion usually seen in court, not onboard a ship, now entering its third month at sea. His red conical hat had lost most of its color but was still doing its job of hiding a large bald spot on the top of Adad's head. His serious, unblinking eyes scanned ahead.

"We need to resupply soon. The water has turned, and the meat is white with mold."

Boaz looked across to Dagon, helming the sister ship just off his starboard side. The man was a beast of war, picked from Queen Dido's personal guards. His dark braided beard and hair were colored almost white by salt. He wore his copper helmet despite the glaring sun and made a short lift of his hand for a greeting. Boaz returned the gesture. They had been through the gates of Hades and had somehow managed to persevere.

"What do you suppose awaits us?" Boaz said without looking back at Adad.

"The sea is fickle, and anyone who claims to know her is fooling himself."

"I suppose," Boaz replied, turning his attention back to Adad.

"Sea devils or perhaps safe passage, only Yamm knows. But I tell you this, we are missing nothing."

"What do you mean?" Boaz asked.

Adad took a breath and pursed his lips before replying. "Carthage. She is still a glimmering pearl cast along the ocean's shore. The people there are still going about their daily lives, and the market is still filled with the smells of coriander and roasting boar."

"Don't forget streets so foul they take your breath away, with thieves and cutthroats hiding in alleys."

"Ah, the good life," Adad said with fondness. "It hasn't changed since we've been gone, but the things we have seen and done…" He paused to stare out at the sea. "We've changed."

Boaz nodded. "We have lived ten lifetimes compared to those in the city."

"Now, we just need to get home to tell our tale."

Tanith interrupted as she approached.

Both men looked over. She was carrying an old scroll and a new parchment in her hand.

"I think we are getting close." She rolled out the scroll. Its edges were worn and tattered. Then, she held out the parchment next to it. "Take a look at this. Here is an old map drawn by an Egyptian expedition many years ago that journeyed down the eastern coast of Africa. They lasted about two months before giving up and heading back."

"So?" Adad said, leaning over the tiller to get a better look.

"So, look at the map. I have been recording the coast as we go. Along this portion here"—she pointed—"the two images align."

"Yes… Incredible," Boaz said, with punctuated excitement. "We are overlapping their original journey."

Tanith nodded.

"Now, all we must do is retrace their steps back to Egypt. Present ourselves to Pharaoh Necho, and we will be greeted as heroes," Adad said.

Boaz chuckled. "I guess the sea devils missed their chance."

As he said the words, there was a change in the wind, and the sail was pulled to starboard.

"Row for your lives," Boaz called. It was the second time he had used those words on this voyage.

Waves crashed over the deck as a howling wind drove them away from land. Sailors held on with grips of steel to anything that would prevent them from being washed overboard. A few had not been so lucky. Lightning randomly flashed from every direction, giving brief glimpses of their surrounding horror in the black night and then taking it away again as the flash extinguished itself into the black liquid cauldron. Oars dug into the turbulent sea, trying to make steerage at any cost. Should the boat get sideways, all would be lost. The mast had snapped sometime back, and their precious sail had washed away with it. The current and wind were in control, but Boaz and his sailors continued to battle for every inch. Adad held firm to the tiller, trying to keep the ship's nose pointed into the huge waves that pounded the ship. They had lost sight of their sister ship early in the battle with the elements. Now it was row or die, a concept simple sailors knew all too well. A large wave hit, and the ship shuddered before half the hull breached out of the water and then plunged back down.

The storm had been raging for more than fifteen hours, and the men had nothing left to give. Arms, backs, and legs were spent.

"Yamm preserve us," Adad cried out just before a wave pried him loose from his grip and washed him into the liquid melee.

Boaz dove for the unmanned tiller, forcing the ship's nose back into the oncoming swells. "Keep fighting! It's our only chance," he screamed into the night.

His words were drowned out as a sudden scraping sound shook the boat and then brought it to an abrupt stop.

"We've run aground on the reef," someone shouted needlessly.

A following wave pulled them off and nearly flipped the ship over. Sailors were flung from Boaz's sight as he shoved the tiller over, hoping to course correct their imminent destruction. A substantial hole in the bottom of the ship began taking on water, and she quickly grew heavy. Another wave hit and took more sailors with it. Once again, the ship ground to a stop.

"Every man for himself," Boaz cried out. Anyone left aboard made a hurried exit into the unknown.

As Boaz reached the hull, the ship twisted again, and he was flung like a cartwheel into the black torrent.

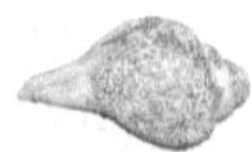

Dark eyes cracked and strained at the impossible brightness of the sun. Perfect white sand dotted with palm tree shadows came slowly into view. A curious-looking tan crab with white claws shuffled past as a sudden bout of liquid coughing racked Boaz. He leaned over and vomited several times before finally sitting up and looking around. His body had somehow managed to find land and survive. Two miracles rolled into one. He felt numb, yet everything hurt.

In the shallows of a small natural lagoon were the remains of his ship, battered, beat-up, but mostly intact. It rocked gently on the easy swells that entered through the outlying reef.

"Oh, that's good news. I thought you were dead."

Boaz craned his head back in the other direction to find Tanith walking up the beach carrying several coconuts. Her dress was ripped and rewrapped, only covering her chest and privates. Her hair was matted, and several obvious scrapes were visible across her smooth skin. Boaz had never seen her look more beautiful.

He watched her walk for a moment. "That's a good look for you," he called out. His voice was no more than a hoarse whisper.

Tanith nodded her head in exaggeration. "For you as well," she replied.

Boaz looked down, realizing his tunic was gone. "Apparently, God has seen fit to return me to this earth just as I was the first time I arrived."

He stood, unfazed by his nakedness, and took a coconut from Tanith. She used her knife to cut off the top, and Boaz guzzled the life-giving liquid inside.

"I think this is an island," Tanith said as she looked down the beach. "I have seen no sign of habitation."

Boaz's eyes followed her stare. To his right, the beach intercepted with a rock face that jutted up into the air. The most curious-looking trees he had ever seen grew along the top. At the lagoon's edge, a large opening into the mountain allowed the tides to flow inside, like a giant rock mouth gulping the seawater. "The crew?"

Tanith's head dipped. "None that I've found."

Boaz nodded somberly.

She took a breath. "I was just about to swim out to the ship. Maybe there is a stray tunic aboard. Wouldn't want the sun to have its way with you." She put down the remaining coconuts and gave his manhood the slightest glance. She moved into the water and looked back, her eyes inviting.

Boaz let a small smile fill his face and then followed. "I'm more interested in the tools aboard. If we can't repair the ship, we can build a smaller one from its timbers."

Disappointment flashed across Tanith's face, then something pulled her gaze down into the hip-deep water. She froze. "Do you see what I see?"

Boaz paused and let his eyes search across the sea floor. The water was crystal clear, but it took a second before he realized what he was looking at. "Gods be praised. The treasure of a thousand kings."

SAUDI ARABIA, 1938 CE

J AWAR'S BACK WAS NOT THE only thing that hurt. His ears were still ringing from the argument he had just endured with his wife, Zubiya. It was not the first time money had driven a wedge between them. Goat herder was not a business for the wealthy, but many generations of the same had sealed his fate. His mind flashed to his five-year-old daughter, Suna. She was the light of his life, and if it wasn't for her and Allah, he would have long ago slipped away in the night and never returned.

Suna had a smile that was so pure and innocent. Uncorrupted by the changing world around her. She made him see things in a fresh way, even the way the wind blew the dried grass. It was all new, thanks to her.

It had been six years since al-Hasa consolidated his world into the Kingdom of Saudi Arabia. The bitter tribal fighting had lasted nearly thirty years, leaving almost everything and everyone he knew dead. Now, there was peace in the land, but life for him had not improved, not until Suna was born.

Jawar had lost his precious wife to the war, a wound that would never heal. When Zubiya lost her husband, they had been thrust together out of practicality, not love. A shared life experience without a real connection. Somehow, Allah be praised, Zubiya conceived late in life, and now their world was more than two aging people struggling toward a slow death. They had Suna, and suddenly, the future mattered.

"Imshi." He called out to his two strongest goats, pulling the hand plow across the hardpack ground. They were just barely able to draw it along, leaving a trench that often looked more like a scratch. Jawar used a long stick, and every native tongue swear word he knew, to coax them along. Behind him, Suna planted lentils, covering each seed by hand. A neighbor had traded him the seeds for one goat, and Jawar was hoping to boost his fortunes with a field of the hardy plants.

His myopic world was so precious to him but so dated to those on the outside. Oil had been found in the desert, and the rich powers of Europe were clamoring to devour it. Goats, it seemed, had just moved another rung down on the ladder of success. The wooden hand plow managed to hit every rock in the small, unyielding field, forcing Jawar to stop, bend over, and clear each one by hand.

He looked up with a squint, wiping the sweat from his eyes. Soon, the sun would be high and too hot for him to continue. The plow came to a grinding halt as the goats strained on the yoke, baaing in frustration.

Jawar moved to the source of the problem, an obstacle against the plow's blade. He squatted down and started to dig the rock obstruction out with a pointed stick, but he quickly discovered it wasn't a rock. The loose dirt revealed the side of a clay amphorae. It looked old, and Jawar slowed down and took his time to dig it out. Unfortunately, the plow's blade had cracked the container. Too bad, as he could have sold it to one of the European foreigners for some much-needed coin.

"What is it, Daddy?" Suna said as she approached, her brown eyes wide with curiosity. Her faded chemise, or long shirt, was smudged with dirt as she knelt.

"Looks like an old oil urn." Jawar continued to dig in the hard ground until he was able to free the urn. The wax seal was loose, and a large chunk of pottery fell off in his hand. His feeling of disappointment at the broken pot faded as he noticed there was something besides old oil stored inside.

Jawar licked his cracked lips, reached inside the jar, and pulled out a solid object wrapped in desiccated animal skin. The fur had long since disintegrated, leaving the leather brittle. He carefully unwrapped the crusty covering. His heart raced as a seashell twice as big as his hand appeared. The shell had intricate relief carvings all over it. It was a style and language he had never seen before.

"What is it?" Suna asked, her eyes wide and her voice high. She leaned over and let her fingers move across the curious black carvings set against the white pearlescent shell. They were delicate and strong all at the same time.

"I'm not sure," Jawar replied.

"Do you know what it says?"

"So many questions, little one, but no, I do not. What I know is we can get coin for it. Get your mother. We are going to town."

Suna jumped up and down with excitement. "Can we get dates?"

"Dates, yes, and perhaps a bit more," Jawar said with a growing smile. Soon, his wife would be very proud of him.

Hazm watched from his camel as far-off figures moved across the barren landscape. The heat waves of the day obscured them into liquid-like aberrations.

"They're heading toward Mocca," said Kanza to his right.

Kanza was an imposing man, and the faded orange turban on his head made him look even taller. The spear in his right hand and the scimitar connected at his waist were the tools of his trade. More effective at close-range fighting than the *Maoukahla*, or long rifle, Hazm carried.

Hazm wore a bandolier across his shoulder filled with extra ammunition. His dusty *Keffiyeh* hid his head from the burning sun.

The last few months had been very good. The arrival of wealthy European oil explorers had given the bandits a new supply and, if they were honest, more interesting work.

Kanza looked over to Hazm.

A round face with lifeless eyes and a hooked nose turned his direction.

Crooked teeth and a cocked head preceded the all-important question. "Are they worth our trouble?"

Hazm squinted his eyes. "Only one way to find out, brother. Come." He spurred his camel to life and galloped off.

Kanza quickly followed.

It took only a few seconds before their target saw them coming, processed the situation, and started running.

"I hate it when they run," Hazm called out as he pulled his camel to a stop and took aim. Just as he had practiced many times, one shot, one hit. A body spun and fell to the ground. A high-pitched shriek followed in the distance. Then the remaining two started running back the way they had come.

Soon, Kanza had galloped past the two runners and herded them back toward Hazm.

Finally, the brothers got a good look at their prize. "They are nothing. We just wasted powder and ammunition."

"Take the child. We can sell her. The mother is too old."

The woman, overhearing this, pulled a hidden dagger from her tunic and let out a blood-curdling ululation as she charged.

Kanza dispatched her with his spear. He stepped off his camel and retrieved the weapon with a sucking sound, leaving the woman to bleed out and die. Stepping over to the young girl, he knelt in front of her quivering form. Then, using his thumb, he wiped away some of the grime on her face. "You smell like a goat, but yes, you are a pretty one. I bet you'll end up working in a palace."

Hazm leaned in his *Mahawi*, or saddle. "We just did you a kindness. What is your name, girl?"

The little girl looked up to the imposing man on the camel, squinting in the bright sunlight. She swallowed the lump forming in her throat and then, in a surprisingly strong voice, answered, "Suna."

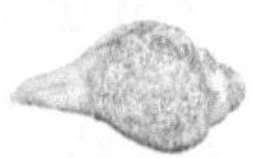

Steam shot from the hood like a miniature geyser. The 1936 Talbot Ten Sports Saloon sputtered to a stop. Dusty leather boots exited the dirt-covered car and kicked a tire in frustration. This was not the first time the British-made car had overheated.

Connor McGree pulled a cigarette from his breast pocket and lit it, letting the inhaled smoke linger and the nicotine do its work. He watched without passion as the small steam geyser slowly died. He was a lanky man with dusty khakis and a matching shirt that were just starting to look worn in.

He had come to the desert for one reason. To make his fortune. Oil was quickly becoming the modern world's new gold rush and, as with any rush, finders' keepers. Connor had studied oil and gas at the University of Aberdeen. His father had reluctantly given him enough money to travel to Arabia and survive for two months before he would have to turn tail and come back home. Home. The thought of it made his face flush. He would rather die in the desert than come home with his hat in hand. He could picture his father lording his failure over him.

At twenty-three, Connor was a lanky Scotsman with a flash of red hair and the temper to go with it. He pulled the fedora from his head and used the back of his arm to wipe the growing sweat from his forehead. The oil well he was currently drilling had yet to produce, and in a few days, he would be flat broke. He tried to chase the thoughts away from his mind as he picked a bit of tobacco from his tongue and flicked it away.

The desert was a greedy place. It took far more than it gave. Life here was forced and manipulated if it had any chance of survival. His biggest problem with it was the dryness. It was worse than a black winter's night in Glasgow. Oh, and the sand. The sand got into everything, from machinery to people, and no amount of cleaning would ever get it all out.

Connor walked to the Talbot's grille and leaned down, surveying the canvas desert water bag hanging there. It was still full, and as soon as his car cooled off enough, he would refill the radiator and be on his way.

His thoughts of home faded as the last of the steam escaped from the overheated car, and he glanced up. A shape on the horizon caught his attention. He stood tall. Shielding his eyes did little to clarify what he was looking at, so he moved closer. Reaching for his Webley pistol to make sure it was still on his waist, he tramped forward.

The form grew in size, materializing into a human. Connor flicked his half-burned cigarette away and ran.

It was an older woman, somewhere in her fifties. She had been pierced just below the neckline, and whatever blood she once contained was now consumed by the desert sands. The gruesome sight unnerved Connor, and he quickly stood up and surveyed the landscape for bandits. Not far away, he spied another lump, but otherwise, the horizon was clear.

He hurried over to investigate. An older man with a single gunshot lay prostrate in the sand. He kneeled and inspected the lifeless man.

Connor had never seen a dead person before, unless you count old Mrs. Perkins, who died in her sleep. Now, he had seen two, both most likely murdered by bandits. It was time for him to leave this place. He started to stand. A hand grabbed his arm. Connor nearly pissed himself.

"*Yusaeid.*" The voice was dry and cracked and difficult to understand.

Connor calmed his racing heart. He knelt and supported the dying man's head. He was fairly confident that the word *Yusaeid* was one of the Arabic words he knew—*help*. "Help? You said help, right? Yusaeid?"

The man nodded imperceptibly. He reached into his thobe and pulled out a delicately carved seashell and held it out. "*Suna. Yusaeid Suna. Suna.*" The words grew weaker with each utterance. As the last syllable fell, so did the shell from his hand. It rolled a few feet, leaving a trail back to the unmoving fingers. He was gone.

Connor leaned down and set the man's head back on the ground. "I'm sorry, Old Timer, but I don't know what *suna* means, God rest your soul." He crossed himself as he stood, his mind already returning to the business of drilling an oil well. He needed to get back as soon as possible. The shell caught his eye. It was a large sea snail of some type. He picked it up, giving the unfamiliar frieze a once-over. There were curious carvings that seemed to be unfamiliar letters circling the outside. Nothing he could make sense of. He tossed it in the air and caught it like an oversized cricket ball before heading back to the car.

"Suna. Maybe that's your name," he said to the shell. "Maybe you'll bring me luck."

CHAPTER ONE

"OKAY, HIT THE LIGHTS." THE cavern suddenly filled with a warm glow that sparkled off the gleaming walls.

Dr. Dani Tran stood back and crossed her arms, admiring the finished product. Her raven-black hair and cream-colored skin encompassed black eyes that reflected the world around her. At five-foot-eight, the Eurasian beauty was striking, with an athletic figure and a razor-sharp mind. "It's incredible," she said, pursing her full lips.

"Yes, I have never seen its equal," Kojo said as he craned his neck, letting in the full experience.

The precious cavern had been rediscovered by the two of them and a man named Cable Janson. He was currently in the States, but together they had overcome several harrowing weeks, fighting for their lives, while unraveling a centuries-old mystery, known as The Eye of Faith or the Pilgrimage of Akon. They had gone up against kidnappers, killers, narcissists, and rebels.

That mystery was now solved and right in front of them. A cavern the size of a concert hall covered in shiny salt crystals, like a giant diamond geode held up to the sunlight.

"Nature's disco ball," Dani said.

"They should do a concert here," Kojo added as he stepped next to Dani. She placed her arm around his waist. Reaching his shoulder would take some doing. At six-foot-four, Kojo's infectious smile towered over most, but what made him so identifiable was his orange beard, white hair, and dark skin, all only a framework for his genetically rare sky-blue eyes. "Cable would love to see this," he said.

"Yeah, a few flashlights didn't do it justice." Dani nodded, remembering when they had first discovered the cavern. She didn't realize how much she missed Cable until she paused to think about it. They had been thrust together via circumstance, but something magical bonded them to each other. The more perilous the situation, the more effective they had become as a team. Out of this unexpected push-pull relationship, respect and love had blossomed. They had found common ground, and now, thanks to distance and the fact there was no cell service in the canyon, everything was on hold. Dani pictured Cable's face, his infectious smile, and his kind eyes. He was intelligent, fun, and maybe even a bit old-fashioned, a rare combination in her book. She let a small smile lift the edges of her lips and eyes.

After discovering the hidden natural cathedral covered in ancient murals, the trio had found a passageway that led to this enormous halite geode. The chamber was a rare phenomenon but not unseen before in nature. What was rare was the size of the crystals. They were small, like a million diamonds, now sparkling in the artificial light.

Broken English shattered the quiet moment. "Good, lights working." A short, round man with a perfectly groomed afro, Marcus Bemnet, entered the cavern. He removed his glasses and meticulously wiped them with his sleeve before replacing them, his judgmental black eyes peering through the lenses once again. He wore traditional archaeologist clothes straight from the 1940s that had no dirt or wear marks. "Magnificent. The world will marvel at our find." He turned, taking the sight in as he spoke. "I have taken the liberty to contact *National Geographic*." He spoke in Amharic, forcing Kojo to translate the Ethiopian words to Dani. "They are eager to come here."

As a representative of the Ethiopian Ministry of Culture, Marcus Bemnet had been placed in charge of preserving the unique site. With each passing day, his ownership of the entire operation grew, and those responsible for actually finding the hidden chapel withered.

Dani had dealt with politicians before and cared little for the man's monologues or grand posturing. Despite it all, she was still kicking herself every day with the excitement of just being here.

Growing up in Austin, Texas, her exotic looks had put her on the social fringe. It wasn't until she attended college that she found her footing and started to feel a part of the bigger picture.

She graduated with a master's degree from UCLA in anthropology and then returned to the prestigious Stanford College of Archaeology for her PhD. Dani had made her postcollege living appraising pots, swords, and sculptures from ancient Egypt and the surrounding areas for the Peak Insurance Company. If it was ancient, 3D, and in need of appraising, she was the go-to.

For her doctorate, she had built a website database that helped translate several ancient languages in the Middle East region. Cable and Dani had used her software to translate ancient Ge'ez from the punt region south of the pharaohs, covering what was mostly Ethiopia in modern days. They had followed arcane clues that had led them to the exact spot where she now stood.

A salt cavern was worth its weight in gold to the ancient world. Now, it was just a curiosity for adventurous tourists. The real find was the attached chapel and the unspoiled murals that covered almost every inch of the walls and ceiling. Paintings that hadn't been seen by human eyes for more than 1600 years.

The fantasy of being on an archaeological dig site was not something Dani had realized before, but here she was, hands in the dirt, mind in the past. It made every day exciting and, more importantly, fulfilling, no matter the circling politics.

After the discovery of the site, the Ethiopian Government graciously added Dani to the group of archaeologists and workers tasked with documenting and preserving the site. She had pulled a few strings, adding Kojo to the team. They had carefully taken videos and stills of every inch of the chapel and the attached crystal cavern. Dani estimated she had about one week left before her work here would conclude. Something she had mixed emotions about.

Ethiopia had long been famous for its churches built into the natural stone. One church, Saint George, was carved from a single rock from the top down. Everything, including the roof, windows, and door frames, were all from one original piece.

This particular church was mostly a natural cavern with only a few carved sections, like the altar and a couple of alcoves, but the brightness and clarity of the murals were world-class. It was located in an obscured slot canyon miles from one of the biggest tourist attractions in Africa, the Blue Nile Falls.

"Marcus?"

The representative from the Ethiopian Ministry of Culture turned to the voice by the entrance.

"You need to see this." The man was one of the workers tasked with enlarging the narrow entrance that led from the chapel to the halite cavern. His voice sounded strained.

"Show me," Marcus said as he followed the man through the tunnel.

Dani could understand the man's emotion, even if she didn't comprehend the words.

"What is it?" she asked Kojo.

"Something's wrong. Come." They followed the two men.

Once out of the passage, they entered the chapel. It was a large domed space. The artificial lights inside refracted every color of the rainbow, lighting up the colorful room. It still took her breath away every time Dani entered.

Off to the right were depicted the nine original saints who brought Christianity to the region. Ultimately making Ethiopia the first state in the world to accept the religion.

Everything seemed in place to Dani as she looked around until a reflection by the front entrance caught her eye. It was water, and it was coming into the chapel.

Two workers suddenly rushed in, rattling off panicked words.

Kojo grabbed Dani by the elbow and started to sprint to the exit. "The canyon is flooding. We need to get out of here and find some high ground." They splashed across the growing pool that now covered half the chapel's floor. "There must be heavy rains in the nearby hills."

Marcus screamed for everyone to get out and ran for his life. Workers and archaeologists paused briefly before gasping as realization hit. Now aware of the danger, they quickly followed.

The entrance to the church was a narrow slit concealed behind a column of sandstone. When Dani first arrived, it had been blocked off with loose rock. Now, it stood clear and open. The workers had even begun to widen the slot, planning to install a door there. Beyond that was a natural pool of calcium carbonate blue water, further obscuring the entrance. Workers constructed a wooden boardwalk stretching across the pool to what was once dry ground beyond.

As Dani exited the gap in the rock, she froze with shock.

Kojo almost lost his grip on her. The usually calm blue pool was churning with current. It was muddy, and the footbridge above was now two feet underwater. Multiple waterfalls cascaded down the walls of the slot canyon, quickly filling the space faster than it could drain. Strangely, the sky was only partially cloudy, with no visible rain overhead.

"Flash flood!" Dani shouted as their tents and supplies were swept past her in the growing fury. "It's pouring rain somewhere above us."

"Should we wait it out in the cavern?" Kojo called out.

"No, that could be a death sentence," Dani replied. "Up. We've got to get up."

Marcus took one look at the turmoil and turned back into the presumed safety of the chapel. Several men followed. Dani had no time to stop them. The water was quickly rising, already approaching her waist and pulling at her. She remembered the entrance to the slot canyon. It was partially blocked by a rockslide. Add enough water to the slow-draining exit, and this place would become a lake.

A few men, who were working outside when the flood started, found themselves quickly overwhelmed and sucked down the canyon at breakneck speeds.

Dani quickly looked around, assessing the situation. There was a small ledge on the cliff face to her left, just above the water. It was four feet long and six inches wide. "No time—come on." She pushed through the rising water, staying close to the rock, and scrambled up to the ledge. Kojo and two workers followed.

As the last worker climbed for safety, he lost his grip and was quickly pulled away before Kojo could grasp the poor man.

Dani watched helplessly as the raging water engulfed him. "We can't stay here long, or the same thing will happen to us."

About eight feet above her was another ledge but even smaller than the one they all now shared.

"There," Dani pointed up, "but we will have to work together."

"Dani, use my shoulders." Kojo cupped his hands together, and Dani climbed up and used his shoulders to access the ridge. She then reached down and helped the worker, who followed her example. He held her legs while she reached down and assisted Kojo.

It was brutal hanging inverted off the narrow ridge. Dani had to trust the man hanging on to her legs to do his part. Kojo was more than twice her weight and used her like a cheap ladder. Eventually, Kojo made it up and returned the favor by pulling Dani's overhanging torso back up to safety.

Dani rubbed the blood back into her bruised legs.

It was at that moment that the rain started, torrential, like a pent-up monsoon.

The rock quickly became slippery, and the visibility nil.

"How long before water get here?" the worker shouted in broken English, his fear evident.

Dani tried to estimate the speed of the rising water. The ridge below them was no longer visible, and the frothing brown water seemed anxious to reach them. She didn't have an answer.

Marcus and three men paused inside the church. It was a respite from the chaos outside. Water still flowed inside, but it was eerily serene. "See if you can find a place to get out of this water," Marcus demanded. A worker waded over to the head of the church toward the altar. It was underwater. Another man moved right.

Marcus watched him, his eyes taking in the nearby electrical generating platform. He realized the situation too late. As water flooded into the machine, sparks flew, and the generator ate itself, gears and shafts failing catastrophically, but not before sending out a surge and electrocuting the nearby man. Fresh water only conducts electricity a short distance. Marcus and the other two men, who were now waist-deep in the flooding church, felt only a tingle before the lights in the chamber plunged them into complete darkness.

The worker by the altar flicked on his flashlight, giving some relief. Its light moved around the room. It found scared faces, the floating body of a comrade, and eventually, the beam tracked the source of a new noise. The water at the entrance was no longer seeping in. It was gushing. Marcus had led himself and these men to their deaths.

Dani's bloodied fingers jammed into a crack small enough to hide a bug. She pulled her soaked body up along the sheer cliff, inch by inch. It was a race between her mediocre climbing skills and the fast-rising water eager to take the last of its victims. The worker who had been integral to their initial climb to safety had slipped just moments before. Dani had not looked down to see what had happened to the poor man. She needed all her focus on the task at hand.

Kojo was slightly ahead of her, encouraging her every move. He had a healthy fear of heights, but with the water following right behind them, fifty feet up seemed like five.

Finally, Kojo called down, "That's it. Nothing but smooth, wet rock ahead."

Dani looked up. There was nothing left to hold on to. "We're rimrocked."

Kojo looked down, confused.

"Stuck."

"That is what I said," Kojo replied.

"For climbers, it's called rimrocked."

"For us, it's called…" Kojo didn't finish his statement. Instead, he looked at Dani with a concerned half-smile and a slight tilt of his head.

Dani looked back up and gave a short nod. They had been through a lot together, even escaped death a few times, and if their number was up, they were better off sharing it.

Kojo's expression grew serious as the water rose past Dani's feet. "It will pull you from the rock. Come next to me."

"There's no place to hold on," Dani said.

"Use me to hold on to."

Dani nodded and continued her ascent, ending up next to Kojo. She was stepping on his toes with her toes and grasping his wrists with her hands. They shared eye contact for a moment. Kojo shuddered as his strength slowly drained, but he ignored it.

Each found renewed strength from the other. Now, all they could do was hope and pray.

"Nine Saints preserve us," Kojo said, in a reverent voice.

The rain only increased. Water continued to work its way up the canyon walls, covering first their shoes and then their hips.

Dani shared an uneasy look with Kojo, who forced a kind, brave smile in return.

The current pulled at the two, making it even more difficult to hang on.

Kojo's hand came loose, and they nearly got swept away before he could regain purchase. His body began to shake with fatigue. Dani considered letting go to save her friend, but Kojo could read her mind. "Don't even think about it. We are in this together all the way."

Then, as if the storm had changed its fickle mind, the water started to drop. The rain subsided, and soon, Dani and Kojo were able to work their way back down the cliff, following the water as it slowly drained out of the canyon.

"Look, I've told you the same thing I told Agent Ascot. Making me repeat myself ten times won't change the story. You should really be talking to Dani. She's the one who was initially taken. She could tell you more about the trafficking operation."

"Dr. Dani Tran is currently out of the country." The agent leaned forward. "Mr. Janson, surely you want us to track down and apprehend those responsible."

"Hold up, right there. Don't try to make it look like I am anything less than appalled and disgusted by slavers. I have done everything in my power to help with your investigation, but I am now late for a meeting. If you have any other questions, please don't hesitate to contact my attorney." Cable stood and left the room before any more could be said. He was angry, but mostly, he was frustrated with the bureaucracy and the agent's need to fill out his paperwork as opposed to following the case.

Cable had stumbled onto a trafficking network in his attempt to rescue a woman he now held very close in his heart. He and Dr. Dani Tran had been through much together during their escape, and now, their efforts to get the word out about the criminal operation was proving almost as troublesome.

Since getting back to the States, Cable had spent more time than he would like to admit in an FBI office, repeating his side of the story. The problem was that the responsible parties were both dead. A convenient dead end for the uninitiated. Cable's knowledge of the human trafficking ring and their operation consisted of two white male faces and the dark hold in the bottom of a ship they had stuffed him into, leaving him to rot. Those men were in the wind, and there was no more information he could provide law enforcement.

As he exited the FBI field office in Denver, Cable let the cold, biting air clear his mind. He had no meeting to get to, but he was officially done with the FBI and their merry-go-round procedures.

As his anger abated, Cable's stomach took over. It was well past lunchtime, and he was starving.

"Are you Cable Janson?"

Cable turned to see a man in a perfectly tailored blue suit coming up the stairs. He had thinning brown hair and a groomed beard with hints of gray. The wind blew his comb-over the wrong way, making one side of his head look bald and the other like an open bird's wing.

Cable measured the words but did not reply.

"I was told you would be here," he said, trying to mend his wild hair.

"Told by whom?" Cable asked, his eyebrows drawn together as he carefully inspected the stranger.

"My name is Logan Minova. My boss has considerable reach. He wants to meet with you."

Cable gave the man an I-couldn't-care-less look and started to walk away. "No thanks."

"Tam McGree. He is the owner of Suna Petroleum." Logan hurried to catch up to Cable. "As I said, he would like to meet with you."

"I said, I'm not interested."

The man seemed suddenly desperate. "It's about your mother."

Cable stopped mid-stride. "What about my mother?"

"I have a car waiting," Logan added.

The metallic dark-blue Maybach turned the corner, not even minding the large pothole. A smooth, quiet ride was just the price of admission for this kind of luxury car. In fact, it might have been a bit too quiet, as Cable's empty stomach suddenly growled so loudly that he felt like even the driver, through the glass partition, could hear it.

"Can we stop and get some tacos or something? I haven't eaten all day."

Logan appraised his passenger for a moment before nodding. "The FBI are not gracious hosts. I know a place that has amazing al pastor."

Cable followed Logan's clicking shoes across the polished stone and past a large formal dining room that could seat twenty. They took a right and then a left before entering a tall wooden door. Inside, floor-to-ceiling windows illuminated a home office like something from the movies. Shelves with collectibles, first editions, art, and statues were all surrounded by rich wood and leather.

A lanky, gray-haired man with stooped shoulders and appraising eyes stepped from behind his runway-sized desk and extended a friendly hand. "You must be Cable Janson. I'm so pleased to make your acquaintance. I'm Tam McGree." He shook Cable's hand like it was a competition.

Cable just smiled politely.

"That will be all, Logan," the older man said, as he put on a pair of black-framed glasses.

Logan left the room and closed the door behind him.

Tam turned back to Cable and forced a polite smile. "Please have a seat." He gestured to a long couch and sat on one end.

Cable followed, taking the spot across from him. "Am I detecting a slight Orkney dialect?"

Tam cocked his head at Cable. "I grew up in Kirkwell. My father married an Irish girl and moved us to Glasgow. I worked very hard to lose the accent, but you picked it out with just a few words spoken. Impressive. Most Scottish natives would not have noticed."

"I have an ear for languages."

"And an eye for cultures, I'm told."

Cable crossed his legs, shifting uncomfortably as he moved his focus to the rest of the room. "Quite a collection."

"Yes, my father was the real collector, much like your grandfather and father, if I am to understand."

Cable lifted an eyebrow, feeling even more anxious at this unplanned meeting and this stranger's knowledge of his family.

Tam made eye contact with Cable, and his smile slowly faded. "I'm sorry to stare, but you have a remarkable resemblance to your mother."

"You knew Dolores, Mr. McGree?"

"Please, call me Tam, and yes, Dodie and I… we were quite fond of each other at one point…" He squirmed a bit, trying to get more comfortable. "We first met in college at UC Boulder. She was a real firecracker with the whole world at her feet and plans to conquer it. I had never met anyone quite like her."

He cleared his throat. "I was dating her roommate, and we just hit it off. Not in a sexual way, mind you. We were two like-minded people who loved to talk politics, religion, and business. All the no-nos for most people. We could argue and disagree, but neither ever took offense…" He paused, then his eyes refocused on the present. "I'm afraid those days might be gone in the world."

Tam looked back at Cable. "I was so sorry to hear of her passing."

Now, Cable felt really uncomfortable. His mother had died by suicide after struggling with depression, and though Cable had eventually come to terms with the tragedy, it was something he didn't like to think or talk about. He still struggled to bring his past and present fully together and preferred to remember only the good days with his mother.

"Sorry to bring that back up. You were very young. It must have been hard."

"Well, thanks for the painful trip down memory lane," Cable said as he started to rise.

"No. Please. That's not why I invited you here… Sit."

Invited? Cable felt like he was one step away from being shanghaied for the second time in a year.

"I am familiar with your recent exploits. Finding the Beite Amharic and the crystal chamber. Quite remarkable."

"Yes, the natural cave church is in pristine condition. The woman and another man who found it with me are there now with a preservation crew."

Tam stood slowly and continued to speak as he walked to his desk. "How much do you know about the Phoenicians, Cable?"

Cable's brows knitted. "The Phoenicians? Ah… Pre-Greek. They were the forefathers of Western Civilization. Owned the Mediterranean at one point and were really good sailors."

Tam reached down and pulled out a leather box. He carried it back to the couch.

"Oh, and they had the first verified alphabet if I recall correctly. Why?"

Tam sat back down. "So, the Wikipedia version."

"Sounds about right."

Tam set the box on the coffee table and opened it. He withdrew a large white seashell covered in black designs. "My father started Suna Petroleum back in the late thirties. He risked everything he had and was effectively drilling a dry hole in the Arabian Desert with enough money left in his pocket to buy his last coffee. That is where his story takes on a mythical element."

Cable tilted his head at the last words.

"Connor, my father, found a curious Bedouin dying in the barren sands of Saudi Arabia. The old man gave him this shell and a name for his company with his dying breath. That very same day, my father's oil well hit paydirt, and the rest is…black gold history."

Tam held up the relic as he spoke. "This shell has become our family's good luck charm, our legacy."

"It is also part of your logo, as I recall," Cable added.

"Yes, indeed." He gazed at the shell as though seeing it for the first time. "At one point, my father had a professor of some sort look at it, and he identified the markings as Phoenician. That was as far as he took it, and this shell now spends most of its time in a safe. I imagine its value as an artifact of the era is high, but its value to my family is much more."

He handed the relic to Cable, who slowly rolled it in his hands, taking in all the intricate three-dimensional carvings and symbols. It was a large sea snail shell about the size of a loaf of bread. "At first glance, it looks like a *dung-dkar* from Tibet, a shell trumpet used in their temples. But these"—Cable pointed to a section on the shell—"look like letters, not symbols, and they are not Tibetan. Phoenician, you say… Hmm. Okay." He handed it back. "It's beautiful."

Tam nodded. Then, he set the shell down and leaned back as he looked at Cable. "I want you to find the origin of this shell. Anything you can. I will pay you handsomely. First-class travel all the way."

Cable glanced down at the shell and then back at Tam. "First class is a place to be seen and admired by those unable to get there. A club I don't intend to ever join."

"Price is not an issue to me, Cable. Name yours. I need to know what story hides behind these markings."

"And you're just now needing this? What? Are you checking off the last of your boxes?" Cable asked.

Tam slowed his sales push on Cable and leaned back, reflecting. "As one gets older, your priorities shift, and things that were once so important become…trivial. While others… priceless. I have more money than I can spend in four lifetimes for me and my family, but I can't buy more time at any price. Perhaps I can buy some answers." He suddenly looked Cable in the eyes. "Name your price."

Cable slowly nodded.

"This shell is just a mystery, not some hidden message that the world would kill for. Please, just get an old man an answer."

"I'm afraid I won't be able to help you, Mr. McGree. Good luck with your search." Cable threw the words out as he stood.

Tam appraised Cable with a look like he just bit into a piece of bad fish. He was not used to people saying no, and honestly, he had expected an enthusiastic yes, but this man apparently could not be bought, which was a strange sensation for him.

CHAPTER TWO

Mona Helal looked out across the Nile. It was an image she never grew tired of. The view gave her strength and passion all in one. The river was always on the move, just like her. It had its moods and its secrets, but most of all, it was life in the desert. A Dahabiya sailed upstream. Its look and design had been unchanged for a thousand years. A new black Revo powerboat blasted past, rocking the older sailboat. The driver was unconcerned with the old man yelling at him behind the tiller. This was Egypt. The ancient and the new smashed together and rarely getting along, except when their national team was playing *fútbol*.

Mona pulled her eyes from the view on the twentieth floor of the high-rise. Her company occupied three levels, and she was considering adding a fourth. Her office was a mix of professional, clean lines with glass and hardwood. Fresh flowers added a distinctly feminine touch. Colorful art and bright fixtures divided the space into two main areas. Three butter-yellow upholstered chairs and a matching couch created a conversation area. A lavender and glass desk with all the work accoutrements dominated the other area. The only personal item in her office was a gold-framed black-and-white photo of a young Mona and her mother that sat on her desk. Both were in matching black hijabs and holding a serious expression to the camera's lens.

Her fitted gray linen jacket was buttoned only at the top, revealing a pink blouse underneath. She had come a long way since the little girl wearing the hijab in the photo. Mona wore custom-tailored slacks and practical heels handmade in Italy. A western-style uniform she had embraced many years ago. Her only connection to her past was her hijab—it was always faster than doing her hair.

Running the most successful construction business in Cairo had consumed her, leaving few outside distractions in her life. Relationships were always complicated for her, and time off was such a bore. Even when visiting her beachfront villa in Alexandria, she kept busy. Mona lived for her work, and work was her life, nothing more.

She was on the back side of forty, and every line and crease that gave her face character was well-earned. Her black, shoulder-length hair was rarely seen, and she kept her eyebrows thin and arched. As a female Arab working in the Middle East, she had overcome more than most to attain her high position. But if anyone knew her true backstory, they would be stunned at her ascension.

Mona started as the daughter of a slave. Born with no rights or freedoms. She was property and nothing more. Her existence was conditional on a daily basis. As soon as she could walk, she'd been given duties. As Mona grew, so did her duties. Once she turned eleven, she was expected to match the other adult slaves' workload. There was no access beyond the walled perimeter of the property, and everything she knew of the outside world came from a few glimpses beyond the wall, a sentence in a passing conversation, or television screens.

Her owner was a wealthy Arab with class and privilege. He had no consideration for those he owned or employed. Owning slaves was perfectly normal and had been a part of his family's heritage for generations. He demanded one hundred percent obedience and punished those who did not comply with a predetermined menu of horrors.

By the time Mona turned thirteen, her owner had made his intentions clear as to what was coming next. Mona's mother could not sit by and watch the same revulsions befall her daughter that she had endured. She would risk everything to help her daughter escape, believing a life on the streets was better than a life as a slave.

On a Tuesday night, when the moon was just a sliver, Mona's mother took her to the back gate. They had two minutes before the guard returned, doing his nightly sweep of the perimeter. The master was away on business, and his return for a weekend with Mona was not going to happen.

She leaned down, whispering, as she grabbed her daughter's shoulders for strength. "My little Jasmine flower, you have grown so beautiful." Her mother reached up with one hand and stroked Mona's straight black hair as she spoke.

At thirteen, she was lean, with just the first hints of curves starting to form. Mona had long, delicate fingers and large, wide-set eyes. Right now, they were filling with tears.

"I know great things are in store for you, but I need you to be brave. Promise me to use your adventurous spirit to keep moving forward. Never look back. Do you understand?"

"I don't want to leave you, Yamma. I can be a good slave," Mona pleaded, a bit too loud.

"Never." The words came out harsher than intended, and Mona's mother paused to let her emotions cool. She grabbed Mona in a vise-like hug and considered never letting go.

Then, in a barely audible whisper, she spoke. "You know our family's story, and I'm counting on you to keep our history alive." She pulled back and handed Mona a small black-and-white photo taken of the two of them. "Take this."

Mona's little fingers moved across the glossy image. She flipped it over. On the back were two hand-drawn symbols that were familiar to her. She looked up through tear-filled eyes to her mother. The symbols were part of a family story her mother had told many times. What they meant, however, was unknown. Two interlocking deltas followed by a sideways crescent moon.

"You have forty-eight hours before the master returns. He has many contacts here and will carpet the city looking for you. Here is some money I have collected. Be very careful with it."

"How did you get money?"

"Don't ask." She leaned back up, letting go of Mona. "I will make sure you are not missed for as long as I can… That will be my gift to you and your new life, no matter the cost." A tender smile slowly lifted her lips and the corners of her eyes. "Always remember who you are and where you came from."

Mona nodded, her eyes flooding, but she didn't have the strength to wipe the tears from her face.

"The best way to stay safe in the bad parts of the city is to run. By the time someone takes an interest in you, you will be long past them."

"I'm a good runner."

"I know. But I want something more for you, my Meri. You must promise me that no matter what happens, you will always push yourself. Climb out of this gutter we now live in. Promise me."

"I promise, Yamma."

Mona knew she would never see her mother again. The punishment she would endure for helping Mona escape would be harsh, perhaps fatal. The last slave who ran off had been quickly recaptured, and both of his legs were broken right at the ankles. The man could only hobble now and was always given the vilest of jobs.

With a hesitant push from her mother, Mona slipped through the gate and started moving away from the compound. She took short, hesitant steps at first, but with each stride, she found her strength. Soon, she was running, like a young deer, through the streets.

The night Mona said goodbye to her mother was truly the saddest day in her existence.

She used her raw emotions to push herself harder and harder. As she ran, tears obscured her vision, but she pushed on. One foot in front of the other, running, until eventually, she was free of Port Said. Mona lifted her chin, breathing deeply. She slowed her pace and caught her breath.

The first rays of the sun warmed the sky. To her left was a never-ending line of oil tankers and cargo ships making passage through the Suez Canal. They seemed impossibly tall in real life, like giant sleeping steel coffins gliding in the desert sun. To the right, homes dotted verdant cotton crops spread out as far as she could see.

Her duty was clear. She must find freedom and fulfill the family's destiny. Mona made her way south along the Suez Canal to Ismailia. A city of roughly five hundred thousand, located halfway between Suez and Port Said. A place where she could disappear.

She needed a drink and found a small street merchant with a grill. As she stepped up to inspect everything, a man bumped into her, nearly knocking her to the ground. Mona gathered herself, selected a bottle of water, and asked for a *hawawshi* or street sandwich. The merchant eyed her suspiciously but started to work on her order. Mona reached into her pocket for her money, but her hand came up empty. She had been robbed. Panic flared, and her first reaction was to start crying, but the words of her mother rang clear, "You must be brave." Mona quickly sobered up and lifted her chin. She needed to be strong. In an unplanned reaction, she grabbed the bottle of water and ran.

The merchant cried out and tried to catch the thief, but the little girl was quick. He soon gave up, not wanting to leave his stall unattended in this part of town. The price of business.

Life on the streets was rough. Mona was just another uneducated orphan panhandling her way along. Homelessness and extreme poverty were no way to live, but she quickly adapted to her new life. Using her young, pretty looks to win handouts, she managed a spot for sleeping under a raised building with two other children and a few rats. What little cash she made scarcely covered the simplest of needs.

One afternoon, the sun was cooking the city more than usual, and Mona made her way down to the canal with four of the other beggars she had befriended. As a total non-swimmer, she was leery of the canal, but after much coaxing from her peers, she ventured in up to her waist. Soon, a water fight broke out, and everyone was laughing and splashing. It was a small moment to be a child again, and they all relished it. What they didn't know was there was a strong undercurrent that followed the larger container ships that paraded up and down the Suez Canal. As one such ship passed closer to shore than the others, an undertow swept all five beggars into deeper water and pulled them under. Two of the five had rudimentary swimming skills and were able to find the surface and swim back to shore. They stood there waiting for their friends, who would never surface.

In an instant, Mona had been pulled under, and no amount of struggling would save her. She fought gallantly to hold her breath, but time and her brain's overwhelming reflex forced her to inhale the warm, green water. It hurt for only a moment, and then her body stilled. It was almost peaceful as her vision dimmed.

As the front door closed, Cable leaned back against it for support. He took a calming breath. It had been a whirlwind of a morning. His eyes took in his childhood home. The three-story red-brick house was in Lakewood, Colorado, just east of Denver. It had been in his family for three generations, and now it was up to Cable to continue its heritage. A house where he had so many memories, some good, some not so much. It had been the place he had escaped from as a young adult, and now, several years later, it was taking on a new meaning. Home.

After his father's recent death, this house was all he had left of his family. Though objects didn't appeal to Cable, this one was worth saving. Living in a big, empty house was not on his wish list, as he was happiest out on the road, exploring and meeting new people and places. Roots were not what he yearned for. He walked to the home office and sat behind the hardwood desk. The room smelled like furniture polish and faded cigars. His mind spun with too many memories.

It was time to plan his next getaway, far from these walls, far from this town, far from this country. He had a notion to visit eastern Russia and then make his way through Mongolia. The war with Ukraine might make that tricky, so perhaps just Mongolia for now.

The doorbell interrupted his thoughts.

Cable swung the front door open to find a beautiful woman in her late twenties. She had perfect blonde hair and a questioning smile framed by dark green eyes. Her almond-shaped face was smooth, and her casual on-trend fashion accented all the right spots, tight, low-rise gray jeans and a white sleeveless top that ended right above her belly button.

It took Cable a second to recognize the face. "Shannon?"

A small, concerned smile crossed her face. "I wasn't sure you'd remember me."

How could he not? *Shannon was the last person he had kissed before leaving for Harvard.*

"Of course I remember."

"I was sorry to hear about your father. He was a kind man."

Cable had less favorable memories of him but kept them to himself. "Thank you. Oh, shoot, please, come in."

He escorted her to the living room, and they both sat on the oversized leather couch.

Shannon's gaze roamed over the dark wood floors with cream walls and the beamed ceiling. "It still looks the same."

"That was something my father requested, that I keep the house, as a family birthright of sorts."

She nodded, feeling just a bit awkward. "Well, he's gone, so now you can do whatev—" Her phone buzzed, and Shannon, Pavlovianly, stopped mid-sentence and looked at the screen for a second.

Cable now had time to get a better look at her. She had fashionable two-tone acrylics, a blinged-out phone case, and lips that seemed much larger than he remembered. All in all, Shannon was on the cutting edge of fashion and vitality, even if some of it was manufactured. She still looked beautiful to Cable, at least on the outside. He tried to remember what it was that killed their relationship. He couldn't think of one single thing, just two young people living in different parts of the country, both too preoccupied with their college lives to keep the flame ignited.

"I heard you were in town, and I wanted to drop by and see how you were doing." Her phone buzzed again, and she did a quick text reply before looking back up to Cable.

Cable watched her. So many memories flashed through his mind. The prom, the drinking, the sex, and the parties. Times, places, and people Cable had left behind.

"So, are you doing okay?" Her phone chimed once more, and a small laugh escaped her lips as she read the message.

"No. I've been given three months to live," Cable replied, curious just how much Shannon was actually paying attention.

"Oh. That's nice." Her phone beeped again, and once more, her attention was split. "We were good together. You and me, and I was wondering if I could buy you a cup of coffee or maybe dinner. You know, just for old times." Her phone buzzed again.

"Wow, you got that whole sentence out without pausing."

"What?" she said, looking back up from her phone, not quite catching the intention of his words.

Her eyes were captivating, but false. Bright blue was not the color he remembered. Cable quickly dismissed the thought. "Shannon, you're right. We had some great times together, and you are a beautiful woman." Cable leaned in. "Very desirable, but I am leaving in the morning for Pankot Palace." Cable tried not to smile at his reference to a location used in an Indiana Jones movie.

"Is that far?"

"India."

"I see. Well, if you ever get back, can I text you?"

"Of course. I would love that." He stood up, signaling the end of the conversation, but Shannon remained on the couch to text another message.

Finally, she looked up. "Oh."

Cable, ever the gracious host, escorted her out the front door.

For the second time in the last hour, Cable leaned against his front door as it closed and let out a long sigh. It had been a day of nos. First the FBI, then Tam McGree, and now Shannon, an ex-girlfriend. "I guess what they say about how things come in threes was right," Cable mumbled to himself.

The phone in the office rang. "Now what?" He was tempted to ignore it.

The voice on the other end of the line was compressed and sounded far away, but mostly, it sounded distraught. "Cable, thank goodness. It's all gone, ruined."

Cable immediately recognized Dani's voice. He was anxious, and a million thoughts flooded his mind. Mostly, how much he missed her. "Dani? What's happening? Are you all right?"

She told Cable everything that had happened to her and Kojo in the last forty-eight hours. The flash flood, the deaths of the workers, the scary cliff climb to safety, and the destruction of the site.

Dani took a long, calming breath like a death row inmate on his way to the gallows. The recent events had her on edge, and just hearing Cable's voice was a comfort. "The government has shut down the whole project for now. I have a feeling no further action will be taken for some time."

"How fast can you get to the airport in Addis Ababa?" Cable asked. There was a pause on the line. He could hear a mumbled question and answer in the background.

"Eight hours."

"Okay, I'll book you both on a flight and—"

Dani interrupted, "Kojo's not coming. He's going to his sister's house after he drops me off."

"Got it. Just one ticket. I've missed you," Cable managed to add. But Dani had already hung up.

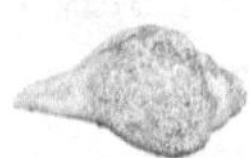

Violent coughing and vomiting came as a natural reflex before there was any kind of recognition. Light followed, and then horrible pain. Her body tried to restart. Deep gasping breaths as a fuzzy brain slowly rebooted.

A voice followed. "Hello, my dear. Thought I'd lost you. It's not every day I pull up a fish with legs in my net."

Mona just gawked up at the man's face, her eyes squinting in the sun's glare. Her senses were slow to return, the last one, smell. Stale fish and tobacco. The face looked older, like someone's dad. With a grubby beard and kind eyes. His collarless brown shirt was tucked into black canvas pants held up by orange suspenders.

"I'd offer you some water, but I have a feeling you are full up." He softly chuckled at his words.

Mona was too afraid to speak. She remembered drowning. Was she dead? Was she now the property of this man? *Once a slave, always a slave?* Perhaps she was one of the heavenly virgins the Prophet Muhammad had envisaged. *It didn't smell like paradise.*

The man seemed unconcerned with her and went about his work. He tightened the sail and turned the boat into the wind.

"By the way, my name is Karim." He gave her a crooked smile and turned his attention back to the bow.

A warm breeze blew across her face as the boat picked up speed. After a time, Mona tested her voice. It was hoarse and timid. "I'm Mona. Thank you for saving me."

"The fate of Muhammad is with you, child. He is whom you should be thanking. All I did was pull up my net."

Mona knew about Muhammad, but as a female slave, she had not been permitted to practice any type of religion. "Thank you, Muhammad?" she whispered.

They glided to a small dock, and Karim expertly dropped the sail and tied off the boat. "Come, you carry the fish. I'll get the nets."

Karim lit his pipe and proceeded to hang the nets up to dry. Mona struggled with two five-gallon buckets of fish. To her right sat a half-finished version of the same boat they had just docked. Up ahead was a small adobe home. It was square with a flat roof. A wooden ladder mounted to the side led up to the roof, where four poles supported a shaded canvas.

"This is my house and my business. I fish in the mornings and build boats after that. Please, come in and make yourself comfortable. There is someone I would like you to meet, Mona."

The door to the small home suddenly opened, and a woman in a black thobe and gray hijab stepped into the sun. Her expression quickly turned to a scowl. "What is with the beggar?" she asked, sternly.

"This is Mona. I pulled her from the sea."

The woman paused.

"Mona, this is my wife, Femi."

Femi looked suddenly confused at her husband's words, and her harsh expression slowly faded when she realized the beggar was female.

It took a few weeks, but soon, Mona was part of the family. Femi had not been able to have children, and Mona had endeared herself. Even the self-abuse Femi often harbored for not being a complete woman faded as her love for Mona grew. Smiles became the norm, and family life flourished.

This was something Mona never believed possible. The sacrifice her Yamma had made would not be forgotten, but more importantly, it would not be wasted.

As one of the rare, educated women in the area, Femi was employed as a teacher at the local high school. She worked hard to encourage the young females allowed to attend school, to instill in them that knowledge was not a crime. She fought prejudices where possible and secretly taught reading and math to anyone willing to learn.

Femi was diligent in adding education to Mona's life, as well. Something the young girl had never been gifted.

Mona consumed knowledge like a dried-out sponge in a running faucet. As soon as she was able to read, books became her window to the world beyond her small home. She would borrow any literature she could get her hands on, from translated classics to local favorites, math, philosophy, poetry, and even occasional fiction.

Mona spent time helping around the house and working with Karim when she was not doing her schooling.

By age nineteen, she had effectively gained a home-schooled college education. She had helped expand her father's shipbuilding business, and they employed two full-time workers.

Things were going well for the Helal family until Femi fell ill. It started as a simple scratch on her leg, but unbeknownst to Femi, that scratch turned to methicillin-resistant staphylococcus aureus, MRSA. By the time they took her to the hospital, no antibiotic could stop it.

Sadly, on a Thursday, Mona and Karim brought Femi home to die. Two terrible weeks they would never forget.

One cloudy night, with distant thunder, Mona lost her adopted mother.

It almost broke her, but Mona managed to put a cast around her heart that no amount of love would ever crack open. She desperately clung to her mother's plea. *"Always push yourself and climb out of the gutter."* She would do just that. No time to wallow in pity or sit on the sidelines crying. With a final whispered 'goodbye' to Femi, Mona stood ramrod straight, determined to push forward and make something of herself.

On one hand, her analytical mind was good to go. On the other hand, she was now cold and calculating, with no room for emotion. It was just a distracting chemical dump in her brain, nothing more.

Karim never saw Mona smile again, but from a business side of things, he watched her excel.

In 2000, by presidential decree, an area of seventy thousand acres was established east of Cairo as New Cairo. This soon-to-be new metropolis was little more than sand and squat houses at the time. Mona's adopted father had seen the vision of a clean, bustling city with gated communities, factories, malls, universities, and more. But mostly, he needed a change. Living in the house where his wife had died was too much. Everywhere he looked, memories followed him like a shadow.

He sold his business and moved to the suburbs of Cairo. There, he sank every penny he had saved into building a small home on a corner lot. Mona had been in favor of the move and worked the numbers side of the growing business. It was not all easygoing, but eventually, the home was finished and sold for a small profit. This led to another venture involving two side-by-side duplexes. The timing could not have been more perfect. As part of the expansion of Cairo, his contracting business quickly flourished.

Unfortunately, it was too much for a heavy-smoking sixty-year-old who had never before known the stress of running a serious business. It wasn't long before a fatal heart attack ended Karim's dream.

Mona picked up his torch and the challenge. Over the next twenty-four years, she turned the three-room operation into a multi-conglomerate.

Now, New Cairo was home to over five hundred thousand people, including her home in Hyde Park. Modern buildings and luxury homes dotted the city, many built by her team. But no matter how new or progressive New Cairo was, there were still plenty of communities to be avoided, especially after dark. This would be her next endeavor, to re-urbanize the bad neighborhoods.

"Ms. Helal, your three o'clock is here," said a voice from the phone's speaker.

Mona stepped closer to the glass. "Send him in," she replied, in a flat tone.

Omari Ur, the Minister of Housing and Development, entered the room with an attitude and purpose. His handmade Italian loafers ticked across the floor as he adjusted the cuffs on his open-collared custom shirt, showing off a full hairy chest. The shirt's light-blue sleeves now just peeked out from behind a Gieves & Hawkes navy coat.

"I thought we had an agreement?" he sputtered as he approached. "Why was I summoned here? I'm the one who does the summoning."

"You thought?" Mona turned slowly from the window and approached the fifty-ish man with black eyes and a greedy heart. "You're not paid to think, Omari." She said his name as if something distasteful was stuck on her tongue. "I asked politely. You refused. I paid you handsomely. You wanted more. I agreed. Now you try to hold me hostage over more money. Enough!"

"Your father built this company, not you. He would never treat me this way."

"My father started this company. I am the one who made us who we are today, not him."

"Women should not—"

"Women should not what?" She glared at the man, not breaking eye contact.

Omari nervously adjusted his collar. An unease grew up his spine, and he found it difficult to maintain eye contact with Mona. As a politician, he knew when he had overplayed his hand, and this was it. "Nothing. I-I will make it happen. Just make sure about the money."

"That will not be a problem, as I no longer require your services."

Omari looked confused.

"I have made other arrangements based on your initial reaction to my request, but thank you for your eventual willingness in the matter. Perhaps another time."

"Another time. What are you talking about?" Amari's voice was clipped and edged with emotion.

Silence returned.

His rage continued to build. "Curse you *and* your father. We have a deal. Who else can get this done?" He stepped threateningly close. "I will have my money, or you will have no building permits ever granted again."

"You sure that's your final answer?" Mona asked.

As if by magic, two large men in suits entered and grabbed Omari before he could reply to Mona.

"What is this?" he squawked as they pulled him, kicking, screaming, and swearing out of the office.

Mona watched with calm disregard. *This is me taking out the trash.*

CHAPTER THREE

"T HANKS FOR COMING TO GET me. I could have just taken an Uber," Dani said as she opened the passenger door.

"Not on my watch," Cable replied as he closed the hood on her luggage and rounded to the driver's side. He dropped into the sports car and leaned over. Dani met him halfway in a kiss that was something straight out of a family reunion, not from a girlfriend who had been out of the country for two months. Cable's pent-up desire and passion did backflips as he watched Dani pull back and turn facing forward.

What's going on? He suddenly felt numb, confused, hurt, and even a bit panicked. Taking a calming breath, Cable started the car. "Sorry about your dig."

Dani didn't reply right away. Eventually, she looked down and said, "Life is so random at times. One moment you're on the top of the mountain, and the next, the rock gives way and you're crashing to the bottom."

It was said with objective distance, and Cable decided he needed to give her some space.

He put the red Porsche in gear and pulled away from the curb at Denver International. The 1965 356C merged into traffic and headed east on Peña Boulevard back toward the city. A light rain had been falling all day, and the old-school wipers mostly marred the view ahead. Cable decided it was a perfect impression of how he was feeling.

At twenty-eight years old, Cable Janson had seen a few things. If he were to ever write up a CV, it would go something like:

Grew up in Lakewood, east of Denver. Played lacrosse and studied martial arts. He eventually became a good student and even played saxophone in a local band named Rottweiler. He worked during the summers as an intern at the History Colorado Center and could speak French and Spanish by the time he was thirteen. Cable received a full ride to Harvard for modern and ancient linguistics and cross-disciplinary studies at the prestigious Radcliffe Institute. Consistently at the top of his class and destined for a high-level academic career.

It was at that point where the CV took a turn. After three years of hard studying, Cable decided to take a semester off. He bought a multi-destination global airline ticket and headed east.

He remembered the ad that had first caught his attention: *24,902 Miles Circumference, 8 Billion People, Over 6,000 Languages, 1,300 Destinations to More Than 190 Countries, One Ticket.*

Cable traveled almost halfway around the globe before deciding the world held more interest and learning than an entire lifetime of college courses. That had been the fork in Cable's path, and that was seven years ago.

Despite globalization's push forward, there were thousands of unique cultures and traditions still flourishing on planet Earth, and Cable was eager to imbibe them. He'd seen a Malagasy tribal warfare dance next to a McDonald's in Nomad, Mauritius, and had attended an Inuit *Quviasukvik*, a New Year celebration that takes place on Christmas Day in Ugashik, Alaska.

Cable had been beaten up in a street brawl in Prague, blessed by a monk in Bhutan, slept next to a camel in the Sahara, robbed twice in Istanbul, and inspired at the summit of Kilimanjaro, and all along the way, he gained many friends and expanded his considerable language skills and cultural knowledge.

Most recently, he and Dani had been kidnapped, thrust into a race for a lost treasure, and thwarted several power-hungry narcissists intent on killing them. It had formed a bond that turned into a meaningful relationship. That was before Dani took a job at a dig site in Ethiopia two months ago, some 8,300 miles away.

Dani stared out at the traffic, not seeing any of it. All she wanted to do was hide away for a few days to recharge. Now, here in the car with Cable, she felt an enormous pressure. She could tell he wanted to pick back up right where they left off, but her plate seemed both full and empty at the same time. She was left feeling unsure what she wanted.

Cable was a marvelous person, unlike anyone she had ever met. His grounded sensibilities and his sharp intellect made him a rare find. He was not caught up in the surface world like so many other Gen Zs she knew. Cable was a man who knew what he wanted—unfortunately, holding down a nine-to-five was not one of those things. Dating the man of her dreams was the most exciting thing she had ever done, but soon, reality would kick in, and what kind of future would they have together? Travel the world living off the kindness of strangers? That sounded fun…for about a month.

Dani let the confusing thoughts fade. Right now, she had to focus on her, then she could ask the hard questions.

They drove across the city to Lakewood, making small talk. The classic Porsche pulled up to a well-maintained three-story red-brick home with three fireplaces and a gabled roof.

The sun was low on the horizon, and the cloud cover made everything prematurely dark. Cable hauled Dani's bags inside and hit the lights.

He set her luggage down in the kitchen and reached for Dani's hands, holding them gently. "Are you okay?"

She looked down for a beat and then eyed Cable. "Sorry, I have been in a funk for a few days."

"Perfectly understandable. Look, you're home now. Just take my room and unplug for a few days. I'm here if you need…anything."

Dani gave a short nod. "Thanks." She gave Cable a hug that lasted almost long enough, then turned for the stairs.

Cable watched her walk away with a furrowed brow. Dani was one of the most amazing women he had ever met. She was intelligent, strong, and confident, with just the right amount of fun mixed in. Her exotic good looks and wonderfully curved body had captivated him since the first time they met. He let his eyes and imagination linger on her backside just a bit.

A soft knock on the front door slayed his growing fantasy.

Dani switched direction, opening the door before Cable could completely recover.

"Hello?" An older man wearing a wide-brimmed hat and raincoat was standing on the porch.

"Hi?" Dani let her greeting hang in the air as she absorbed the sight of him.

He removed his hat, revealing gray, swooped-back hair. Her presence seemed to startle him for just a second before he made a visible effort to recover his composure. "You must be Dr. Dani Tran? The anthropologist who helped find the Beite Amharic."

"Ah, yes, but I'm an archaeologist," she replied.

"That's right, my apologies. My name is—"

Cable interrupted before he could continue. "His name is Tam McGree from Suna Oil, and he wants us to find the origin of an artifact in his possession."

"Suna Petroleum, and yes, I do. Please, call me Tam. I came to plead one more time for your help, with my hat in hand as it were. I'm afraid I might have come off a bit too strong when we first met."

Dani looked between Tam and Cable. "Yeah, that'll do it." She gave Cable a smirk. "Please, do come in."

"But…" Cable glared at her.

"I brought this as a peace offering." Tam handed Cable a college-era Kodachrome photograph of his mother, father, and Tam. They were all smiling with goofy expressions.

Cable stared at the picture. They all seemed so happy. He tried letting his vision of the past and its skeletons go, but a single happy photograph would hardly do the trick.

Dani showed Tam to the living room and gestured to a chair.

He paused at the collection that was displayed on the left wall and put his glasses on to give it a better look. "Very eclectic collection."

"It's more of a family history than a specific era or culture," Cable said, a bit defensively. He was still somewhat upset that Dani had let this man into his home.

Tam turned and took a seat. "Well, that is the best type of collection. Our personal connection to the past is a small window into our future."

Cable tried not to roll his eyes.

Dani gave Cable a sharp, darting glance.

"Thank you for hearing me out. I'm afraid I was a bit overzealous with thoughts of August's son working with me."

"You knew Cable's father?" Dani asked.

"Yes, very well." Tam began to lay out his request once more, the artifact, its history, and what story it might hold. Only this time, he focused on Dani.

From blackness came a familiar fuzziness that was hesitant to leave. As the man's vision slowly cleared with time and a few blinks, his view transformed into an ant's perspective. A faded and worn jute floor stretched out to infinity. A popcorn ceiling covered in three decades of stains hovered far above. His brain was sluggish, and making sense of his surroundings seemed arduous. With time and effort, he eventually sat up with a liquid wobble, the floor's woven pattern etched into his cheek. The sound of broken glass was the first thing he recognized, followed by a dull pain in his hand. Blood wept from a fresh slice on his palm. He wiped off the excess on his dingy pants and looked down, realizing he had sat up in broken glass. Instinctively, the man reached for the largest chunk with the label still intact. SangSom rum. The recollections of bad liquor, regrets, and even sorrow tussled to the surface.

He put his good hand on his forehead, willing the pounding and memories to stop. It didn't work. A foreign reflection in the room's full-length mirror grabbed his attention, and he jerked back reflexively. The unfamiliar stooped creature glared with bloodshot eyes, dirty clothes, a pitiful beard, and a drawn face covered with dried mystery puke. An involuntary injured hand pulled through the matted hair, leaving a thin trail of blood behind.

Jon Chibi was a thirty-three-year-old former captain in Japan's Ground Self-Defense Force or Special Forces Group. A former fiancé to the lovely and very connected Akari Tanaka and a former good guy. Now Jon was living at the bottle's bottom in a rented room in Patpong, the seedy part of Bangkok, where few foreigners ever ventured.

A shell of his former self and a mere shadow of a human, Jon had chosen this location as his final destination.

His mind slowly spun with the events that had brought him here. Events Jon would never forget. Yuzhno-Kurilsk.

The word filled his head with the past.

Crouched behind a small stone wall, Jon adjusted his throat mic. "This is Alpha Actual. I'm in position." He then took a quick peek over the wall and ducked back down. Two armed guards roamed this side of a large stone home some thirty yards away. The structure looked just like in the briefing, a wood-and-stone two-story building with a traditional *kirizuma*, a blue-tile gabled roof. Small windows glowed in the moonless night, with little landscaping lights dotting the yard and pathways.

"Two tangos with weapons. West side," he added.

A quick reply followed over the radio. "Alpha Three, I got one tango east side, also armed."

The other members of his team checked in as Jon pressed his back to the cold stone and let his mind wander.

It had been a long time coming, but finally, the last of the Aum Shinrikyo doomsday cult was in his sights. The cult was responsible for the deadly Tokyo subway and Matsumoto sarin attacks. The death toll had taken thirteen innocents, including Jon's father. It had gutted the Chibi family and flipped everything that was important to a young college grad on its ear. The attack was largely responsible for Jon's current career path.

The leaders responsible for the original attacks had finally been executed after a long-drawn-out legal battle.

Jon had followed closely as the cult splintered and eventually reformed under a new name, Hikari no Wa. Different name, same game. The problem was they had all but disappeared, not the terror they promoted but their base of operations.

It had taken authorities years to locate and gather enough evidence against the group to activate Captain Jon Chibi and his Special Forces squad. They specialized in domestic terror and organized crime and had a reputation that made even the Yakuza take note.

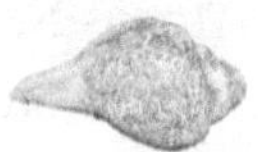

Kunashir Island, part of the Kuril Island chain that reaches from Japan's northern island of Hokkaido, continuing upward toward the Kamchatka peninsula, had long been in a territorial dispute between Russia and Japan. Russia had recently placed hi-tech weapons and stationed soldiers on several of the islands, despite Japan's protests. Near-deadly flyovers from both sides only raised tensions, and politics between the two countries came to a complete standstill.

Yuzhno-Kurilsk, with a population of just under ten thousand, was Kunashir Island's largest city. The people were mostly self-sufficient and lived their day-to-day lives despite the unrest that hovered over them. The island was a tranquil land with a deadly ticking clock.

The squad had arrived in the cover of darkness along the empty beach north of the small town in two RHIB fast-attack boats. It was a quick march up and around the sleepy seaside township to the target property on the west side.

The Hikari no Wa had cleverly reestablished themselves in this neutral zone of sorts. It provided close access to mainland Japan and protection from the aggressive Russians, who encouraged their actions against the imperial status quo. With a haven from which to operate, the group had grown and ramped up its operations. A planned coordinated attack on the Kyushu Railway Company was mere days away.

Jon was well aware of his mission parameters and the importance of stealth. They were to get in and collect up the group's leaders, then get out without alerting the locals or the island's Russian babysitters.

For Jon, taking down the Hikari no Wa terror group would be the end of a long, emotional trail that had garnered many sleepless nights and a growing angst that he held on to with both hands. Right now, he could feel those hands tightening just thinking about it.

"Alpha Actual, I say again, do you copy?"

Jon shook away his distracting trip down memory lane and refocused. "Good copy, in position. All teams, sound off."

Each team leader responded that they were in position and ready. Alpha Two was to his left, and Alphas Seven and Five were on the right. Jon gave them a nod and waited for a return.

"This is Alpha One, go, go, go," he said over the radio, lowering the Gen 2 Night Vision with an integrated gas mask over his face. He raised his suppressed Howa Type 20, took aim, and fired two controlled bursts into the man on the right. He then shifted his weapon left, but the soldier next to him had already dispatched the other guard.

Almost immediately, the lights in the home were extinguished, and unsuppressed gunfire from inside returned.

Jon dove back behind the stone wall as rock fragments splayed through the air. The soldier next to him was not as lucky. His head rocked back suddenly, leaving a twitching body in the grass.

Jon scrambled to Alpha Seven, but there was nothing he could do. "Seven's down."

He and his team had no illusions as to what they might be up against. Radicalized followers who were willing to die for the cause.

A breathless voice cracked across the comms. "This is Alpha Four, heavy resistance on the south side. Soldiers… They look Russian."

What the Special Forces Group wasn't expecting was heavily armed Russian soldiers protecting the compound.

"Gas 'em," Jon ordered. Immediately, several gas canisters were fired through the home's windows. Jon watched as gray smoke filled the building, and the shooting became erratic. The CR gas was a recent development in Japan for non-lethal applications. It was much more effective than standard military CN tear gas and required a class III or higher gas mask to prevent exposure, as the active particulate was microscopic. It was also more effective at incapacitating the opposition.

"Going in," Jon called across the radio as he hurdled the stone wall and sprinted for the house. Bullets sprayed in his direction, and Jon returned fire as he moved. Alpha Five, to his right, let out a 'humph' and fell. Alpha Two, next to him, paused to help. Muted screams could be heard inside the building as the gas did its job.

"Stay on mission," Jon yelled back as his body slammed against the wall of the structure. He pulled a flash bang and tossed it into the window to his right, then ducked back. A bright flash followed, and a concussive blast blew out the remaining shards of glass in the window frame. Alpha Two dove into the house, and Jon followed close behind.

Inside the home, his night vision struggled to see through the smoke. He was in a kitchen complete with a large table and steel kamado oven. A barrel flash from the right was returned by both Jon and Alpha Two. The shooter collapsed, and Jon continued forward, clearing the room. "Clear."

He paused to inspect the downed man—six, maybe six-two, athletic build, with black tactical gear. An AK-12 lay next to the body. Jon rolled him over. A lifeless face stared back through the smoke, definitely Russian. Jon dropped a swear word and stood back up. "Be advised this is Alpha One. We have Russian soldiers on the scene."

Alpha Two looked anxious. "What do you wanna do, boss?"

Behind his gas mask, Jon made a frown and a decision. "This is One, change of plans. No witnesses. I say again, no witnesses." He waited for the other teams to respond and then prepped to clear the next room.

A sudden concussive blast tore the house from its foundation, sending blue roof tiles as high as three hundred meters. It was not the sort of explosion you see in the movies with the big orange fireball but rather, a building was standing one second, and the next, it was a scattered kaleidoscope of toothpicks and pebbles.

Before Jon could follow Alpha Two into the next room, a table unceremoniously flung in his direction, picked him up, and knocked him out into the yard, smashing him hard into the grass. It took several minutes for Jon to collect his wits and catch his breath. He slid out from under the battered table. His hearing was gone, and he stumbled erratically.

The other side of the table was covered in embedded shards. It had saved his life. He glanced back at the home. There was nothing left. Shredded bits of rubble mixed with human remains. The arm of one of his men lay in the grass next to him. Jon leaned over and retched.

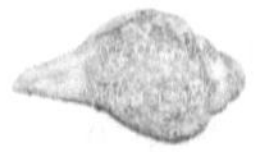

Tears blurred the musty apartment as Jon looked around desperately, finally finding an unfinished bottle lying sideways on the ratty rattan coffee table. He reached for the neck and pulled it back to his wanting lips. A couple of deep chugs preceded a short wait as the drug worked its magic. *Let the dulling begin.*

Tears began to fall as thoughts of his lost team threatened to overwhelm him—brave fighters who were connected on a level few could imagine. The all-too-familiar anger returned. The politics and cover-up that followed in his mission's wake. It was sickening.

Japan didn't have the balls to face Russia, and Russia was too busy fighting a losing battle with its neighbors to act against Japan. 'A terrible training exercise accident.' He told that lie to every family on his squad. *Why had he lived when the rest had died?* It left an unhealable wound.

Jon left the service shortly after and bounced between a few private contractor jobs. The focus they required helped distract him, and he always did his best, but survivor's guilt wormed its way deeper and deeper.

Frantic eyes searched the room, landing on the one thing he had yet to pawn. A ceremonial Tanto, or short sword, given to him by his commanding officer for valiant and brave actions in the face of the enemy. To Jon, the sword represented impotence and loss, but today, it held freedom and release.

Fingers probed past the moldering fast-food containers and gripped the hilt, pulling the sword toward him. He slid the blade from the sheath and held it up to his face. A sad reflection bounced off the pristinely polished surface. Brown eyes filled with guilt looked away as hands gripped the sword and slowly turned the blade to his midsection. It would all be over soon. No more pain, shame, or regrets. No more, anything. Just a proud warrior doing his duty to his ancestors.

Seppuku, or ritual suicide, originated with Japan's ancient samurai warrior class. It had long been a voluntary action to restore honor once lost. Jon would atone for his actions and join his brothers.

A buzzing to his left broke his meager focus as he placed the tip of the sword on his abdomen. It seemed to increase his head's pounding, and Jon closed his eyes, willing the sound to stop. His phone's battery should have long since died, but like an alarm clock, only action would deter the incessant buzzing. He pressed against an invisible force that seemed to hold his sword at bay. *Buzz.* A drop of blood from the tip of the sword ran down his stomach. Sweat popped out across his entire body. *Buzz.* He tried again to push the blade into his torso, but it wouldn't budge. *Buzz.*

Jon cracked an eye to the sound. *Buzz.* Then opened both. *Buzz.*

Finally, he lowered the Tanto and reached for his phone.

"What?"

A familiar voice. "You busy?"

"I was in the middle of something, yes."

"Well, drop what you are doing. I have a gig." The phone went dead as its last speck of power hit zero.

Jon tossed the cell phone across the room and looked back at the sword lying loosely in his other hand. Then his eyes moved to the nearly empty bottle on the floor.

Omari Ur was still upset. His forced removal from Mona Helal's office did not sit well with him. He let his mind wander with the many ways he could retaliate for her injustice. As Egypt's Minister of Housing, he could practically shut her down.

He adjusted his shirtsleeves by pulling and rotating each one, a tic he was unaware of. He quickly crossed the intersection at Abdulaziz Al Saud and Mohammed Farid Wagadi, a plan forming in his mind.

Omari cut through an alleyway that dropped him at one of the many ferry terminals along the eastern side of the Nile. Traffic this time of day was horrendous, and the ferry, though old-school, cut fifty minutes off his commute back to the capital. Time he would put to good use planning his next steps. The forty-foot blue-and-white boat pulled to the dock, and a line of soon-to-be passengers waited as it unloaded. It was an open-bow concept filled with bench seats. A striped canvas canopy was held up with a pipe rail system, obscuring the sun. In the bow sat a small, enclosed helm for the captain and the controls.

Omari watched as an aged woman with two chickens struggled down the ramp. He had no empathy for the sight. The old had no place in his modern world.

At fifty-two, Omari knew his strengths and weaknesses. He was not a handsome man. A large nose and ears framed small black eyes, all topped with a receding hairline. This had only partially contributed to his single status. From a young age, Omari learned that love was always better paid for—no strings or attachments.

Politics was his game, and Omari played better than most. He had maneuvered himself into a prominent position in the government with a combination of luck, timing, and smarts. A position that allowed him to make a significant income through the Egyptian bribery network. If you wanted permission to build anything in Cairo, Omari Ur was the man to see. He could get things done.

He stepped to the back of the boat and took a small bench seat in the rear. This would give him some privacy to think, as all the other passengers would have their backs to him on the other benches facing forward. He watched with mild curiosity as a short, round man with a cowboy hat moved his way, eventually taking the seat next to him. Omari slid over a few inches to make room, hiding his annoyance. The familiar sound of a cheap Bic lighter clicked, followed by an obvious inhale. A second glance found that the man's face matched his body shape, round. He had no hair anywhere, including eyebrows and lashes. *Alopecia,* Omari surmised. His bright yellow tunic was as blinding as his seemingly ever-present white smile, as the man exhaled a blue cloud of smoke that drifted on the wind.

Omari let a soft, frustrated sigh out as the boat jerked slightly, beginning the return trip to the other side of the Nile. Conversations sprang up around the boat as they pushed against the strong current, heading for the western terminal.

Omari closed his eyes and let his brain clear. He would get back to his office and cancel Mona's building permit for starters. Then, he would work out a plan to destroy Mona and her company. He had many important friends who would love nothing more than to watch the shrew burn.

That would be a stern reminder to her who truly held the power in this country. *With no ability to build new construction, let's see how fast her business crumbles. She'll come begging to me, and it will be my turn to throw her out on the street.* No uppity, power-hungry woman would push him around. He let the thoughts simmer. For the first time since leaving Mona's office, the corners of Omari's mouth curled up.

Omari had spent most of his youth playing soccer in the streets of Cairo. He had a good head for math and a personality that melded well with others. His non-threatening looks matched a cool, calculating confidence that helped him get ahead. After graduating from Ain Shams University, he leveraged his way into politics, and after twenty years of doing others' bidding, he finally got his chance to call the shots. The president himself had nominated Omari to the Egyptian Ministry of Housing. It was a posting that held both prestige and power. Omari filled the role perfectly. If he played his cards right, a cabinet position was very possible.

With his anger subsiding, Omari slowly opened his eyes. They were almost halfway across the river. A casual glance to the left revealed several Nile crocodiles drifting past. It always amazed him how these primeval creatures found a way to survive, no matter what civilization threw at them. The prehistoric-looking reptiles seemed well-versed in adapting and overcoming man's modernization.

A sudden prick of pain hit Omari's neck, and he slapped at it. He rubbed his neck and looked for the bug that had bitten him, but there was nothing. Something had definitely bitten him. The strange man sitting next to Omari was watching him with that unwavering smile and cold, soulless eyes. *What just happened?*

"Did you just poke me?" Omari accused the man.

The man nodded back with excitement. No apology was given.

Omari, being much larger, reached out to grab him. "Who do you think you—"

His arms suddenly felt heavy, and they never made it to their intended target. Omari's head spun with disorientation. His face filled with confusion as the little man inched closer, speaking softly. "I have given you a cocktail of Adenosine and a few other special ingredients. Your heart is now beating irregularly and rapidly slowing."

Omari tried to look at the man's face, but his head lolled back.

"Now, it won't stop completely, but the beats per minute will practically put you in a coma." He chuckled at his words.

Every muscle in Omar's command seemed to take enormous concentration and effort just to nudge them. It was like he was swimming in wet cement. His senses were working fine. He could feel his heart slowly bucking like a broken teeter-totter.

The man leaned closer and whispered in Omari's ear. "Compliments of Mona Helal."

If Omari's eyes could shoot up, they would have. The old she-devil had outplayed him. *How could she have known his intentions?*

He watched helplessly as the small man took out his phone and snapped a few shots.

"Smile. Oh, not in the mood, I see… Pity." The man then hooked Omari's legs and levered him up and over the back of the railing. The small splash was hidden by the churning water from the propellers.

Omari tried to yell out, but he had no energy for it. It was all he could do to hold his breath and keep his eyes open. The ferry moved away, and he was swept downriver, all the while that insidious man in the cowboy hat just sat smiling and watching. He even let out a little wave.

No one on the ferry turned around to see what had happened. For the passengers, it was just another uneventful river crossing.

Omari took another lungful of air. He was using his filled lungs to just keep his mouth and nose above water. Hopefully, someone would spot him and pull him from this liquid hell.

The first bump came from behind, but Omari couldn't turn to see what it was. The second one came from below, and it included teeth. A jolt of pain around his ankle. Omari was jerked under the water and then released. Panic surged as he very slowly floated back to the surface, unable to kick or swim in any capacity. Eventually, he breached, gasping for new air. Omari took a large breath to refill his lungs when suddenly, an intense pressure around his middle forced the air from him.

The crocodile locked onto its meal and pulled down. It began its death roll, designed to incapacitate and drown its prey. The meat was soft, and it was only a few moments before its prey was ripped in two. The crocodile stopped spinning and opened its jaws to reacquire the top half of its meal. With the attack complete, it was now time for a well-earned dinner.

CHAPTER FOUR

H E HAD CONSUMED NEARLY HALF a bottle of aspirin, washing it all down with the last of his rum. The dark Aviators did little to hide the blinding sun from Jon Chibi's bloodshot eyes as he ventured out of his apartment for the first time in a week. His stomach swirled with bile and acid, forcing what little concentration he had control over to be focused on keeping everything in there, down. Following his recharged smartphone's directions, Jon wobbled his way to a small streetside café in the heart of Patpong.

A small, red metal table with two plastic chairs, just clear of the oncoming traffic, opened up. Jon sat with an uncontrolled plop. His elbows found the corroding surface of the table, propping him up. Hands supported his heavy head as he tried to catch his breath from the exertion of just getting there.

The sounds of an active city pounded in his ears as locals and tourists migrated in a chaotic ballet with no end to the first act in sight. Rotting vegetables, burnt diesel, and day-old fish mixed with the oppressive heat and humidity. Soon, Jon's pits were dripping.

Unaware of the bouncing action his right foot was engaged in, he tried and failed to focus his mind on the upcoming meet. His surroundings blurred past with an unearthly lean to the left.

"I've seen worse," a voice directed his way commented, "...in the morgue."

Jon didn't bother to look up as an American ex-pat named Marshal, with long hair and broad shoulders, took the seat across from him. He had the last hint of a military bearing that was losing its edge to the comforts of city life. His beard was a mix of brown and gray, and the concern on his face was palpable. "Two Thai teas," the man ordered in perfect Thai to a short woman in all black as she passed, holding a plate of food for another customer.

It took a moment, but eventually, Jon lifted his head, making a face like he had just bitten into a lemon.

Kind, empathetic eyes stared back, no judgment or malice evident. "When's the last time you ate?"

No answer was returned.

"Never mind, it's none of my business." Marshal continued as if speaking for both of them. "Oh, speaking of business, I have a job for you… 'Thanks, Marshal. I could use a little work right now to distract me from my pathetic existence as a man way too focused on the past and not on my future.'"

Jon managed to lift his middle finger.

"Well, Jon, you are welcome. Happy to help."

"You always were a *gesu jarō*," Jon mumbled.

"Don't bring that Japanese tone on me. I'm the one trying to help you. Though, for the life of me, I don't know why," Marshal retorted.

"It's because I saved your life."

Marshal slowly nodded. "Yeah, a couple of times. And now, I'm trying to save yours."

Jon looked up. "Thanks, Marshal."

"You sure you're up for work? It is a bit of a milk run, but the last thing they need is a security man with a death wish." Marshal gave Jon a hard stare, waiting for an answer.

Jon stared back and decided it was time to come clean. "No, but right now, I need this."

Marshal considered the words, trying to decide. Eventually, he let out a breath he was holding. "Here are the particulars." He slid an envelope over to Jon, then gave him one more cursory glance, pursing his lips. "Hope your passport is current. Call me when you are done. We'll find a safe way to celebrate."

The Thai teas arrived at the table, and Marshal leaned back in his chair, taking a tentative sip. His friend was hurting, and apparently, right now, there was nothing he could do for him except provide a distraction. So, a distraction it would be. He let out a slow sigh, placed a 100 baht note on the table, and left. "See you around, Commander."

Jon watched as Marshal melded into a throng of passersby. He pulled the envelope closer and took his time opening it with shaky fingers. There was an airline ticket, address, and phone number, along with $10,000 US dollars. That would buy a lot of rum… He pushed the reflexive thought away and refocused. The address was not familiar to Jon, but apparently, he was going to America.

The first thing she removed after stepping into the large entry were her shoes. Mona Helal loved the feel of cool marble against her bare feet. She padded toward the open design kitchen and took a right at a tall, carved door. She stepped inside, letting the door auto close. The room was small compared to the rest of the house, but its design was unique and purposeful. A domed ceiling was supported by hand-carved granite columns stretching to the floor. Straight ahead on the wall was a realistic oil painting of a woman who looked much like an older Mona. To the side were several glass shelves that supported a collection of Middle Eastern artifacts covering several centuries.

Mona stepped up to the portrait and stared for a moment. The weight of the day seemed to drain from Mona's body, and soon, a look of consternation was replaced with a rare smile.

"Thank you, Mother."

Every day was a gift, given by her mother's sacrifice, and that made it imperative that Mona thank her as she pushed herself further. Up and up.

The serene moment was interrupted by a buzzing in her pocket. Mona slowly opened the phone and said nothing.

"I am here."

"Good. Let yourself in. I'm in my sanctuary."

The short man with the cowboy hat entered the room a few seconds later. Deniz Laurant removed his hat and ran his fingers across his bald scalp. He instinctively reached for a pack of cigarettes and then thought better of it. His impossibly white teeth flashed as he gathered himself. "I have reached out to Colonel Ayad. It seems that Omari Ur has disappeared." He let the information hang for just a beat. "He was last seen boarding a ferry…then nothing."

"He had outlived his usefulness anyhow. How soon before we have someone to replace him?"

"I mentioned your suggestion, and the Colonel was keen to comply."

"See that he is compensated for his efforts."

"Of course," Deniz said with a growing grin.

Mona looked over to the short, bald man. "Those veneers are ridiculous."

Deniz's smile broadened even more. "You have your quirks, I have mine, and I happen to like my smile. The whiter, the better. You would be surprised how it can disarm even the most guarded person."

"I suppose," Mona accepted. "Deniz, have I ever told you about my mother?"

"I only know that she means very much to you."

Mona stepped up to the portrait. "She set me on a journey. One that is still ongoing. I owe her much, and every day I am not on that journey, I am breaking a promise. A promise that I would gladly kill to keep." She turned back to Deniz and locked him with her steely gaze. "No more delays, understand?"

"Yes, my Sidi."

"Now, why are you here? I hope it's not to gloat over your recent actions."

"Of course not. As always, I am at your service." He waited for Mona to respond with a subtle nod, then continued. "You recall the picture with the symbol you shared with me?"

Mona gestured for Deniz to sit in one of the two baby-blue upholstered chairs in the room. She followed, sitting across from the short man and leaning forward with an expectant look. She recalled giving a copy of her most precious possession to the man three weeks ago with a promise of discretion and a hope for results.

The small picture her mother had given her was all that she had left of her previous family. Mona had tried many times to track down the whereabouts of her mother and the man who owned her, but that quest had been nothing but a dead end. She could clearly remember the day she had left her behind, never to hear or know what happened after that. *Was she still a slave, alive even?* The small black-and-white photo she had been given was etched in her mind. Even the color portrait that hung in this room had been created from the small picture. Mona also remembered the two symbols drawn on the back of the photograph. Symbols she had yet to discover their meaning. Mona paused her thoughts and refocused on Deniz.

"I must admit I have had no luck with the photograph, but I might have a lead on your symbols. In Haifa," he said.

Mona seemed confused. "Israel? We have no business there."

"A professor at the university there specializes in ancient symbology."

Mona's expression suddenly softened. "How soon can you leave?"

"I've been thinking," Dani said as they walked up the path to the stone estate's front door.

"About?" Cable asked.

Dani had used her time alone in bed the night before to consider her situation. She needed a new start, something that utilized her education and passion. She was done appraising family artifacts for Peak Insurance Company. What Tam had laid in her lap seemed to fill the void she was feeling, and every instinct said she should grab this opportunity. How Cable fit in was still a bit foggy, but she hoped that would work itself out.

She decided to voice her intentions. "We should use some of that money we got from our last adventure and start a business together doing this exact sort of thing."

Cable looked at her like she was nuts. He was still not exactly happy she had agreed to work for Tam McGree. "Working for rich people? I'm out."

"No," she said a bit defensively. "Finding and connecting artifacts and relics to their origins. Do you know how many random artifacts and heirlooms have either lost their provenance or are not connected to a culture or their history at all?"

"That's a thing?"

"It's a thing." She could feel the passion in her voice taking over. "Not to mention the oddball and one-off relics like the Dropa stones or the Antikythera."

"I'm more of a day-by-day guy, not really interested in starting a business—"

Undeterred, Dani interrupted. She had an excitement and energy that Cable hadn't seen since she returned from Ethiopia and the dig site. "Think of each job as an adventure into the past and the culture tied to it. You have the culture and language skills, and I have the archaeological and artifact skills."

Cable shifted from one foot to the other.

"We would have to travel, do research, and meet all sorts of people."

"Last time we did that," Cable said, "we almost got ourselves killed."

"That was different. We didn't have much of a say. It turned out to be a trial by fire, and I'd say we made a really good team," Dani said as she pressed the intricately forged doorbell.

Cable waited for more of an explanation.

"Look, if you don't want to do this, I understand, but don't be difficult for difficulty's sake. Think about it."

Cable started to reply, but the front door opened before he could.

Logan Minova stood there, all business. "Good, you're here. I've got you all set up." He turned and headed back into the house.

Cable started to open his mouth again, but Dani stepped inside before he could. Was he never going to get to explain his side and concerns? Apparently not. He followed them through the huge door, closing it behind him.

"Mr. McGree is away on business, but he insisted that I give you anything you need," Logan said, as he walked without looking back. He opened a door and showed them inside. It was a clean, open space with large windows and a long wooden worktable in the center. A few office chairs were in one corner, and sitting in the middle on a small purple velvet cloth was the Phoenician shell.

Dani immediately gravitated toward it.

"The Wi-Fi and password." He handed Cable a small, printed card. "I'm sure I don't have to tell you to handle that with caution," he said to Dani.

"Of course. We'll be very delicate."

Logan watched for a few beats as Cable and Dani got out their computers and began to set up. He quickly grew bored. "Kitchen is fully stocked, help yourselves," he called out as he left the room.

"I still can't believe you talked me into this," Cable groused.

"Look, you don't have to be here. Go. I got this…" Dani stepped over and placed her hand on top of Cable's.

They locked eyes for a moment. Dani was the first to break contact. "I'm not proud of the way I reacted to losing my…" She faltered. "The dig was really important to me. I wasn't just an appraiser making money for someone else. I was doing real science, real archaeology. It felt… I felt *real*…and now this." She pointed to the shell. "This is just as real."

"Dani, you can do whatever you put your mind to. You are amazing…talented…beautiful. You don't need me to start a business."

"I think what I need right now is to find the origin of Mr. McGree's artifact." She looked down and then back up. "I'm sorry. I was a bit of a mess when I got back." She stepped closer. "I've been trying to find my footing again. This job is offering that to me, but I'd prefer not to go it alone. Cable, I need you… I want you." She pulled Cable into an embrace and kissed him.

This was not a family-reunion kiss. This was what Cable had been waiting for. He pulled her close, and they each explored the other's mouth. After a much-needed moment, they separated just a bit, eyes locked on eyes.

"All you had to do was say so," Cable whispered.

"I think I just did."

Cable pulled her back, and this kiss lasted even longer, hands roaming, eyes closed, passion flaring.

After a time, they paused to catch their breath.

"Okay, you got me, but before we go and start a business, let's see how we do on this project first."

"That's fair." Dani's eyes lit up and then took on a devious slant. "I'm more interested in finding out if this table can support the weight of two people."

Cable cocked his head. *Did I hear her right?*

Dani lifted Cable's shirt over his head.

Yes, I did.

"Are you sure?" Dani had been a bit all over the place the last couple of days, and Cable didn't want to take advantage of her instability.

"I'm sure," Dani whispered, looking right into his brown eyes.

"Ah, there is a very good chance Logan could pop in here at any time," Cable said.

"Good. Let's give him something to talk about." Dani ran her finger across a small tattoo over Cable's heart. It was a north star with compass rose made from his mother's ashes. It was a great reminder to Dani what Cable was all about and why she cared so deeply for him. She started unbuttoning Cable's pants, and Cable tossed his shirt in the corner.

There was no stopping them.

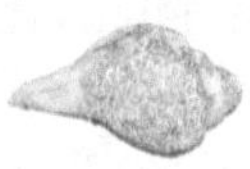

"I'm hungry. Let's see what this stocked kitchen looks like."

Dani looked over at Cable as he pulled up his pants. "We haven't even started working yet."

"Keeping you happy is a lot of work. I'm famished," he said.

"Keeping me happy? I'm the one who practically had to throw myself at you."

"And…it was worth every second."

They shared a silly smile that reminded Cable of the photograph Tam had given him. He threw on his shirt and headed for the door.

Before he could get there, it opened, and Logan stepped in. He looked to Cable. "Everything all right? I thought I heard a disruption."

Dani turned bright red, but Cable didn't miss a beat. He walked past Logan, heading for the door. "It was nothing. Just breaking in the table before we get to work."

"Wait, what?" Logan looked from Cable to Dani for an explanation.

"He's kidding." Dani quickly recovered and followed Cable out the door. "Which way to the kitchen?"

"Um… It's-it's just down the hall…on the left."

Cable whispered to Dani, "Nice disruption."

"Yes, it was."

After a snack of smoked salmon and hummus with some white wine, the two refocused on their task. Dani picked up the shell and began digitizing every symbol with her phone. She then re-created an exact digital replica, slowly rotating it on the screen and checking the original for discrepancies.

Cable began a search for experts on Phoenician culture. He sent emails and partial photos of a few of the symbols from the shell to each. He then tried to source the origin or location of the actual shell itself via several databases.

"It looks like a type of sea snail, but nothing in these databases matches. If I were to guess, it is similar to a Murex Snail but much larger."

"Isn't that the snail the Phoenicians used for making Tyrian purple?" Dani asked.

"Yeah, but we dead-ended at that."

"So much for the easy way," Dani replied.

By mid-afternoon, they had a pretty good sense of their next steps, and all of Cable's apprehension about Dani's previous actions were gone. It was amazing what a little direction and some intimacy could do.

Logan popped in every now and then unexpectedly, but each time, he seemed disappointed that they were busy working.

Cable and Dani shared a secret smile, knowing he'd missed his only chance.

At one point, Dani asked for a 3D printer, and Logan delivered one a short time later.

She went to work loading parameters, and soon the machine was working away, creating an exact plastic duplicate of the shell.

Cable paused from his research. "There are earlier writing systems such as cuneiform, but the first letter system that did not use pictographs is thought to have originated from the Proto-Canaanites."

Dani looked over. "Didn't the Phoenicians adopt this base system?"

"Yeah, and it's not like anything we have experienced in the past." Cable spun his laptop around for Dani to see his screen. There was a grid with a collection of unfamiliar symbols. Some had an English translation next to them, like the letter 'T.' Others had nothing. "It has symbols for some sounds and symbols for some complete words. A few are still not known, according to this article. As sophisticated as the Phoenicians might have been in their time, there are not a lot of examples that have survived."

"They are the basis for the Greek alphabet," Dani added. "I see several familiar symbols."

"That's correct. Phoenicia is credited with the birth of Western Civilization."

The next time Logan entered, she handed him the original shell. "You can put that back in the safe. We have everything we need for now."

Logan stepped over to the 3D-printed shell and picked it up. "Wow, it looks identical."

"It is," Dani replied as she handed the original shell to Logan. He held both shells up and marveled.

"You guys should consider doing this for a living," Logan said as he left to put the original artifact back in the safe.

Dani smirked at Cable. "See, told ya."

He smiled. "You wouldn't need new shoes by chance, would you?"

Dani's eyes narrowed as she looked up at the unusual question.

"I think we are going to Rome."

"Ah, yes. I hear shoe shopping in Rome is a must."

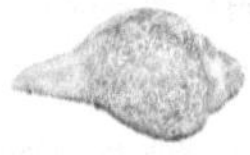

Jon Chibi stepped into the elevator at 1801 California Plaza. He pressed the button for the fiftieth floor and moved to the corner. A young blonde woman pressed a number Jon couldn't see. She positioned herself in the opposite corner, absorbed in something on her smartphone. Jon tried not to stare at her by looking at his blurry reflection in the polished brass walls that lined the lift. His black dress shirt fitted with charcoal slacks and a sports coat framed a dour expression that lately had become a permanent fixture. He shifted from one foot to the other, trying to control his jangling nerves.

The woman's soft brown eyes lifted and looked him over. A small smile escaped her curious face. Apparently, she liked what she saw. Jon tried to smile back, but the grimace he mustered frightened the woman right back onto her phone. He suddenly longed for the peacefulness of an empty room and a sharp blade. The elevator dinged, and he shook the destructive thoughts away.

Suna Petroleum's corporate offices occupied the forty-sixth through fiftieth floors of the modern skyscraper in downtown Denver. The rest of the company was spread out across the globe. Gas and oil were a "must have" for every country, requiring at least a modicum of representation for an international conglomerate like Suna.

Tam McGree's office was in the corner of the building, giving a view of the entire southwest of the city. Snow-capped Rocky Mountains and fertile valley plain, now covered with houses.

Jon didn't bother to look at the view or around the spacious office, with its modern appointments. Instead, he kept his eyes locked on the older man in front of him rising from a polished runway of a desk.

"Commander, good of you to make the trip on such short notice," Tam said as he reached his hand out.

Jon returned with a firm handshake. "Jon is fine. I'm in the private sector now."

"Yes, of course. Jon, it is. So, you come highly recommended. I have had some dealings with Marshal in the past." Tam returned to the chair behind his desk as he spoke. "He helped me clean up a few problems with some wells we lease down in Indonesia. A bunch of rice-sucking terrorists tried to…"

Jon stood there, hardly listening to the man yammering on. His mind was suddenly focused on the liquor cabinet prominently displayed on the left wall. His mouth felt dry, and every instinct in his body was screaming for him to deck this old dude and dash for the Dictador 2 Masters

Château d'Arche rum bottle he spied among a collection of many other high-end liquors.

"Well, anyhow, they got what they deserved." Tam paused, realizing Jon was not making eye contact. He glanced in the direction he was looking. "My apologies. Where are my manners? May I offer you a drink?"

"Ah, no, thank you," Jon forced himself to say.

"Oh, okay, then please take a seat. You'll put a crick in my neck staring up at you." Tam gestured to one of two high-back leather chairs across from him and watched as the Japanese man in his mid-thirties moved to the chair. His straight hair was fashionably messed up with several days' growth of a splotchy beard that would never fully fill in. He had strong cheekbones and a proud chin, but his eyes seemed puffy and undisciplined. Not what he was expecting based on Marshal's description.

Jon sat, and his eyes slowly locked on the highly polished wood desk. He reached out a hand and slid it across the wood finish. "This by chance wouldn't be Dalbergia wood."

"Impressive. I was gifted this desk by the president of Venezuela. I helped him out with a few wells in the Maracaibo area. As you may know, Dalbergia sawdust is poisonous, and few people are willing to build with it. This is one of the larger specimens you may ever see."

Jon slowly pulled his hand from the stunning wood. "I used to be a bit of a home woodworker, and I loved to find rare samples of wood and use them in my projects. Your desk is quite magnificent."

"Well, thank you, Jon. You are one of only two people who have ever identified the origin of my desk." Tam let the words settle before continuing. "So, I guess we should get down to business. I am engaged in something a bit out of my power band. You see, I have this family relic, and I have hired a young couple to research it for me. It is something very dear to my family and this company."

Jon seemed confused. "A relic, sir?" In the private sector, he was more adept at carrying a weapon and clearing out trouble in faraway lands or handling security for VIPs.

"Yes, something my father acquired. A good luck charm, as it were." Tam placed both palms on his desk. "Anyway, I need someone to watch over my researchers and keep them safe while they track down its provenance. Unfortunately, they have already left the country, so you will have to play catch up."

Jon picked up on the direction of the conversation. "Watch over them, but first and foremost, protect your interests, as well?"

Tam smiled. He could always count on Marshal to send him the best and brightest. "Precisely. I do not know where their journey will take them, but should it be in a direction that casts a negative light on me or my company, I will need you to…well…"

"Contain it." Jon finished the sentence for him.

Tam just nodded. "See that you take every precaution."

"They will be safe with me, sir, as will your reputation."

"Thank you, Jon. It takes many good deeds to build a good reputation."

"And only one bad deed to lose it," Jon added.

Tam made a pained expression, but it was lost on Jon as he stood up. "I will show myself out."

"My associate Logan Minova has all the details, including bios on my two researchers," Tam said as he leaned over and shook hands with Jon. Before he left the office, Jon's eyes indulged in one last longing scan of the high-end rum.

CHAPTER FIVE

O N TOP OF A RISE known as Mount Carmel, overlooking the port city of Haifa, sat one of the most prestigious places of learning in the world. Founded in 1963, the University of Haifa was known for encouraging higher education for all. It catered to an unusually high mixture of Arab and Israeli students.

Across from the Eshkol Tower was the Hecht Museum of Archaeology and Art, a multi-story block building housing some of the region's finest relics.

Deniz adjusted his cowboy hat as he walked through the open lobby with its artificial light and hard surfaces. He passed two Bronze Age carved alabaster coffins. The translucent stone shimmered in the open display.

Taking the stairs to the right, he followed a hallway to a door with a sign in three languages. The Arabic at the bottom read, *offices*. He removed his cowboy hat, ran his hand across his bald head, and pushed through.

Dr. Adah Hadassa was a short, thin woman with black eyes and light brown hair. Her smile seemed reserved, though her handshake was anything but.

She showed Deniz to her office and sat behind her piled desk. There were papers stacked everywhere, and several artifacts with labels were used to hold them in place. She made no mention of her mess, only sat with a harried humph, looked Deniz in the eye, and asked, "How can I help you?"

"Dr. Hadassa, as you may recall from our phone call, I work for a client who is trying to reconnect with her heritage."

Dr. Hadassa interrupted. "Please call me Adah, and if she is trying to reconnect her heritage, you may have been misinformed. My work here is in Roman and Persian alphabets and symbology, not genealogy. You might try Dr. Yadida over at the Heritage Genealogical College."

"Actually, I was hoping you might be able to shed some light on these." He passed a piece of paper over that had two hand-drawn symbols on it.

Dr. Hadassa pulled some readers from her desk and meticulously placed them on her narrow face. She studied the two drawings for mere seconds before glancing back up at Deniz and removing her glasses. Two upright equilateral triangles were overlapping slightly at the base. Next to that was a lazy *C* with its ends pointing to the sky. "Two deltas and a ship or maybe a cup? What about them?"

"I was hoping you might be able to shed some light as to their origin."

"The delta is the fourth letter in the Greek alphabet, though it has links before that in both Hittite and Phoenician culture." Her old days as a professor at the university kicked in, and she found her groove. "It has been seen in both Mycenean and Norse mythology, as well as linked to the late Babylonian empire. The delta is also used in early math, but that is not in my skill set. These symbols could also depict a place like a mountain with two peaks next to a bowl or lake…maybe a ship." She then turned the paper upside down. "These two reverse deltas are known as nabla. The Phoenician symbol for harp and the upside-down cup could represent a hill or the Ayin symbol for an eye."

Deniz frowned. He didn't like being lectured to, especially by a woman. It reminded him too much of boarding school.

"So, in modern language, it says eye, two harps, or double D cup."

Dr. Hadassa's face flushed. "Well, that's not how it actually works."

"I understand that." Deniz eyed the skinny woman like there might be something more.

She reflexively placed an arm to cover her flat chest. "I'm sorry, these are very common symbols, or letters…or numbers. Honestly, I'm not an expert in the pre-Roman era. I have an acquaintance, however, who might get you closer to an answer. She and I met at a conference last year."

"Can you at least put a rough date on their usage?" Deniz tried flashing her a smile, but it came out more like a grimace.

Dr. Hadassa looked up, calculating in her head. "So, 1000 BCE to, say, the eighth century CE." Her words had an edge to them now.

Deniz's hopeful face dropped slightly. He wanted to reach out and slice the uppity woman's throat and be done with it, but he was being paid to not leave a trail unless necessary, so he quashed the urge.

"I'm sorry I couldn't be of more help, but without more information… Here, give her a call." She let the sentence fade to silence as she passed a name and number to the man who was now giving her the creeps. "Now, if you'll excuse me, I am behind on my paperwork."

"Yes, of course," Deniz said as he reached out and picked up the card before leaving the office.

With the amount of paperwork piled on her desk, Dr. Adah Hadassa would be busy for at least a month.

Deniz twirled his cowboy hat as he retraced his journey through the museum. It was an unconscious practice that had recently developed when his mind was focused far from the present. He had collected the hat off the corpse of a CEO in Damietta a couple of years back. The man had considered himself a flashy oil baron, but in reality, he was just a middleman for the Saudis and Alexandria Petroleum. A competitor from West Bakr Petroleum wanted the contract and had paid Deniz to make the middleman go away. If complete and total confusion could be bottled and sold, Deniz could have tripled his money, based on the look the man had given him as Deniz plunged a knife between his ribs.

Deniz had watched, fascinated, as the man's raised eyebrows slowly dropped, and he melted to the floor. Then something interesting happened—the man's cowboy hat popped off and rolled right to Deniz's feet. Deniz declared it a sign, and that hat was now his signature attire.

As he pushed through the exit doors of the museum, he pulled out a cheap lighter, rolling a flame to life. A quick inhale and the tip of a cigarette glowed. Deniz held the smoke in his lungs for a moment, getting a full nicotine hit before blowing it into the breeze. He dialed his smartphone and waited.

"What did you find out?" a familiar voice probed.

"Nothing we didn't already know, except one possibility. They might not be letters."

"What are you talking about?" Mona asked.

"Perhaps you have been overthinking this. It might be two mountains next to a lake."

Silence filled the phone for a few seconds. Deniz knew better than to fill the dead space. Clients with objectives would sooner or later tell you what they really wanted. So, he just kept walking in the warm sunshine.

"So, where to next?"

Deniz looked down at the card in his hand. The address was for a museum in Rome. "I'll text you the details." The phone clicked off before he could finish.

Rome. The word painted a picture of food, fashion, old-world architecture, and mythology all wrapped up in a modern metropolis. A place where any given block could contain first-century ruins, next to sixteenth-century Gothic columns, beside modern steel and glass. Dani, however, was just grateful for the small wall air conditioner that rattled a soulless tune behind her as she watched with fascination as Oriani Gioelli went through many adjustments until her three pairs of new shoes were a perfect fit. Gioelli was known to the locals as the friendly shoemaker. He had treated Dani and Cable like family, and his attention to detail showed in everything he made.

Cable had taken the time to get his well-worn walking boots resoled.

Dani had indulged herself. She stepped from the small shop with three shopping bags in tow and a smile that slowly faded as the furnace-like air hit.

Central Italy was experiencing a late fall heat wave. The normally crowded streets were relatively quiet, as the temperature maintained a constant 100 degrees.

They crossed the street, dodging a moped in a hurry. "Don't look at me like that. One of these pairs is quite practical," she said, holding up a bag. "Besides, I'm having fun playing your average tourist."

Cable shot Dani a patronizing glance as they turned at the piazza. "You could never be an average tourist," he said, taking in the view.

Dani took Cable's hand as they walked. It felt right. "I'll take that as a compliment." Her face brightened even more.

Cable couldn't take his eyes off her.

Dani's shiny black hair was loosely curled and framed her face perfectly. But it was her eyes that captivated him the most. Black pools that somehow seemed to draw you in…captivate you. They were all-consuming, with intelligence burning in them, making it seem like they could sense any hidden truth. She was a remarkable woman—smart, funny, and with just enough drive. She was the most interesting and captivating person he had ever met.

He closed his eyes for just a beat. If only this moment would last.

She turned to Cable. "Okay, I got my new shoes, so now we can go get your soup-ly or however you say it."

Cable dismissed his inner thoughts, forcing himself to be present. "*Supplì*, and it's an Italian street food with roots going back over 150 years."

"I'm not eating a 150-year-old root."

"Funny. You'll love it." Cable grinned at her playful banter.

"Aren't you the guy who ate fried camel spiders on one of your trips across the Sahara?"

"They taste a lot like lobster."

"I'll pass."

Cable hailed a cab that took them southeast to the San Giovanni district. Dani exited the cab with a small amount of apprehension. Cable had been fifty-fifty on the foods he'd introduced Dani to. One time, he had convinced her to try crickets at a famous Mexican restaurant. That had been a total bust, as was the *casu martzu*, or larvae-infested sheep cheese. Truth be told, Dani was more of a burger-and-a-beer kinda girl.

The air here smelled of poorly burned diesel and freshly baked bread as they passed row after row of small shops and cafés lining the narrow streets. A whiff of espresso hit her nostrils and then faded. A small shop with a line out the door proudly displayed a sign above, *Casa del Supplì*. They waited in line until Cable finally ordered four Supplì Classico, *fagottini al prosciutto cotto e mozzarella*.

A few moments later, four oblong balls the size of bull testicles arrived. Cable handed Dani several napkins. "You will need these."

Dani curiously watched as Cable took a bite. Melted mozzarella stretched like old-fashioned telephone wire between Cable's lips and his food. Inside the rice croquette was a ragù sauce with prosciutto ham. Cable seemed to forget his surroundings as the explosion of flavors hit his taste buds.

Dani followed suit, quickly losing herself in the marvelous flavors. "OMG."

They ate standing up, just outside the café, not a word spoken between them.

Their next stop was an appointment with the assistant curator, Arrius Florin, at the Villa Giulia, or Museo Nazionale Etrusco, Rome's national museum. It had an entire section dedicated to Etruscan and Phoenician culture.

It was two minutes till three when Cable and Dani clicked across the marble floor of the museum's lobby. They followed an impossibly tall, thin man in a sweater and pressed jeans, his Roman nose seeming to lead the way. They passed an octagon-shaped staircase leading to the second floor.

The centuries-old, large U-shaped building was a museum in itself. Cable and Dani let their eyes scan each and every display as they walked. Originally built for Pope Julius III, the Roman Gothic structure's interior was updated with modern wood and stone. The trio moved past a group of tourists gawking at an exquisite life-sized clay exhibit, the Sarcophagus of the Spouses, in a large glass enclosure. The couple was still in a tender embrace that had endured since 520 BCE. Hundreds of artifacts filled hallways and walls. Copper, bronze, gold, wood, pottery, and stone. Anything that could last the ravages of time and a looter's grasp.

Their guide pushed through a door with an Italian sign.

Cable leaned to Dani. "*Solo personale autorizzato*, Authorized personnel," he whispered.

They moved down an all-white hallway and out a back door. The small piazza surrounding the ancient building was well maintained, with a collection of tables and chairs along the left. On the far side of the open square were two armed museum guards standing on either side of a metal door.

As they crossed the open space, Cable noticed two construction workers up above to the right. They were repairing the cracked masonry along the roofline.

A rapid exchange of Italian between the guide and the guards pulled Cable's attention back. The guards did a quick pat-down and then gestured for them to pass.

Cable stepped into the room. It was dark, except for two pinpoint LED flood lights mounted on a green box that moved robotically in the middle of the room. It hummed and snapped above what looked like a gold tablet lying on a specialized surface of the machine. The room had a strong odor of ozone, with a faded hint of disinfectant.

The guide cleared his throat as an introduction. From the shadows came a plain-looking woman in her mid-thirties with violet hair and a small digital tablet in her hand. Her eyes scanned Dani and then Cable as she removed her white cotton gloves. "You were friends with Dr. Hilary Lavigne?"

Cable felt a jolt of electricity blast through him at the mention of the name. He had developed strong feelings for Hilary on a dig off the coast of Kuwait City a few years back, but he had also watched helplessly as she was murdered. The guilt of that experience still haunted him.

"Yes, I was… I'm Cable Janson, and this is Dr. Dani Tran."

"Dani will do. Pleased to meet you."

"Dr. Arrius Florin, but please, call me Arri." She glanced at the tall man trying to follow the English conversation. "Thanks, Collum. I got this," Arri said in Italian.

The tall guide gathered himself and left.

"Hilary and I were classmates at the Sorbonne in Paris. She was an amazing person… Such a loss. That is, in part, why I work here in the museum, much safer than a foreign dig site."

A moment of silence followed.

"Is that a Core+ inspection camera?" Dani asked.

"Yes, it is. Are you familiar with it?"

"I had a chance to use one at Stanford." Dani moved closer to the green robot-looking arm with a box on the end of it. That's when she noticed the artifact the Core+ was inspecting. She spun to look back at Arri. "The Pyrgi Tablets?" she said almost reverently.

"What's that?" Cable asked.

Arri gave a quick explanation. "They're 2,500-year-old gold tablets with brief texts from two dead languages."

Dani added, "Kinda like the Rosetta Stone only for Phoenician and Etruscan."

"Amazing," he said as he moved in for a closer look. The bright gold sheet was covered with symbols etched into the soft metal. It had old, ragged holes in the corners, where it was probably nailed to a wall at some point.

Arri pressed a tab on her tablet, and the Core+ stopped. She then flicked on the lights.

Cable blinked back the glare, taking in the room. It was a small laboratory/workshop with shelving and worktables. Everything was very white and very clean.

"Yes, every ten years or so, technology advances enough that we take the time to reinspect certain artifacts that might have more of a story to tell," Arri said.

Dani added, "Its hyperaccurate inspection of 3D objects can tell us so much more than a picture can. Hesitation marks and micro grains left behind, maybe even some old DNA if the original cleaning didn't destroy it."

"Yes, I'm afraid I'll be in this room for the next month. That's also why there is security outside. These offices are not protected like the rest of the museum." Arri paused after her comment, remembering why she had visitors. "Now, I believe you have something for me?"

"Oh, right." Cable took off his backpack and removed the bubble-wrapped seashell. He placed it on a side table and unwrapped it.

"May I?" Arri said, gesturing to the artifact.

"Of course," Dani replied.

Arri held up the shell and inspected it.

Dani and Cable watched as her expression soured.

"What is this? Plastic?"

Dani stepped forward. "Oh, sorry, it's a facsimile of the original."

It took just a second for Arri to realize Dani's words. "Oh, got it. For a moment there, I thought you two were some kind of scammers... A 3D model makes perfect sense. Keep the original safe and travel with a duplicate." She flipped the flashlight feature on her tablet and took a closer look at the myriad of inscriptions on the shell.

"Are you able to read it?" Cable asked after a few minutes had passed.

"Most of it. You were right. It is Phoenician, but a few of these symbols I am not familiar with. They might represent a family crest or maybe directions." She pulled up a chair and sat down, seemingly lost in the shell's message.

After a time, she began to write down symbols in order.

Dani watched, as a few moments later, English equivalents followed. "Boaz?"

"That has no meaning to me," Cable said.

"I think I have heard this word before," Arri said, standing up and trying to remember. "We'll have to go back to my office. If that doesn't work, an old colleague of mine is probably the most well-versed person I know on this subject. I was think—"

Just then, the door opened, stopping Arri mid-sentence. Two men stepped into the room.

Arri was about to object when she realized they were both wearing clear plastic masks that distorted their features, and one of them was holding a pistol.

The man with the gun spoke Italian with a strange accent. "My name is Tobias. Do as you are told, and you just might survive this."

Cable translated for Dani.

Arri went as white as a ghost and started to tremble. "Wh-where are the guards?" she said feebly.

"Keep talking, and you can join them," Tobias replied.

Cable took Arri's arm and pulled her behind him, shielding her.

"Now. Back up and sit on the floor with your legs crossed. Preferably in that order."

As Tobias contained and controlled the room's occupants, the other man went straight to the scanning table. He grabbed the gold tablet and then looked around for the others—nothing.

Arri wanted to protest, but words failed her.

"Where are the other two tablets?" Tobias demanded.

Arri couldn't help herself. Her eyes flittered to the drawers along the left wall.

"Check those drawers," Tobias said to his partner.

A few moments later, he found the other two tablets and began packing them up.

"Okay, lie down on your stomachs. Feet together. Hands behind your back." The partner then zip-tied everyone's hands and feet.

Tobias suddenly took an interest in the shell lying on the side table. "This looks interesting." He grabbed it and started to leave, then stopped suddenly, turning back. "If anyone comes out of that door in the next ten minutes, they will get a bullet for their trouble. Understand?"

No reply.

"I will need an affirmative answer from each of you, just like emergency row passengers on the airlines." He smiled at his cleverness.

The pistol pointed first to Cable, who returned, "Yes."

Dani quickly caught on to Cable's response, as the gun moved to her. "Yes."

"Y-yes," Arri stammered, her eyes shutting tight, as the pistol moved her way.

"Excellent. You have been wonderful hosts."

The lights suddenly went out, and the door opened and closed.

Cable craned his neck back. He could just make out the thin, light line at the bottom of the door. "They're gone."

"*Dio mio!*" Arri exclaimed, trying to catch her breath. The whole experience had been nerve-racking. She had almost died, and one of the museum's prized possessions was gone, all on her watch. Her emotions threatened to consume her.

Cable rolled over to a table and used the edge of the metal leg to pop his zip ties. After rubbing his wrists back to life, he felt his way over to the wall and turned on the lights. He then quickly found a pair of scissors and freed the two women.

As he headed for the door, Arri cried out, "Not yet. It's only been like five minutes."

"Arri, it will be okay. They are long gone, and the sooner we get some help, the sooner the police might be able to catch those guys. Did you notice? His Italian had a Greek accent."

"No. I was too scared… Sorry," Arri replied.

As Cable reached for the door, it suddenly swung open. A man in khaki cargo pants and a green Henley rushed in. He was ruggedly handsome with genuine concern on his scruffy face. "Are you okay?"

"Yeah," Cable replied, carefully.

"Cable. I'm Jon. Outside, I need your help." The Asian man said the words like he was used to giving orders and dashed back outside before Cable could protest.

Cable followed.

Jon was kneeling over one of the guards, assessing his injuries. It took Cable just a beat to see what had happened. Two split-open bags of cement lay on the ground. Both guards were covered in cement dust and unmoving. Someone had dropped the heavy bags from above and obliterated both guards. Standing a few feet away and speaking rapid-fire Italian into his phone was the tall guide who had led them here… *Collum.*

Cable quickly knelt next to the other guard and checked for a pulse. It was thready, but the man was still alive. He brushed off the cement dust that covered the man's face and leaned him up. "I've got a pulse."

"Same here," Jon replied.

"The Carabinieri are on their way," Collum said as he twitched nervously, his eyes unable to focus.

"Thanks," Cable replied before looking at the new man. "Who exactly are you, Jon, and how do you know my name?"

Before Jon could reply, two museum guards sprinted across the piazza. When they saw their fellow guards lying motionless on the ground, they started screaming and pulled their pistols, pointing them with menace.

Just then, Arri and Dani exited the door.

Chaos ruled for a brief time, as the two armed guards couldn't decide who to point their guns at. The girls' hands shot up, and Arri rattled back in Italian, trying to defuse the situation.

Eventually, the guards lowered their weapons.

Ambulances took the guards to the hospital, and a captain in the Carabinieri, the state police in charge of museum theft, spent the next three hours debriefing everyone.

By the time they were released, it was dark.

Jon convinced Cable and Dani to go to dinner and share a few bottles of wine to decompress. He had promised to explain everything.

Arri recommended a café just over the nearby Tiber River, Ristorante Cacio e Pepe, a family-owned traditional Roman trattoria with a casual dining experience and first-rate pasta. A circular table by the window was just opening, and they all sat with a feeling of relief.

They started by ordering two bottles of Frascati, a local white wine that remained a favorite of the locals.

Dani swirled the wine in her glass and inhaled the aroma, savoring the bouquet for just a second before downing her glass in one large gulp.

Cable refilled her glass, feeling like doing the same thing, but there was a stranger at the table, and he wanted answers. He waited for the waiter to depart before demanding to know what was going on. "So, you owe us an explanation. Who are you, and why are you here?"

"My name is Jon Chibi. I am a logistics officer hired by Tam McGree to help support your search."

"What?" Dani was right in the middle of taking another swallow of her wine.

Cable's eyes narrowed for just a breath. "You mean you are here to babysit us and make sure nothing blows back on Suna Petroleum."

"You're very perceptive. That is part of my job, but I am here to help protect you, as well, and I am excellent at what I do."

"Logistics officer? We're not in the military," Dani said with concern on her face.

"No, but until we know what is waiting for us out there, it is better to play it safe. Especially after what just happened. As I understand it, you two had some real trouble last time you ventured out into the—"

Dani had heard enough. She jumped in. "Ventured? I was kidnapped."

"Like I said, trouble. I'm here to prevent that from happening again. Just let me handle all the transportation and security, and you two focus on the science. If we all work together, we can complete this mission and do it safely."

"Mission?" Cable rolled his eyes.

"We're perfectly capable of taking care of ourselves," Dani countered.

"I know. I read your files. Your recent exploits in Ethiopia were impressive. But when it comes to bullets versus artifacts, bullets tend to win."

Cable realized the man was right. He had seen that firsthand and had no desire to do it again. "Your accent… Southern Japan?"

"Impressive. I grew up in Okinawa. Learned my English from the soldiers' children stationed at Camp Hansen… We played a lot of soccer together."

"I see."

"I take it we don't have a say in the matter?" Dani said, slightly calmer, but still clearly unamused.

"I've been hired by the man who hired you, so until he says otherwise, you now have a colleague."

Dani took another guzzle of wine.

"And I have other skills that might come in handy if you happen to run into another piece of business like today," Jon added.

Cable turned to Dani. "Dani, I don't think it's a bad idea to have someone watching our backs. We both know the birthplace of Phoenicia is Syria, and if we must go there, it's not a safe place for Americans right now."

Dani slowly nodded. Cable was right. She had no interest in getting shot at again. "Fine, but stay out of our way." She gave Jon a less-than-friendly look. "We do the research, and you do whatever it is you do. We may be stuck with you, but neither of us has to like it. I'm going to go back to work and pretend like you're not even here."

"Okay by me," Jon said. His head was pounding after all the back-and-forth. He needed to find some more aspirin, but what he really wanted was a drink of their wine.

Dani took out her phone and emailed the images of the skull to Arri. Now that Arri's current project was in the wind, she might need a distraction, and Dani made sure her text encouraged her to indulge in just that.

Cable glanced at Jon. He noticed his wineglass was upside down. "You're not drinking?"

"Not currently," he replied cryptically.

CHAPTER SIX

ARRI FINISHED ANOTHER SHOT OF grappa. Her nerves were still jingling, but the high-octane liquor was doing its job to numb them. After the Carabinieri finished with her, she spent another two hours being drilled and ridiculed by her boss. At one point, she exploded in his face, screaming about the useless guards who were the ones supposed to prevent this sort of thing from happening…not her. She had stormed out of his office and straight home to her apartment in Prati, just East of Vatican City.

Unsure if she still had a job and filled with adrenaline, she found her couch just as the tears flooded. Heavy sobs racked her body as she finally let her emotions loose. After a time, the crying faded, and she was feeling good enough to reach for her next remedy. Shaky hands poured the first shot, and she downed it in one swig. The fiery liquid seemed to course through her body, so she poured a second.

Arri had had an idyllic childhood. She grew up in a countryside estate just outside Cortina. Her summers were filled with hiking and mountain biking and her winters skiing. She was fearless. At age six, she was downhilling a single track and lost control. She crashed her bike into a tree, puncturing a lung and breaking several bones, including her spine. As she lay there wondering if anyone would find her before she died, Arri had been overwhelmed with a single thought: *The world is a dangerous place. It can take you at any time.* She spent three months in traction. The doctors were certain she would walk with a limp for the rest of her life.

During that time, she fell in love with reading. Any book, any topic, that would keep her from the reoccurring visions and nightmares of the crash that constantly haunted her. She found herself escaping more and more into the safety of her books. By the time she was thirteen, she was well-read but no longer an outgoing, adventurous spirit.

Her father had played soccer for Lille and was always busy managing his finances. Some days, he was happy, others, a royal grouch. Arri's mother was the main force in her life. An educated woman, she pushed Arri to expand her knowledge. Even though she eventually was able to walk without a limp, she shied away from anything too physical. The fear inside her grew, sometimes taking control and leaving her helpless. Over time, Arri found herself with few friends and few life experiences. She was happy just studying, reading, and staying home.

In college, her mother tried to influence her daughter's path even more. At nineteen, Arri had had enough. She picked up a part-time job, found a roommate, and left home for good.

Her roommate worked hard to get Arri out of her bubble and encouraged her to have a life. For a time, it was working. That is until the roommate met a German boy. One night, she packed her things and never returned. Arri quickly fell back into her safe routine.

Come graduation with a doctorate and honors, Arri's parents showed up, hat in hand. It was awkward at first, but slowly, both parties calmed, and a conversation started, then weekly phone calls. Now, after nearly ten years of living on her own in the city, Arri missed the simpler life of her childhood…her family. She planned monthly visits back home to sample the good old days and recharge.

Right now, she could go for some good old days, but before she could pour a third shot, her phone beeped.

Arri dug through her pockets and found her smartphone. The message was not her termination notice, as expected, but several pictures of the seashell the two Americans had brought her before all hell broke loose.

A short text followed. *In case you need a distraction.*

After all that had happened that day, a small thought blossomed, and she realized it was exactly what she needed. She set the grappa down on the coffee table and moved to her laptop in the kitchen.

Mosaico was a Roman courtyard café adorned with stylish umbrellas and soft lighting. It was the Hotel La Ville's go-to breakfast spot. Cable pulled out a chair for Dani, and they sat at a patinaed copper table near the fountain. The sounds of the city were muted by the thick stone walls surrounding them and the constant trickle of water. The warm morning air was already filling with humidity. Cable took a menu from the waitress. "*Grazie.*"

Dani played with her coffee cup.

"What's up?" Cable asked as he watched her adjust her cup placement on the saucer for the tenth time.

Dani looked up. "Just thinking."

"About us?"

"No," she said, a bit too defensively. "Well, yes…in a way."

"You wanna talk it out?"

"Cable, I don't think we should—"

"Good morning," Jon interrupted with a smile, as he strolled across the black-and-white patterned concrete floor, taking a chair.

"Hey," Dani said, with a flatness that did little to hide her contempt.

"Hope I'm not interrupting."

"No," Cable lied.

A ding pulled Dani to her phone, and after a moment, she looked up. "Well, this is unexpected, but I guess Arri needed a distraction last night." She held up her phone screen for a second. "I got three pages on the symbols from the shell and a brief history to match. She says it's about eighty percent accurate, in her opinion. She goes on to recommend a colleague who can take it to the next level, Professor Lombardo."

Dani looked back at her phone, hitting the highlights. "Boaz expedition around bottom of world. All dead. Treasure of a thousand kings. Rising sun to land's end. A mystical place. Then there is this double delta and a sideways *C* or wide *U*." She paused, still looking at the screen. "There are several of these words with question marks, by the way." She showed Cable the screen.

Jon leaned over to get a look.

Cable looked closely before saying, "The last two might not be letters at all. The overlapping deltas could represent two mountain peaks and the *C* a cup or valley, and what's your guess on Boaz? A name?"

"That's a real possibility," Dani replied.

The waiter approached and took their order. As he walked away, Jon was the first to speak. "Treasure of a thousand kings. I like that part. So, Mr. McGree's shell is a treasure map?"

"That would be a large assumption," Cable said. "Not every treasure map leads to treasure, and not every treasure is what you expect it to be."

Dani added, "One man's treasure is another man's trash. It's often true, especially when you add thirty centuries to the mix."

"I'm not sure that's the saying," Jon added. "I just can't believe you two are not more excited. We have a bona fide treasure map. Treasure of a thousand kings. Which way do we go?" Jon seemed lost in the momentary fantasy of it.

Dani and Cable shared a look. They had been through this before, and the thought of a repeat performance made them both second-guess their purpose here.

Dani decided to clarify their search to Jon. "This is like looking for a single eye of a needle in a haystack full of needles. I wouldn't get your hopes up."

"Come on, guys. We can do this," Jon said, his eyes gleaming with the possibilities.

"Until we get more information on the translation, we would just be spinning in circles," Dani said as she shook her head slightly and looked back at her phone. She pulled up some additional historical information that Arri had included.

"Phoenician records mention Queen Dido sending a Boaz and a small fleet on a quest."

"So, Boaz is a name. Two collaborating sources, that sounds promising," Cable said.

Dani looked up from her phone. "Yeah, you rarely get that with anything pre-BCE."

Their breakfast arrived, and all three hungrily dug in.

After a few spoonfuls of a very fluffy omelet, Dani finished reading the text. "Historically, there is no further mention of them."

"Until now," Jon added, through a mouthful of food.

Cable and Dani could only nod at the thought.

After a moment, Dani glanced back at her phone and read the next part. Arri recommended they visit another expert for a comparison of her translation. That made perfect sense to her. She set the phone down and looked over at Jon. It was time to see if this man lived up to his hype.

"I'll call Logan and see if he can print us up another copy of the shell. I still have the 3D file we used for the first one. Jon, I need you to get Logan an address he can use to send the duplicate. We need to see a man about a horse."

"We need to use the restroom?" Cable asked, suddenly confused.

"No, the man we need to see is Professor Beppe Lombardo, and apparently, he is currently excavating a horse and chariot in Tharros."

"Okay, but I will need more information than that," Jon replied.

"Tharros. We will need accommodations and a way to get there."

"Never heard of it."

"It's on the island of Sardinia about two hundred miles west of us," Cable said. "You'll love the locals and the *Su Porcheddu*."

Dani shared a brief smile with Cable before looking back at her phone. She read the last part of Arri's message. *Good luck. Stay safe, Arri.*

Safe... If only. Maybe Jon Chibi was a good add, after all, she thought.

It was early, really early, as Deniz picked at the lock on the door marked 3C. It was an old-school single deadbolt, maybe from the eighties, and it hadn't been well cared for. He paused to squirt a small stream of lubricant into the mechanism and tried again. This time, a satisfying click rewarded his efforts. Deniz had found that between the hours of two and four in the morning most people, even party people, were either too wasted or in their full REM sleep to cause a problem. It was the perfect time, in his mind, for a home invasion.

He silently stepped inside, pulling the door closed. It was a well-cared-for space with a mix of modern and older furnishings. There were obvious female touches throughout, but mostly, it spoke of a lonely existence.

Deniz refocused on the task ahead. He removed his shoes and padded down the short hallway to a door at the end. He pushed inside. A dim glow from a streetlight outside exposed the sleeping form on the bed. Purple hair splayed across the pillow as the woman took slow, deep breaths. He padded over and sat on the body, pinning the arms. At five-foot-four, he was a short man, but strength came in many sizes. Deniz's muscled legs clamped down on her like a vise.

He was surprised at how long it took for the sleeping woman to wake until he smelled the alcohol on her breath.

Eyes fluttered open in confusion as the inability to move seemed to overwhelm her. It took a few seconds, but eventually, she opened her mouth to scream.

That's when Deniz placed the barrel of his H&K VP9 in her mouth. At that point, her eyes shot open like saucers, and her scream died in her throat.

"Dr. Arrius Florin, I am not here to harm you, but your office said you were taking some sick days, and I didn't have time to wait for you to come back. So, I popped over for a quick Q&A... Understand?"

She didn't.

"Okay, let me start with, I'm going to remove my gun from your mouth, but if you try to call out, I will shoot you in the face. Do you understand now?"

A feeble head nod followed.

"Okay, good." Deniz kept his H&K pointed at her as he slowly removed himself and stood. He tossed a robe that was hanging on the back of the door to the bed. "Put that on, and remember, nothing funny." Deniz watched as the confused woman in her underwear put on her robe.

She had a serious hangover, and just getting her arms in the sleeves seemed like a challenge.

Hopefully, he could get what he needed from her.

Arri's mind was trying to process her situation. It had only been two days since the attack at the museum, and now this. *What was happening?* She slid from the covers and clumsily donned her robe. The world around her seemed to be dipped in molasses. Her brain was pounding, and she couldn't focus on the simplest of tasks. Tears filled her eyes, making everything worse.

The man used his gun to direct her to the kitchen.

"Make us some coffee. It looks like you could use it." Deniz proceeded to put his shoes back on while he watched her every move.

The fear index in Arri's body was banging at an eleven, competing with her high blood alcohol level, and she had a hard time measuring the grounds.

It seemed like hours before the coffee was finally ready. The man at the table seemed unfazed. She poured them each a mug and placed them on the table as she plopped in the chair across from her tormentor. Hands trembled as she took a tentative sip. The hot brown liquid calmed her, slightly.

"Dr. Florin, I have it on good authority that you are an expert in ancient alphabets and symbology. You see, a colleague of yours recommended I speak with you, so here I am."

"A colleague?"

"Yes, Dr. Adah Hadassa." He passed a piece of paper with two hand-drawn symbols on it across the table.

It took Arri a moment before she remembered meeting Dr. Hadassa at a conference in Paris. Arri picked up the paper and stared. Not seeing the symbols. "You could have just called. I would have gladly helped you," she said in a timid voice.

"I'm on a bit of a time crunch." Deniz tapped the barrel of his pistol on the table to get Arri's attention back on track. "What can you tell me about those symbols? And I won't ask again."

Arri forced her mind to focus on the paper. There were two overlapping deltas. Next to a wide-body U.

"Understand that you must consider the source when translating these. I am an expert in the Etruscan era and, to a lesser degree, Phoenician. That slants my response. These look Phoenician to me, though I have not seen overlapping deltas quite like these before."

"I'm losing patience, Doctor. Do you want a mouthful of lead?"

Arri panicked, trying to find something that would appease this monster. "I-I recently came across an artifact with these exact symbols on it." She reached for her laptop.

"Slow down," Deniz warned her as he stood and came around the table to see what she was reaching for.

Arri carefully opened her laptop.

"Enter the password very slowly," Deniz ordered as he watched.

She logged on. Images of the shell popped up on the screen.

"Stop. What is that?" Deniz said, pointing to the screen.

"As I was saying, I recently came across an artifact that contained these exact symbols. Look." She zoomed into a section of the shell. Sure enough, the symbols matched.

"What is this from?" Deniz asked, his excitement almost showing.

"It came from a large seashell with these Phoenician symbols etched around it in black."

"A shell? Where is this shell now?" Deniz demanded, his excitement hardly contained.

"It was taken."

"Taken…by whom?"

"There was a recent robbery at the museum. The shell was taken along with other priceless artifacts."

"Who took the shell?" he insisted.

"You would have to talk to the Carabinieri about that."

"Do you know what it says?"

For the second time in two days, someone had pointed a gun at her. It was weird how familiar the second time around felt. Arri was starting to feel her debilitating fear subside. It allowed her mind to take a step back and assess her situation. This man just wanted answers, and she was in a position to give them. Hopefully, answers would motivate this creep to leave. "Only bits and pieces," she lied. "But there is a colleague of mine in Sardinia, Professor Lombardo, he is an expert on these symbols. I was going to send them to him."

Now, all she had to do was wait for her assailant to leave, and then she would alert the authorities, Cable, Dani, and Dr. Lombardo. After that, Arri was going to go home and visit her parents. She needed to get away from the city.

"I see," Deniz said, as his left hand moved across his chin. "Write down as much as you know, and if you want to see the sunrise tomorrow, don't leave anything out."

Arri carefully drew several of what looked like non sequitur letters in a row on the piece of paper she'd been given: *B z s rch b tt m w rld d th t g r.*

She then went back and filled in the missing vowels, taking her time before writing each one down. It was important to slow down if she was going to sell her message.

"That's it?" Deniz tried reading the words. "Boaz search bottom world all dead."

"Without the professor's help, the rest would be mere conjecture."

"What does that mean?"

"A guess."

"Oh." Deniz stood back from the table and processed his options.

Then, in a flash, he grabbed Arri's hair and slammed her head into the table. He put his H&K against her temple. "If you're lying to me."

"No. Please." Arri's fear came pouring back. Her plan vaporized with the pressure of metal on her skin. She was about to give in and tell this man everything when he suddenly released her.

"Okay, stand up."

She did.

Deniz used his phone to snap a picture of her computer screen.

"I'm going to tie you up and leave you in your bathtub. Tomorrow morning, I will call it in, and you can go back to your life. If you make any trouble or try to get help, I will come back in the night and end you. Understand?"

"Yes," Arri managed.

Deniz guided her to the bathroom. On the left was an older claw-foot bathtub with a hooped shower curtain.

"Step into the tub," he ordered.

Arri leaned over to get into the tub.

Deniz abruptly thrust his whole weight down on her head, impacting it on the edge of the porcelain tub. Arri went limp and dropped to the floor.

Deniz quickly stripped her naked and set her halfway into the tub, face down. He then closed the drain and turned on the water. He splashed a little on the floor as he waited for it to fill. Once there was enough water in the tub, he turned it off and submerged Arri's unconscious head.

It took a moment before she started to revive from the head impact. Her first instinct sucked in a lungful of water.

"There you go, take it all in. It won't be long now," he said with encouragement.

Deniz held tight until Arri's feeble attempts to fight back stopped. He stepped back, surveying his handiwork. A nod of satisfaction preceded his taking a few pictures for the album. Finally, it was time for a ciga-rette. He lit up, savoring the first inhale. Then he grabbed the woman's laptop and stealthily exited the building.

The hand-carved cave turned into a WWII bunker, and now an aging warehouse sat under the highway bridge that crossed above the canal into the city of Karystos. A small cliffside access road wound around an ancient Greek ruin, ending at a turnaround too small for a modern truck. From there, a tall, arched entrance made of weathered wood and double sliding doors led inside. The view of the aquamarine Aegean Sea was breathtaking, and all but ignored by the man who stood outside leaning against his Defender 110, enjoying a Cuban cigar. The blue-gray smoke danced on a gentle breeze as he exhaled. His unbuttoned silk shirt revealed part of an enormous gold Greek Orthodox cross held by a matching heavy chain. Nico Xander was a man of many talents, most of which the Greek government frowned upon. Organized crime was only effective if you were truly organized. Nico's operation was that and more. The problem for Nico was that he had yet to truly hit the big time.

Yes, he had a few million stashed away for a rainy day, but nowhere near the level of the guys running Athens. They were big-time mobsters.

A flat black VW Touareg with a police lightbar on top pulled slowly into the turnaround. The driver's side window lowered, and Nico sauntered over. "Sheriff, how's business?"

The local sheriff looked up at the imposing man. Nico was just under six feet, but he had extremely wide shoulders, and his open shirt revealed a fashionable mob boss's hairy beer belly. He leaned in and smoothed his thick mustache. The handle of a Glock pistol could be seen poking out of the top of his black slacks.

The sheriff glanced over. "Nice and quiet."

"Excellent, let's keep it that way." Nico looked up and scanned the horizon before pulling an envelope out of his back pocket and sliding it into the car.

"Of course." The sheriff took the envelope and tucked it into his uniform. "But don't run any stop signs, just in case." He gave Nico a half-smile.

"I respect the law."

"Hmm… Until next month," the sheriff muttered as he put his car in reverse and backed out along the narrow road.

"Looking forward to it," Nico called out as he watched the car vanish around the turn. He spun and slipped through one of the warehouse's doors.

The cool inside cavern was lit with an overhead row of hanging China hats bolted into the bare rock. Stacks of boxes and rows of shelves filled the space going back into the mountain nearly a hundred yards.

Nico's operation, at its heart, was black-market goods. Those included cigarettes, alcohol, arms, antiquities, and recently, thanks to a new tax, olives. Anything that could turn a profit and keep him off the state police's or Hellenic police's radar.

A few moments later, the door opened and closed, and a man stepped into the light.

"Tobias, my friend." Nico took Tobias in a brief hug, and then they *La Bise*, or cheek kissed, before separating. "Good to see you."

"I noticed the local sheriff was here. Getting his monthly stipend?"

Nico took another slow puff on his cigar, savoring the sweet smoke. "I prefer to keep my friends and enemies close, and money ensures they are one or the other. A man who does not appreciate money has no place in my world." He leaned his hands on an empty processing table in front of him. "So, how was Rome?"

"It was just as I planned. In, out, and no one the wiser. The authorities will be chasing their tails."

"You take unnecessary risks, my friend." Nico took a newspaper and slid it across the table. It was open to a large article with a picture of three golden tablets. Tobias read the title *Daring Museum Raid.* The subtitles held more interest. *Greek national, possibly known as Tobias, wanted for questioning.*

"You have to stop using your name."

"It will not come back on you, boss. I am but one of a hundred thousand Tobiases in southern Europe."

"I would kill you right now if I didn't love you like a brother."

Tobias's instinct was to react negatively to the threat, but he knew that was just how his boss reacted to things that he didn't like.

Before the argument could heat up, the rumbling of a van coming to a stop could be heard outside.

"Ah, right on time," Tobias said, looking at his watch. He opened the door just as a DHL delivery person was getting ready to knock. He signed for the four boxes and returned inside, setting them on the table. "Happy birthday, Nico."

"Four? I thought there were only three." Nico took out a folding knife and cut the tape seam on each box. Three of the boxes were identical, and one was nearly twice as large.

Tobias raised his hands to his sides but said nothing.

Inside the three identical boxes came three identical brown paper-wrapped hardbacks about the size of a coffee-table picture book. The titles were identical. Greek Mythology.

Nico lifted the book. "Heavy reading?"

"The heaviest."

He opened the cover and flipped a few pages to find one of the gold Pyrgi Tablets inside the hollowed-out book. "Marvelous." Nico opened the other two packages, laying all three tablets out on the table. "Marvelous times three. See that it gets repackaged for our buyer."

"Of course. It will happen today."

Nico rubbed his hands together greedily. "Great job, Tobias." He then turned and opened the fourth package. His hand pulled out a strange seashell with black writing all over it. "Interesting." He examined the shell for a moment. "It's plastic?" He set the shell down, suddenly uninterested. "What's the deal here?"

"Hang on, boss." Tobias picked up the shell and turned it over. "Look at this." At the bottom of the shell was a small tab of material. "This is where it was removed from a 3D printer. I believe this is a replica of a genuine artifact."

"So?"

"So, why was it in a museum behind a door with armed guards?"

Nico took the shell from Tobias and looked at it more carefully. "Perhaps the real value is in what it says."

"That was my thought as well," Tobias said, with a growing grin.

"Okay, get it translated. I want to know what we're dealing with here."

CHAPTER SEVEN

THE PRE-ROMAN RUINS OF THARROS were extensive. Stone buildings and streets for hundreds of yards in all directions. Many of the structures were crumbling, and several had bushes growing from them. At first glance, it was a tourist stop that had long ago been excavated and then forgotten. It sat on a thin peninsula on the western side of the island of Sardinia and, at one time, was a thriving city that covered the entire area.

"I present, Tharros, colonized by the Phoenicians around 800 BCE." Dani stepped next to a large number mounted on a post, with her hand outstretched.

The number corresponded with a brochure that came with the cost of admission. The brochure was written in four languages—Italian, German, English, and French—all of which Cable spoke fluently.

The sound of waves crashing on the nearby western shore carried on the sea breeze. Small, white, puffy clouds sailed on a blue sky overhead. A large square surrounded by stone walls poked up through the earth in front of them.

"Seems to have lost some of its splendor since then," Jon said, eyeing the ruins. It looked more like a boulder pile to him.

Cable matched the number to the brochure and read the description. "This used to be a Thopeth."

Cable and Jon looked to Dani for more information.

"An open-air commonplace that was sacred to the Phoenicians."

"Those look like Roman columns over there," Jon said, pointing at two white columns rising above the ruins.

Dani smiled at his interest. "Well done. Corinthian and the Phoenicians may have started this city, but it is layered with many eras over the centuries."

"Come on, the dig site is over that way," Cable said.

As they walked, Cable let Jon move ahead and sidled up next to Dani. He whispered her way, "You never got a chance to finish your thought at breakfast the other day. Whatever it is, I know we can work it out."

"Okay, but can we talk about it later?" Dani said.

"Sure." Cable let her move ahead before continuing. Whatever was bothering Dani, he felt helpless to fix it. Maybe it just needed time. That seemed to solve most of his problems. That, or picking up stakes and moving to the next village.

They walked down a path to a roped-off area. Jon lifted the rope, and they ducked under.

There were three large tarps supported by poles above an excavated area. Several workers down in a pit were focused on a task, while others seemed engrossed in their jobs around the camp.

A young man covered in dust climbed out and brushed himself off. Fine dust carried away in the breeze. "Can I help you?" he asked in Italian.

"I'm Cable Janson, and this is Dr. Tran. We are looking for Professor Beppe Lombardo."

"Ah, the professor. He is in Oristano at the Wild West."

Cable looked confused.

"He has a standing date with a steak there every Monday."

Cable thanked him for the information.

"Incredible."

Both men turned to see Dani looking down at a partially excavated chariot sticking out of the dirt.

The dusty man rattled off some Italian, and Cable translated. "He says it's possibly a ceremonial chariot, once connected to three horses."

Dani smiled as the three left the dig site in search of the Wild West.

"There is something right about getting your hands in the dirt," she said as they got back into the rental car and headed for the small town of Oristano. Jon drove as Cable looked up their destination. "Old Wild West Steak House," he read, as he programmed in directions.

"Not exactly what you would expect from an island off the coast of Italy." Dani laughed.

"Spaghetti Westerns," Cable said. "Back in the sixties and seventies, Italian Westerns became a big deal. Several even made it to the American cinema. They have a certain style and campiness that gave them their name."

"Spaghetti Westerns, huh? Makes sense," Jon said.

The Old Wild West Steak House was an end cap at a modern strip mall. The front of the restaurant had a faux barnwood saloon feel, jutting out from the steel building.

Jon parked the baby-blue Citroën C1, and they all headed for the door.

Inside was a rustic American Old West dream envisioned by an Italian decorator. It took only a moment for Dani to identify Professor Beppe Lombardo, the sole diner in the restaurant.

He looked up as they approached. "Ah, my American friends, please come over and join me," he called out in perfect English while gesturing with a steak knife in his hand. "Sardinia is a small island. Gossip moves here faster than a hungry cheetah."

Quick introductions made the rounds, and they all sat, now using first names.

"Monday is my steak day, and I do everything in my power not to miss it. I'm too old to be eating this heavy late at night, like the locals do, so I make it a late lunch, and I'm good to go for the rest of the day."

A bored waitress came over and passed out menus.

"The Americans and Argentinians have the market cornered on a really good steak. It's the Japanese who have perfected it, but A5 wagyu is not something you find around here."

Dani peered over her menu at the seventy-ish man with a full mop of curly, long gray hair and a Van Dyke beard to match. Small, deep-set eyes were framed with many years of sun damage and a few liver spots. He wore a khaki, long-sleeved shirt that looked threadbare as he unapologetically stuffed another piece of steak in his mouth. She smiled at the thought of spending your whole life digging for answers to the past.

"I recommend the porterhouse medium rare. Oh, and to clear up the confusion on your faces, I taught at Columbia for seven years." He leaned forward and lowered his voice. "I'm afraid I fell in love with American food. Twinkies—now that is something I would kill for. No chance you will find them around here, let alone on the mainland. I think they are banned in Italy…maybe all of Europe."

After a moment, they placed their orders, and Beppe looked up. "So, what can I do for you?"

Cable reached into his backpack and produced the second replica of the Phoenician shell. It had been waiting for them in a FedEx box at the hotel when they arrived the night before.

"Hmm." He tapped the shell. "This is a replica?"

"Yes, the original is back home in a safe," Dani answered.

Beppe nodded his approval. "I heard about the business in Rome, very nasty. I don't know what the world is coming to. Luckily for me, my worries are mostly behind me." He smiled at the thought, then refocused on the shell.

Dani slid over the translation Arri had sent her.

Beppe pulled his smudged glasses out of his shirt pocket and inspected both.

The room seemed extra quiet for a time. Their meals arrived, and everyone dug in. The professor, however, had pushed his plate aside. He was mesmerized by the shell and its markings.

"Most unusual. At first glance, it looks like a Tibetan *dung-dkar* prayer shell, but there is no doubt about it, these are Phoenician symbols." He set down the shell. "Well, I agree with everything Dr. Florin has written here. I am familiar with Queen Dido. This shell might be Boaz's legacy or a very good hoax. Without the original shell to test, I can only guess." He reached out and took another bite of steak. "Give me some more time to study it and come see me tomorrow at one. It's Taco Tuesday. Well, more like Tapas Tuesday. I have convinced a small Spanish café to dabble in the Mexican arts. They can't quite get the tortillas down, but it's as close as you will get on this island."

"Hello?"

"I have good news and great news."

Mona tried to clear her head. Seconds ago, she had been riding a stallion across a vast desert. Now she was in a dark room, under her covers with her head on her pillow. The glow from her smartphone was intense, and she squinted against it. "Deniz?"

"Yes?"

"It's—" Mona looked at her phone's screen and frowned. "It's four a.m."

"I am sorry to have woken you, but I am certain you will want to hear what I have to say."

Mona fluffed a pillow and sat up. "Well then, get on with it. Enough of your posturing."

Deniz cleared his voice. "You told me of a shell covered in writing that your grandfather found?"

"Yes."

"And of how it was stolen, your grandparents killed, and your mother sold into slavery. How she only remembered two of the letters."

Mona reached over and turned on the small lamp next to her bed. "Deniz! Please stop with the ridiculously painful walk through my family's history. I am well aware of the past. If you—"

Deniz blurted out, "I found it."

"W-what? You found what?" Mona stammered.

"The shell. I have found the seashell. It still exists, and the symbols on it are from an ancient language, and two of them match the ones on the paper you gave me."

Silence followed. Mona placed her hand to her mouth. The words seemed impossible to comprehend. It had been a lifetime of searching with no results.

"Hello?" Deniz asked.

"Yes, I'm here. Tell me everything."

Deniz recounted his experiences over the last few days. He decided to leave out the mention of a treasure or the part where the purple-haired woman had a slip-and-fall accident in her bathroom. There was no reason to give the woman more power than she already had over him.

"So, where is the shell now?" Mona asked.

Deniz flicked a cigarette to life, pausing to inhale the pungent smoke. "That's just it. It was stolen from the museum. It's gonna take me some time to find that trail. I do, however, have a picture of the shell and the symbols."

"Send it to me immediately."

"Of course. It should be in your inbox already. I also have a lead as to how to get the letters translated."

Mona opened the screen on her phone. Several pictures of the shell covered in symbols appeared. The second image held the two symbols she had carried with her since childhood. Her family's long-lost legacy was no longer lost. The shell had been carefully described to her by her mother. Her heart seemed to tick up a few beats as a warm sensation filled her body. A promise made to her mother was finally being fulfilled. A rare smile crossed her face. There would be no going back to bed now.

"Deniz, you have done well and will be rewarded accordingly. Follow your lead, and let's see what was written on the shell, but most importantly… I. Want. That. Shell. It belongs to me. My family found it and sacrificed everything for it. I don't care who you have to kill or pay. Just get it back."

Deniz stomped out his cigarette. "Yes, my Sidi."

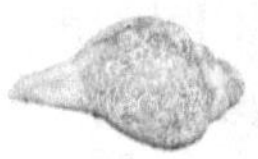

The phone rang for the…he'd lost count today and answered it before checking the caller ID, which would have said *unknown*. "Detective Rossi." The up-and-coming detective in the Carabinieri financial crimes division was sitting at his desk with his boots up.

A voice that sounded like gravel pouring from a bucket spoke. "Detective, I'm calling on behalf of a mutual friend of ours, Don."

The unexpected call made Rossi pull his feet from the desk and suddenly sit straight. He yanked off his glasses and replied. "I'm sorry, I think you have the wrong extension. Can I get your number, and I'll have him get right back to you."

Rossi quickly wrote the number down and hung up. He then stealthily pulled a burner phone out of his bottom desk drawer and left the Rome Police Headquarters. Stepping outside the melon-yellow concrete and glass four-story building, he dialed the number and tossed the paper he had written it on. The gravelly voice returned to his ear after just two rings.

"Can you talk?"

"Yes," he replied.

"I have a job for you."

Rossi just listened. That was his job and a big part of why he had risen so fast in the ranks. Do what you are told and don't get caught doing it. A simple mantra learned firsthand as he watched his training officer beaten to death in front of him for not following it.

Sweat started to bead on his forehead as he listened to his orders.

"That's not a case I have access to."

The reply was not kind.

"Yes, sir."

More directions followed.

"I will do it," Rossi said, as the conversation ended with an abrupt click.

Just then, a thin man in well-worn clothes stepped up to him. "Detective Rossi. This is for you." He handed Rossi a small package and walked away.

Rossi hefted the package. It felt empty. He stashed the burner in his pocket and returned to the building. Once back at his metal desk, he opened the package. Inside was a smartphone memory stick about the size of a fingernail. A small note said: *Turn on the phone. Plug this in. Ship.* There was an address at the bottom.

Rossi put both items in his pocket and left his desk for the fourth floor.

The detective area, covering major crimes and the recent death of one Dr. Arrius Florin, was busy on a recent murder near Vatican City.

He stepped to the evidence board and found a small section relating to his newest assignment. Reading down to the bottom, he found the word *accidental*, and it was circled. This case was closing or already closed, and no one would be the wiser that there might have been foul play. That was good.

"Rossi. What brings you up here?" a large sergeant walking into the bullpen called out.

Rossi nearly jumped before he forced himself to calm down.

"I'm checking up on case B230816. I-I have a friend who was close to the deceased," he lied.

"Oh yeah, real shame. First, she gets robbed at the museum and then does a swan dive into the edge of her tub. They say bad luck comes in threes. She didn't make it that far."

"That's a shame," Rossi parroted.

"Body's been released, and her personal effects have already shipped."

"To her parents?"

"Ah, let me take a look." He moved some files around until he found what he was looking for. "Yep, Mr. and Mrs. Florin. They're up in mountain country."

"Thanks, I'll let her know."

"Hey, when you gonna stop playing around at financial crimes and come work with us in major crimes?"

"I don't like the sight of blood, but that's what I love about you, Sergeant, always looking out for others."

"Get outta here."

Rossi drove north along the A27 out of Venice. The weekend traffic was unusually light, and the first signs of winter speckled the landscape with snowy patches. The Italian Alps were a natural barrier to Austria, known as the Dolomites or Pale Mountains. The small tourist town of Cortina, home of the 1956 Olympics, was nestled at the top of Valle del Boite, surrounded by large, craggy peaks. The Florins lived on a small farm along the Campo di Sopa, a one-and-a-half-lane road southeast of town. The quaint butter-yellow stucco-over-brick structure was two stories tall with small, brown-framed windows and a flat roof. Built in the late 1800s, the family had done a good job of maintaining and modernizing the structure without losing its original charm.

Detective Rossi stepped from his car and focused his mind on his next task. After a couple of knocks and a badge flash, he was ushered into the living room. It was a mix of antiques and modern comfort, with limited sunlight due to the small windows.

Rossi hit all the high points. *Sorry for your loss, just following up, wanna make sure we didn't miss anything, etc.*

The couple seemed truly sad at the loss of their only child and hung on his every word.

"I wonder, if it wouldn't be too much trouble, could I have a look at her cell phone?"

Mrs. Florin gave him a curious expression.

"If there was any foul play, and I mean *if*, there might be evidence of it on her phone. Since the investigating detective ruled it an accident, they simply had Tech unlock the phone and do a cursory check. In order for me to sign off on their findings, I need to do a deeper dive, but they shipped everything here before I had a chance."

This seemed to do the trick, and Rossi's banging heart slowed a bit as Mr. Florin carried an open box over.

Rossi looked through the few pieces of evidence inside. A wallet, a phone, and a gold necklace. He inspected the necklace briefly. It was a simple heart on a chain.

"I gave that to her when she graduated," Mr. Florin said, as tears formed in his eyes. "She was a simple and smart little girl. Had her head on straight. I always thought…" The words failed him, as sobs and tears, not for the first time, flowed. Mrs. Florin soon joined him, creating a somber background tune as Rossi powered up the phone.

A low battery warning flashed as he covertly slipped the memory stick into the bottom of the phone.

He let the grieving couple continue, doing his best to portray empathetic eyes.

After a few moments of pretending to look carefully at the phone, he pulled out the memory stick, powered down the phone, and returned it to the box.

"There is nothing here that looks suspicious. Again, I'm so sorry for your loss."

Rossi let himself out and quickly drove to the nearest mail service center. As the memory card, packed and ready to be shipped, left his hand, he could feel his nerves calming. How he was going to keep doing this on a regular basis was beyond him, but that was a worry for another day.

Time for a big lunch and a long drive home, he thought.

After dispatching the woman from the museum, Deniz left Italy behind and flew to Tangier, a port city in northern Morocco. It was never a good idea to linger in an area after killing someone.

Having spent a good portion of his childhood on the streets of Tangier, he knew how to blend in and even get away, should it be required.

He tossed the butt of his cigarette out the window of the taxi. The smell of spices from a passing market brought back thoughts of his youth. It was not far from these exact Moroccan streets that Deniz had suffered and cried many nights as a child. As an unusually short child with alopecia, Deniz had been the target of bullying and downright hostile abuse. He was the go-to kid in school. If you have a problem, take it out on Deniz.

He had tried to run, but his short legs made him too slow. He had tried to fight, but as soon as the fight went to the ground, he was outweighed and soon thoroughly pummeled. He tried going to teachers, but nothing was ever done. Finally, Deniz found a solution—hide. He would hide for lunch, hide for recess, and hide after school until it was safe to leave. The maintenance basement became his haven, a place to not be seen or heard. Deniz could peer out the small ground-level windows from behind the plumbing pipes and watch the other children till it was safe to come out.

Home wasn't much better. His strong-willed father ruled the house with an iron fist. His disappointment at how Deniz had turned out was often shared with both Deniz and his mother. The emotional and often physical abuse was like a thick fog in the house, heavy and constant.

One day, while Deniz sat on an old box crate eating his lunch, the janitor came into the room unexpectedly. Deniz jumped up, readying himself to flee.

"Relax, I'm just looking for a spanner."

Deniz slowly lowered himself back to the crate and continued eating, both eyes tracking the invader.

"I've been watching you," the old man said.

A shot of fear coursed through Deniz, freezing him in place.

"Hiding down here, afraid of the other kids. I've seen it before." The janitor stopped looking for the spanner and turned back to Deniz. "You seem like a bright kid to me."

Deniz watched as the old man grabbed a box and took a seat next to him.

"What is your name, son?"

"Deniz." He squeaked out his name.

"I'm Toraz."

Deniz already knew that. Almost every kid knew the name of the old janitor who roamed the halls and classrooms.

"The Leopard of Juybar."

Deniz looked at the man with confusion.

"Reza Yazdani, an Iranian-born wrestler. He was known as the Leopard of Juybar. At only five-foot-four, he conquered many challengers, all of them much taller. He took gold in over eight major tournaments, including several World Championships."

Deniz stopped eating.

"He was truly magnificent, and do you know what his secret was?"

Deniz shook his head.

"He was very short, so first of all, they underestimated him. He used his height against them. Leverage. It can topple even the tallest of challengers."

"Leverage?"

"Yes. You will learn about it in science. Your brain and your determination dictate where you end up. Not your height, not others', understand?"

Deniz nodded, his enthusiasm showing.

"What goes on in school is but a moment in your life, but what goes on in here," he pointed to his head, "lasts a lifetime."

Deniz looked up, making eye contact.

Toraz continued, "What you *can* do and what you *will* do is up to you."

The words echoed in Deniz's head long after the bell rang.

The first chance Deniz got, he went to the library and looked up the Leopard of Juybar. Sure enough, the very short wrestler had done all those things.

Deniz started to look at himself differently. What people did and said around and about him lost all power. He would be destined for greatness, and greatness had no barriers.

After finishing school, he made his way out of North Africa and headed east into Egypt, where he could disappear into the masses. Living on the streets was no picnic, but Deniz eventually found a path for his skills and aptitude as a fixer for several clients. His background, combined with his low moral code, was exactly what a desperate CEO or politician needed. No job was too difficult or too illegal.

The squeaky brakes on the taxi pulled him back to the present, as his cab stopped in front of an older concrete apartment complex. Deniz quickly paid the fare and headed up to his room.

He sat down and scratched an errant itch on the crown of his hairless head. This flat was one of three safe houses he maintained in northern Africa. It was off the beaten path in the small suburb of Malabata. From his window, he could see a football stadium across the street that looked more like a dirt field with lines. He double-checked the functionality of the two security cameras that would alert him before someone got too close. The battered Formica tabletop matched the small counter that held a chipped sink, a new one-cup coffeemaker, and a stained hot plate. There was nothing else he needed for a kitchen.

On the other wall was an old tube-type TV with a local news show on channel 2M TV. The signal was filled with static, which Deniz quickly tuned out. He slid a panel off the back of a battered bookcase to reveal a small hidey hole behind it. There were several stacks of euros, two alternate passports, a few weapons, and two small PE9 packs with timing detonators. It was the South African version of C4 plastic explosive. His first instinct was to grab the H&K and three loaded mags. Flying on public airlines these days didn't allow for weapons of any kind, and he always felt vulnerable, especially after his recent exploits. He felt a calm surround him as he slipped the pistol into his waistband. Next, he grabbed one of the explosives before resealing his hidden stash.

Deniz opened Arri's laptop and powered it up, connecting it to Wi-Fi. This was the first chance he had to really dig into the museum employee's files. After looking more carefully at the pictures of the shell, he browsed through her iMessages. The last one caught his eye. It was a more thorough translation of the symbols on the shell. Had the woman deceived him? He was certain she had told him all she knew. Maybe she was trying to protect someone. The translation was sent to a Dr. D. Tran. *Hmm.* He forwarded everything to his phone. He would send the contents to Mona, but not right away. It would be good for her to think he was working hard on her behalf. Three more days, at least.

Deniz read the translation: "Boaz, leader expedition around bottom of world. All dead. Treasure of a thousand kings. Rising sun to land's end. A mystical place. Then a double delta and a sideways *C* or wide *U*." He compared that to the original message Arri had given him. It contained half the information.

She had lied. Deniz considered himself a very good judge of human behavior. He had felt sorry for the lonely woman and her existence and made quick work of his interrogation. He had made a mistake. Something he would not do again. Luckily, the truth had still come out.

Next, he dug into her contacts and pulled up Dr. D. Tran, the recipient of the text. Only a phone number appeared, with a note at the bottom: Cable Janson.

He did a quick Google search. There were some fifty Dr. D. Trans. Most had some social presence online, but there was nothing that caught his eye. He tried the same search again with Cable Janson. This showed fewer results, but again, nothing obviously connected to the shell.

He tried a combination of Tran and Janson together. This produced three articles about a trio finding a lost temple in Ethiopia. The third person was a man named Kojo. He zoomed in on a picture in the article. Kojo and Dr. Dani Tran were standing inside a natural cavern temple, smiling. Restoration operations were going on behind them.

"Gotcha," Deniz mumbled to himself.

A fourth article popped up. It was all about a flash flood that destroyed the renovation efforts of the temple by the Ethiopian Government. It clearly showed the man in charge, Marcus Bemnet from the Ethiopian Ministry of Culture, and his sad demise. Now, he just needed some leverage.

Deniz looked up the country code for Ethiopia, 251, and started dialing.

CHAPTER EIGHT

TACO TUESDAY WAS EXACTLY AS described. Tapas with a Mexican flavor. That's not to say it wasn't good. It was excellent, and even the salsa had a nice kick to it.

Cable cooled his mouth off with cold Peroni Nastro. The café was tiny, with four small tables. A rotund woman in her sixties watched with a smile as the four patrons gobbled up her latest attempt at Mexican food.

Dani looked up as Professor Beppe Lombardo set his fork down and cleared his throat.

"I am satisfied that the symbols on your shell are real. They tell a story that is quite remarkable. In 570 BCE, Pharaoh Necho commissioned the Phoenicians to circumnavigate Africa in hopes of opening it up for trade. Queen Dido of Ancient Carthage, in turn, assigned one of her best military captains to the task."

"Boaz?" Cable guessed.

"Right. In fact, there is a brief mention of Boaz in an Egyptian scroll dated the same time. We also know that Boaz and his fleet sailed west from Carthage and then turned south along the coast of Africa, based on a record found from Queen Dido's court. That is the last they were ever mentioned, as far as we currently know. Your shell tells us that Boaz ran into trouble, *all dead*." He slid out several sheets of printed paper. There were re-creations of both Ancient Carthage and the unique design of

Phoenician warships. One page held Bappe's translation, and he pointed to the section he was referring to.

"But someone left the shell behind as a marker. They found some type of *treasure in a mystical place*." He pointed to that section now. "If you put on your Phoenician hat as you think about that, it could be many things and/or places."

"What about *the rising sun to land's end*?" Dani asked.

"Your guess is as good as mine."

"Travel east, *the rising sun*, to where the *land ends*," Cable said.

Bappe pulled out another page. It was an outline of Africa. He drew his finger counterclockwise around the continent. "So, to travel east, you have to get to at least here, agreed?"

All three nodded as the professor's finger moved south and then east, as the upside-down bell-shaped landform curved back.

"But this is not land's end. You have to travel south again. And now you reach the bottom and start to head east once more. Is this land's end?" He continued up the other side until it started to widen again. "And now you are heading in a mostly eastern direction. Is this land's end? The fact is, if you zoom in on the continent, there are hundreds of places where land juts out and then abruptly cuts back the other way. Is one of those land's end?"

Jon couldn't hide his disappointment.

"As you can see, we don't have enough information to even guess with twenty-five percent accuracy," the professor summarized.

Dani had been anticipating this dead end. The odds of really finding the answer to a centuries-old question were always slim.

"That is all we can gather from the words. These two symbols here," he said as he pointed to the connected deltas and the sideways *C*, "are not words, so I'm guessing they are your next clue."

"We were thinking they might refer to a geologic formation," Jon said, trying to be helpful.

"That is a very good possibility," Bappe said. "The real question is where to start looking."

The silence that followed lasted too long for Jon. "So?" he prompted.

"So," Bappe said, "you need to make a trip to Ancient Carthage in hopes of finding out more. That is the only play I see from here."

"Shoot, I forgot to bring the time machine," Jon said, with a heaping of cynicism.

Dani felt like they had gone as far as they could. "Well, we are certainly grateful for your help, Professor Lombardo. This was a hopeless case without your and Arri's help."

"Yes, well, how is Arri? We haven't spoken for nearly a year. Is she still with Museo Nazioale Etrusco?"

Dani and Cable relayed their experience with Arri, unaware of her demise.

"This is our second 3D copy of the shell. They took the other one," Jon pointed out.

"Oh, dear. I'm glad you are all okay. Please send her my love."

"I'll be sure to tell her. I promised to keep her updated on our progress," Dani said, echoing the sentiment.

Jon showed his thanks by using Tam McGree's credit card to pay for the meal.

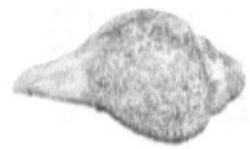

Tobias watched as the memory stick of Arri's cloned cell phone downloaded to the new burner phone in his hand. Now, it would work and act just like the original. He waited for it to update from the cloud, populating with apps and contacts. He checked the voicemails. Whoever owned this phone was not much of a socialite. Tobias had spent several hours formulating a plan to fulfill his boss's wishes. Find out about the shell.

In some ways, he had brought it on himself. If he had just tossed the plastic artifact instead of inspecting it, he wouldn't be where he was now. He had first reached out to several Greek historians with no luck as to what the symbols were. Then an idea, born of desperation, struck. If the girl in the museum was investigating the shell, maybe she knew something about it. That's when his real brilliance paid off. Tobias reached out to a man he had done previous business with. A man very well connected in Italy, bent nose and everything. The connection led him to one of the mob-controlled detectives in Rome, and the rest was straight out of the gangster 101 playbook.

He had purchased his ticket to return to Rome, but soon after researching her address, he found her obituary. Rome now appeared to be a bust. As her phone's data loaded back up on the clone, nothing of value appeared in the call log or voicemails. This girl was a real loner.

Tobias was never happy with dead ends, and he banged his hand on the table before leaning back in his chair. He placed his hands behind his head and spun slowly, thinking. His mind drifted back to an earlier time.

Tobias was Albanian born with a long history of violence. His grandparents had fought in the Greek Civil War for the Provisional Democratic Government in 1949. His parents inherited their anti-establishment zeal and participated in several skirmishes against the Greek ruling class. Tobias's grandfather was killed in the battle of Athens, during which the ruling class left the country seeking refuge in Egypt. His father seemed to lose his passion for the fight and shrank back into running his uncle's pharmacy. A small rectangular shop in a quaint northern town.

Tobias had seen the fire in his parents and wanted to pick up the torch and carry on, if for nothing else than to avenge his grandfather.

His father, however, had other plans. At age thirteen, Tobias was sent off to a strict boarding school where his energies could be channeled and refocused. It worked for a time. Tobias had quickly risen to the top of his class, but school learning soon lost its charm, and Tobias snuck out one night for good.

He bounced around from town to town for a time until he had an epiphany. On a moonless night, after a few too many drinks, Tobias found himself leaning against a crumbling wall for support. A loud noise rumbled up the street, jarring his molars. A bright light flashed across his eyes, temporarily blinding him. An AMX-13 tank appeared with two troop carriers. Just before being blinded by the powerful searchlight, Tobias had seen a faded poster on the wall next to his head. He reached into his worn pocket and pulled out an antique silver-plated Dunhill lighter, bringing it to life with a practiced flick. It was the one thing he had taken from home, his father's lighter. A keepsake and a memento from a different time.

He waited as his bloodshot eyes adjusted to the orange glow before reading the poster. Join the French Foreign Legion, Honor and Fidelity. At the bottom, a single statement caught his eye: No Questions Asked.

At that moment, Tobias's hammered brain knew how he would avenge his grandfather. He would let someone else pay to train him. Then, he would beat them at their own game.

He staggered into a recruiting office and, before he had completely sobered up, was on a bus to the nearest training camp.

Three brutal years later, Tobias was finished with the Legion. He had learned what he needed and risen as far up as he wanted.

His corrupt commanding officer, who fancied himself as a reborn Napoleon, cut every budget item possible to line his pockets. The men were underfed, underequipped, and underappreciated. Conditions were at an all-time low.

One night, his commander made a fatal mistake. Tobias was assigned as the officer of the night watch. He would take this opportunity to leave this dreadful place, but not before making a statement. Tobias crept into the sleeping French officers' area and killed every single one. For his final act as a legionnaire, he plunged a knife into his heartless commander's chest. He watched with fascination as the man's eyes bugged open in alarm and then shrouded with confusion before flickering closed.

Tobias left the desert behind and headed back to Athens, where he used his newfound skills to help him move up the criminal ladder, eventually getting a permanent position up north in the Xander family business.

The door to the warehouse slid open, and Nico Xander strolled in with a half-eaten baklava, honey sticking to his fingers.

Tobias pulled himself from his thoughts of the past.

"How goes it?" Nico asked, with a mouthful of dessert.

"I hit my first dead end, but I'm sure—" The cloned phone beeped. "Wait a minute." Tobias scrolled through the texts. A recent message caught his eye. There were pictures of his artifact and several pages of notes. Tobias carefully studied everything.

The connection in Italy to the bent cop had cost him a favor and €10,000, but as he gaped at the phone's screen and read the words, he realized it was worth every Euro.

"*Alfentikó*. I think I found something," Tobias said, as he cast the information to his laptop for better viewing. He spun the screen toward

Nico and leaned over to tap the down arrow. There was no way he was letting his boss's sticky fingers on his keyboard.

After a few minutes of viewing, Nico's jaw slowly lowered. "A treasure map to untold wealth. Am I reading this right?"

"Yes," Tobias said, with excitement just spilling out.

"So, where do I go to get this treasure?"

"The directions are a little vague. But I have a lead. Professor Beppe Lombardo. He is in Sardinia."

It was early when Tam McGree's private cell phone began buzzing. He took another sip of his espresso and reached to hit the button. It was a FaceTime call. He hesitated and ran his fingers through his hair before answering. "Ah, my intrepid explorers. How goes things?"

"Well, we translated your shell for you," Cable said, instead of a greeting.

"Oh really? That's marvelous."

"I'll send you all the details, but listen to this." Dani relayed the translation, what they had learned so far, and the connecting history.

Tam listened in amazement as the story of his father's good luck charm was revealed. He seemed out of breath when he spoke next. "Well done, you three. I am most impressed. Know that a bonus will be forthcoming. So, what are the next steps?"

"Next steps?" Cable seemed confused for just a beat. "We were hired to translate your artifact, and we have. There are no next steps."

"But what of the treasure? Surly the shell's story is only half told without an ending."

Cable couldn't argue with that logic. "There are a thousand places we would have to look and no guarantee any of those would be right," Cable said. "There is just not enough information."

Silence followed.

"I'll tell you what. You three have impressed me with what you have discovered so quickly. Give me two more weeks. Think of it as a paid vacation and see if you can't complete the story. If you do that for me,

I'll double your fee, and if we do find treasure, you can split a twenty percent finder's fee. The rest can go to charity."

Cable was about to say no when Dani, reading his mind, held up a finger to him and answered. "Keep in mind this quest for answers is kinda like building a sandcastle with a pair of tweezers. One grain of sand at a time. We might find our next clue, or we might not even find the beach."

Tam nodded. "I understand, but also, consider what one little grain of sand can do under the right tutelage… Say an oyster, for example. That tiny speck can grow into a very valuable pearl."

Cable rolled his eyes and shook his head in surrender.

Dani placed her hand on his shoulder while still making eye contact with Tam. "Okay, two weeks, but then we're finished."

"Agreed. Thank you all for your hard efforts. Talk soon." Tam hung up before Cable could say his piece.

Dani gave herself a small smile. She was committed to finishing this job. It was something her dad had instilled in her as a young child. Growing up in Austin, Dani's father, a retired sergeant in the army, ran the family business, Tran-sit Construction.

He was always pushing her to finish strong, no matter how hard things became. He did it when she started pee-wee soccer and right up until the day she left home.

Every summer, they would take a month off and go somewhere. Usually, they went to their houseboat on Toledo Bend Reservoir, but one summer, the Tran family went to Israel and Egypt. Dani saw all the holy sites and did the pyramid thing. She was fifteen years old at the time, and the majesty of physical history, standing the test of time, changed her forever.

Since college, Dani had dreamed of seeing the world and discovering its secrets, and that was exactly what she was doing now.

She opened her laptop and navigated to the files on the shell. She did a quick text update to Arri and finished with a snap down of her laptop's screen. "Jon, see if you can get us to Carthage."

"Is that still a place?" Jon asked.

"It's near Tunis, in Tunisia. Like 150 miles due south of here," Cable clarified.

"On it."

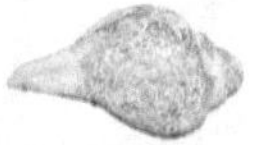

A small 8v8 soccer game kicked up dust on the worn field across the street. Deniz watched for a while, letting his mind drift, as he worked a cigarette down to a butt. He rubbed his weary eyes with his palms and turned from the window.

The call to the new acting Ministry of the Interior in Addis Ababa, Ethiopia, revealed a lot. It was funny how some people just couldn't keep their mouths shut when they thought a reporter was doing a story about them. It was an old ruse, but it had paid off many times for Deniz.

The single-cup coffeemaker was soon steaming and dripping caramel-brown liquid into a chipped mug. Deniz sipped as he returned to the worn table and his stolen laptop. Surprisingly, his neighbor's pirated Wi-Fi was decent, so far from the city.

Deniz took a moment to memorize the images he had collected of Dr. Dani Tran. There were fewer options for Kojo and Cable Janson, but he was sure he would now recognize them on the street. Their backstories did little to connect them in any way to the museum girl, Arri, or the shell. Next, he did a deep dive on Professor Beppe Lombardo. He was mentioned in the text to Dani, and Deniz wanted to know everything he could before confronting him. There was a lot of information to digest. Did the professor find the shell, or was it one of the kids?

The pursuit of details or history about the carved shell had produced nothing, including a deep dive into the museum's website. *Where had it come from, and why was Arri sharing her findings with Dani? Was Dani working with her old partners in Ethiopia or on her own? Was Professor Lombardo the man behind it or just another source of information?*

Too many questions and no real answers. He leaned back and let his frustration show.

His job was to retrieve the original shell for Mona, not follow treasure hunters on a wild goose chase. But what if the goose wasn't wild…

What if they really had a chance at the treasure? The fantasy bounced around in his mind for a bit. He made a good living but not the kind of money that truly sets you free. This could be that kinda money.

Perhaps he could do both, Deniz considered. Retrieve the shell for Mona and find the treasure for himself. The problem was that he had no idea where to go next. His only clue was four people, and he had no idea where they were.

For now, Mona didn't need to know anything about the treasure.

He needed to confront the professor and find Dani Tran, then he would have his answers, and this time, no mercy.

He picked up his phone to call a friend in Interpol at the Cairo office. Maybe he could get a passport hit from an airport. At the same time, he logged into Expedia to book a flight to Sardinia.

Arri's stolen laptop suddenly pinged. Deniz stopped dialing and looked over. A text message updating Arri on Dani's progress popped up. *Seriously? Am I that good?*

Deniz let a smile burst out for an answer, and he quickly hung up and started to pack. Thoughts of visiting the professor were now completely gone.

Tobias had flown in Nico's plane many times. It was a Diamond DA42 Twin Star, a sleek twin turboprop with a prolonged nose for fuel and cargo.

Nico complained every time he had to use it, as it was not a jet. What he really wanted was a G6, like his counterpart in Athens. Honestly, though, the plane did the job, just a bit smaller and slower.

Especially smaller today, as they had a full load. Flying the plane was Jason Asker, also a member of Nico's gang. He was a wiry man with snake-like reflexes and a studious mind. His short, buzzed military hair topped a dour disposition.

Nico took the copilot's seat, imagining himself capable, should something happen to the pilot. That was a crock.

Sitting in the rear seat with Tobias was Nico's favorite heavy, Jude Kontos. He was a giant of a man with halitosis, a shaved head, and a penchant for violence equal to the giant chip on his shoulder.

Jason had to correct the controls to maintain a level flight every time Jude was aboard.

Tobias looked at his boss in the copilot's seat. At fifty-five, Nico Xander still played the single life. There had been a few women over the years, but nothing ever stuck. Nico saw his relationships as transactional. Sex was no different. He seemed to prefer renting his love and flaunting his wealth and power throughout the small towns he controlled in northern Greece. Always wanting more but never quite getting it. If this treasure was real, it could open things up for Nico in a way he probably couldn't imagine.

Tobias had worked for Nico for nearly ten years now. Nico's dad had taken him on as a sort of sounding board for his son. Help him to make good decisions and keep him out of trouble. It was not easy at first. Nico grew up in the family business, and his entitled frat boy attitude made everything messy.

Nico's dad had worked hard to try to pass down most of his good traits, but sons will be sons, especially spoiled ones. When Nico's father passed, the operation stood on shaky feet for a time. Like a pendulum, his actions and moods seemed to go from one extreme to another as he tried to find his place. Those were dark days.

Finally, Nico settled into the role he now played.

With a lot of help from Tobias, the Nico Xander mob now ran like a well-oiled machine. It was Tobias's greatest joy, as he found his passion in the structure and smooth operation of things.

They touched down in Cagliari, Sardinia, after a bumpy ride across the Mediterranean. The plane taxied to a private area, and a customs agent met them as they exited. After a quick inspection, passports were stamped, and the foursome were good to go.

"How far to this Professor Lombardo? I want some answers, and fast," Nico said, his mood still foul from the long flight.

"We'll need to rent a car and then maybe an hour," Tobias said, hoping to calm his boss a bit.

As they headed for the small private terminal, Tobias's phone pinged, or rather, his cloned phone pinged.

Tobias pulled it out of his pocket and peered at the message. "Ah, hold up."

Everyone stopped walking.

"We're in the wrong place. We need to course correct to Tunisia."

"What about the professor?" Nico asked.

Tobias looked up. "We now know what he knows. He's irrelevant."

Nico stared at his number two for a second. "This better not be a waste of my time."

"Alfentikó, it is a treasure hunt, not a treasure find. Right now, we are tapped into the people leading the search, but that could dry up at any moment. If we lose them, our hunt is finished."

Nico let the words sit for a beat. "Jason, get us refueled and a flight plan to Tunisia." Nico looked to Tobias for more information.

"As close as you can get us to Carthage," Tobias replied.

"Carthage," Nico ordered. "We'll wait in the lounge."

The private terminal lounge turned out to be two parallel benches with no back support. Something else for Nico to complain about.

Forty minutes later, they were taxiing down the runway.

Cable watched the whitecaps dance past the small porthole window, bending his knees with the motion of the ship to maintain his position. The wind had picked up, and the forty-plus-hour ferry ride from Sardinia to Tunis was starting to seem like a bad idea. The Tunisian Ferry was built like a small cruise ship with none of the usual amenities. The three stories above the waterline contained tiny berths, a simple lounge, and a cafeteria. Cars, trucks, tractors, and equipment were loaded via a drive-up ramp to the lower sections while passengers boarded via a steep gangplank.

The gray water reflected the cloudy skies and Cable's mood. He was trying to find his place in this new adventure with Dani. His usual loner self and travel via the whims of the day were a far cry from the structured business life he was now leading.

Dani, on the other hand, seemed to thrive on the structure and was very adept at scheduling their days and next steps. Cable loved watching her smile and eyes twinkle as the quest pulled them in uncertain directions. She was determined to find the ending to the shell's story.

He reminded himself for the hundredth time, *Just go with it, relax, enjoy the ride. Do what you can to help, and the rest will work out.*

He packed his thoughts away for now and left the cabin. He needed some fresh air.

Outside, the wind cut diagonally across the steel bow. There was no rain, but the smell in the air predicted it soon. Cable noticed Jon leaning on the port railing and stepped over.

Jon, without looking, said, "Nice day to kitesurf."

"If you say so," Cable said as he leaned his forearms on the railing next to Jon.

The wind was the only sound for some time.

Cable finally broke the silence. "How did you get into this business…? If you don't mind me asking."

"No. I was an officer in Japan's Ground Self-Defense Force. Did my time and got really good at it. Bad intel and politics got me out. I loved what I did, so it just seemed natural to keep doing it."

"That sounds rehearsed," Cable said.

Jon looked over at Cable. "That bad, huh?"

"Yeah."

Jon let a small smile cross his face. Then, as quickly as it had appeared, it was gone. He took a deep breath. "Honestly, I hated being out. I didn't have a good exit, and being a civilian slowly ate at me… You asked why I don't drink. It's because I am afraid. The bottle took me down a dark path, and it would be so easy to go back there… Some days, I *want* to go back there. Then I look at you and Dani, and I see how good two people can be together. Working in unison, peeling back the layers of forgotten history. It's noble and intriguing. I envy you two."

"Us? We hardly got our act together," Cable countered.

"You're wrong. I can see it, and it's beautiful."

Cable was taken aback. Had he been so busy fighting against the process that he failed to see all the good that was now part of his life? He had left for Harvard to get away from his father and left college to get away from the status quo. He was not comfortable blending into classic societal norms, but how long could he just keep running away? That was a question he had been afraid to ask.

"You two are good for each other."

Cable slowly nodded, letting the thought simmer.

"I work best when there is a task. Start to finish. I think of nothing else till it's complete. I guess I become the task, in a way," Jon said. "And when it is done, I struggle to find my identity. Lately, that condition has taken me to some bad places." Jon's eyes misted just a bit at the thought of how close he had come to ending his life. "I once had someone like Dani in my life, and I lost her. Don't make the same mistake, Cable."

Jon was right. Dani was an exceptional woman. If only he really knew where he stood with her. Maybe that was why she was being standoffish at times, because of him and his insecurities.

The rain finally came, forcing both men back into the ship's interior.

At dinner, Jon seemed unusually chipper. He sat down, rubbing his hands together. "So, what are our next steps?"

Dani watched with fascination. "My, someone is in a good mood. Did you find a special cruise friend?"

"No. I didn't find a special cruise friend… I just finally pulled my head out." He turned to Cable, smiling. "You should try it sometime."

Cable turned red and quickly buried his face in a menu as Dani's eyes bounced between them. She decided to table the question and move on to a quick update of their next steps, as she saw them.

After dinner, Cable followed Dani back to their berth. She plopped on the double bed and kicked off her shoes, then laid back and extended her arms in a stretch.

Cable sat next to her and suddenly wished he had drunk more wine at dinner. "Dani."

She glanced his way.

"I just want to say that I think your plan of us working together is a good idea."

Dani shot up into a sitting position. "Really? You mean that?"

"Yeah, I mean it. We are good at what we do. Though a lot of the credit goes to you."

"Nonsense. You make connections I never could. Not to mention your cultural and language knowledge. I could never do this without you."

"Thanks. Look, I don't know how to say this, so I'm just gonna say it. What we've been doing is great, this whole thing… It should be perfect for me."

Cable ran his fingers through his moppy hair. "Nobody can hurt you if you don't let anyone in. My father taught me that in his own way. But I am… What I'm trying to tell you is that I really care about you. It matters, what we have." He gestured between them.

Dani placed her hand on his arm.

Cable turned and looked down. "I just needed to say it, that's all."

"Cable, my whole adult life I have been in control of me. I'm the one who decides what's best for me, not others. I could be with you as long as it was on my terms and I was doing okay with everything, the partnership…the emotions…the sex."

Cable smiled.

"The more time I spent with you, the scarier it got. One minute, I was angry. The next, I was an emotional wreck. I felt like I was losing control. Losing myself. That's why I have been all over the place lately. I guess I was hoping you would run away from me and that would solve all my problems."

Cable shook his head slightly as he looked into Dani's eyes. They were glistening.

"It turns out I was gaining, not losing. This new person I was becoming was a stronger, better, more complete version of me." She wiped a tear away. "I don't want to hurt you like that anymore. Because… because I love you."

Cable pulled Dani close, and they hugged tightly, auras slowly mixing. Then he pulled back and looked her in the eyes again, only now his eyes were tearing up as well. They kissed passionately, letting their love guide them.

CHAPTER NINE

ENIZ SAT ACROSS FROM THE terminal, watching the last of flight AZ1590 exit the plane. Nothing. He was sure he had arrived in Tunis before his quarry, but this was the second day with no results. There was no way they were flying private…was there? He looked at his phone. The next flight was tomorrow, same time. He took a moment and updated Mona on his progress. Keeping her anxious and excited about his progress was an important part of maintaining his newfound leverage over her. He stubbed out his cigarette and dropped it outside his car next to a growing pile in the street. Deniz had driven all night from his safe house to Tunis, and he was sure he had beaten Dr. Dani Tran here. His only option now was to come back and try again tomorrow. As he exited from the terminal, a poster ad caught his attention. *Tunisian Ferry Lines: Travel in style to many ports of call.* The ferry, of course. Deniz quickly looked up the schedule on his phone. The trip from Cagliari took just over forty hours. He had twenty minutes to get to the ferry terminal. Deniz stomped on the gas.

Cars and trucks drove down a large ramp in the back while passengers exited out the side. Deniz had found a parking spot where he could observe both through compact binoculars. When about half the passengers had disembarked, his target appeared. Dr. Dani Tran. She was with Cable Janson, and they walked hand in hand down the gangplank. *Was that something new?* he wondered. There was no sign of Kojo, but an Asian man in front of them hailed a taxi, and all three got in. Deniz only got a glimpse of the man, as he'd been focused on the couple. "Who are you, my friend?" Deniz mumbled to himself as he put his car in gear and followed discreetly. They moved east along the ocean, and they turned left on R23.

The Golden Carthage Hotel was a modern concrete building, complete with Moroccan arches and re-created ruins sprinkled throughout the premises. A circular fountain surrounded by a collection of flags from several countries stood sentinel to arriving guests.

The cab pulled up and expelled its passengers.

Deniz pulled to a curb and watched as they disappeared through a revolving door into the lobby. He parked his car and casually walked to the bellhop. A short conversation and a wad of cash secured his silent services, and Deniz left the three-story white structure in his rearview mirror.

As soon as the door to their room closed, Cable and Dani fell into an all-consuming kiss. "I've been waiting all day to do that."

"Me too," Dani replied, slightly out of breath.

Once the passion part of their relationship was checked off, Dani and Cable got down to business. From the photos they could see on various websites and Google searches, most of Ancient Carthage was nothing but crumbling walls.

"The city has changed hands so many times through so many wars, finding what we need seems impossible."

"That's where I come in, making the impossible, possible," Cable said with a smirk.

"I like the optimistic sound of that, but don't expect me to sit here holding my breath until that happens."

"There are other activities we can be doing that require you to hold your breath."

Dani smacked Cable on the arm.

"I'm talking about swimming. The Mediterranean is right there, and it is one of my favorite oceans," he said, pointing to the view out their window.

Ten minutes later, they were bobbing in the warm, robin's-egg-blue sea.

"If I didn't know better, I would say you are a bit of a perv, Mr. Janson."

"Lucky you," Cable replied, as he flipped on his back.

Dani splashed him with water. Then conceded, "Yeah, lucky me." She swam over and kissed him for good measure. "So…after our two weeks are done, what next?"

"I've been giving that some thought. If you're still keen on the idea, we should do exactly what you proposed. Start a business together documenting and connecting artifacts and relics to their origins."

"That might require us to work for some rich fat cats," Dani said.

"I'll manage…" He pulled her close. "I can't keep wandering the world in search of something special when I already found it," he said, with a smile in his eyes.

Dani responded with a kiss…a long kiss.

They bobbed and swam for the next half hour before Dani complained of getting raisin syndrome.

His phone buzzed. Deniz smashed out his cigarette and cleared the phlegm from his throat. Looking at the screen, he had wondered how long his boss would wait until she became impatient with his progress. Now he knew—forty-eight hours.

He leaned back on the hood of his rental and hit the green button.

"What's new?" Mona's voice seemed strained, so Deniz came right to the point.

He gave her a quick update, including his trip to Tangier and the bribe he'd given the bellhop to keep him informed of Dani and Cable's movements. He still had no information on the third man, other than a name passed to him from the same paid hotel source, Jon Chibi.

"They're at the Carthage Museum right now, and I'm just outside waiting."

"Don't you think you should go in and see what they are looking for?"

"They are the experts, not me. I intend to follow them to their conclusion and obtain the artifact and its message. I have no skills to take on a historical journey of this sort. I'm more of a pop-in-with-a gun-and-take-what-I-want sort a guy."

"Yes, you are. Just remember, this isn't about some quest. My interest lies solely in getting the shell back to the Helal family. I took a chance on you, Deniz. Don't make me regret it, or worse, do something about it."

Deniz stood up from the car's hood and began to pace. "Save your threats. I am doing everything in my power, all for you. Besides, have I ever let you down?"

Mona seemed appeased.

"Keep in mind, your shell is much more than a physical artifact. It has a message as well. That might be pivotal to your birthright."

Mona let the words sink in. Was Deniz in this for his own gain or hers? He seemed intent on following the Americans to their final destination, but the reason escaped her. "Have you been able to translate the symbols?"

"Only a few words," he lied. "It speaks of a journey around Africa."

"Interesting. Make sure you don't lose them."

Deniz didn't bother to reply as he killed the call.

Inside the museum, Dani's eyes scanned from display to display as they walked. Most of the dramatic artifacts belonged to later periods like Roman. The Phoenician section was small by comparison. An incense burner in the shape of the God Bá al, two sarcophagi of the Priest and Priestess, and several steles were the highlights. Lots of tools and pottery filled the rest of the exhibit.

Any clue, no matter how small, could hold the answer.

Dani didn't know exactly what she was looking for, but she would know it when she saw it. Patience was something her professors had reinforced multiple times.

Jon scanned the area, looking for threats. His historical knowledge about the era was nonexistent.

Cable paused for a second, thinking he saw something worthwhile on a partially broken vase. On closer inspection, he dismissed it.

After determining that the area was secure, Jon spun toward Cable. "So, what's the story with the Phoenicians?"

Cable paused his search. "Quick history. The Phoenicians started in Tyre, modern Syria, around 1200 BCE. By 600 BCE, they had expanded to pretty much rule the entire Mediterranean, from North Africa around to Spain. They were master shipbuilders and navigators and excelled in trade. The one thing that fueled the empire was Tyrian purple."

Jon looked confused.

"You've heard of royal purple?"

"Yeah, European royalty liked to wear purple back in the day," Jon said.

"Well, the Phoenicians developed the process for that purple, and that dye was worth a hundred times its weight in gold."

"And no one else could make…purple?" Jon asked, with disbelief.

Dani stepped over and added her two cents. "No one could match it. This purple was bold and saturated. Even the few samples remaining from the era still hold their color. They discovered a specific species of sea snail that produced a rare enzyme needed for the formula. Its process was a well-guarded secret. Even modern-day science has yet to duplicate the formula."

"And the Phoenicians used that dye as the basis of their substantial trade," Cable said.

"Ultimately killing millions of those snails on their way to becoming an empire," Dani finished.

Jon shook his head. "An empire built on snails… Crazy."

"But true," Dani said before turning back to her hunt.

"So, what happened?"

"Ran out of snails," Cable threw out flippantly. "Our last treasure hunt ended with a cave filled with salt. It was far from the ocean, so it was worth a fortune back in Roman times but only a curiosity nowadays. Time changes everything."

"Including the price of seashells," Jon added.

"Hey, guys."

Both Cable and Jon stopped talking and stepped over to where Dani was scrutinizing a white piece of rock.

"It's part of a stele," Cable said, as he got closer.

Dani clarified for Jon. "Stone monument."

"We ran into these in Ethiopia. Look at that." A white carved stone with a pointy top and jagged broken-off bottom hung on the wall. In the center was a depiction of a sailing vessel above swirling circles representing the ocean.

"It's a Phoenician warship," Cable pointed out, as he studied the carvings in the limestone.

"I'm more interested in that," Dani said, gesturing. At the bottom, where the stone was broken at an angle, were several worn symbols. She pulled out the papers Professor Lombardo had given them and found the one with the translation. "Here." She held up the page. Three of the last symbols in the stone matched the three on the page. "It spells B-O-A."

"Boaz?" Cable ventured, finishing the word. "This might be a dedication stone to his voyage."

"And it would mean nothing without this," Dani said, holding up the shell's translation. "We need to find where this came from." To the right of the wall-mounted stele was a collection of pictures showing the excavation and people who had rediscovered it.

They all studied the pictures and information that came with it.

"It says here, Site Archéologique Carthage," Jon said.

"That just means Carthage Archaeological site. That's pretty vague," Cable said.

Dani pulled her phone out and did a quick search. "Except that is the actual name of one of the three main ruins out on the point." She took several pictures of all the information on the wall, including the stele.

"If we hurry, we'll have a few hours before sunset," Cable said as he turned to leave.

The drive from the museum to the ruins was brief. They pulled into a small parking lot adorned with a dozen Tunisian flags, positioned in front of a contemporary gate and ticket booth. Cable seized his backpack as he slammed the car door. A weathered man, whose life had clearly been spent under the sun, accepted their money in exchange for a torn ticket. The air was warm, accompanied by a gentle ocean breeze that followed them through the entrance. The expansive site was largely overgrown with weeds and wildflowers, featuring several mature trees scattered throughout. A few tourists wandered the grounds, exploring the remnants of the past. Ancient, stone-paved roads, bordered by crumbling walls, crisscrossed the complex. At the center, a small hill stood with the tallest walls, which even included a few door and window openings.

Dani paused to take it all in. "This looks mostly Roman to me. They pretty much smashed Carthage during the Punic Wars. It was common practice back then to rebuild on top of or modify whatever structures were left after the fighting."

"Let's see if we can locate where the stele was taken from," Cable added hopefully.

They moved up the hill across ancient stone pathways that had been trodden on for millennia. Weathered, narrow stairs led them up to a courtyard once part of the palace grounds. It was a good fifteen feet above ground level, surrounded on two sides by tall stone walls. The other two sides had a low retaining wall, giving them a magnificent view of the Gulf of Gables. In the center, several Roman columns still stood tall against time. Flying above it all was a red Tunisian flag with a crescent moon and five-pointed star.

Dani held her phone up with the pictures taken from the museum. She turned slowly in a circle, looking for a match to the picture of the stele being hoisted up by a group of archeologists. "There," she pointed.

An alcove near the southeast corner of the square seemed to catch her attention. Dani moved closer, followed by Cable, while Jon kept his head on a swivel. She held her phone up and compared the image to the reality in front of her. A faint weathered pattern that replicated the stele's original position in the alcove was just visible. "This is it," she whispered almost reverently.

Cable stepped forward and examined the now-empty recess. The bottom sill was uneven. "It looks like someone has repaired this section of the wall."

Sure enough, the bottom ledge of the alcove had a repair that tried to mirror the look of the stone.

"I'll wager the rest of the stele is long gone, or maybe it's below this patch," Cable said.

"The way the original was broken off at the bottom, the remains might be nothing but crumbs," Dani added, trying to hide her disappointment.

Jon stepped over to see for himself. "You said the Romans built on top of the Phoenicians' original structures?"

Dani nodded.

"What's left of your stele could still be below this courtyard."

Cable was already ahead of him. He leaned out over the small retaining wall, straining to see below. After several failed attempts to find what he was looking for, he said, "I got something."

At the bottom of one wall was a small, arched aqueduct, mostly filled with dirt. Several tall weeds grew up around it, obscuring the view.

Cable led them down to inspect it. The years had filled the aqueduct with dirt, but the very top was still open. "We might be able to worm our way inside with a little digging." He looked around. Three tourists were walking away to the left, and one local by a staircase was absorbed in taking selfies. Otherwise, no one was in sight. "We'll need to come back at night and chip away at the concrete up in the alcove and dig out this entrance to know for sure," Cable said, letting a plan slowly form in his mind.

"I'm sure there will be at least one guard on duty at night," Jon added.

"Do you think you can handle him without anyone getting hurt?"

Before Jon could answer, Dani ducked past the weeds and dropped to her knees. She started pulling some of the loose dirt away from the entrance before squirming belly down into the aqueduct. Jon and Cable were speechless for a beat as her feet disappeared. Cable quickly collected himself and followed. Jon did one more security sweep with his eyes. Only one tourist was visible, the selfie guy, and he was facing away. He echoed Cable's actions.

Deniz pulled into a dirt lot next to three other rental cars near the back. He sat patiently in his car as Dr. Dani Tran and company walked to the entrance. He removed his cowboy hat and donned a traditional maroon chechia. No need to stand out here. After a few moments, he grabbed a small canvas messenger bag and followed his marks into the site, just another local appreciating his country's culture.

He adjusted his upside-down bowl hat on his head and grabbed his cell phone, before lighting a cigarette with the dying butt of another.

Pretending to be absorbed in the ruins around him, Deniz covertly watched as his targets made their way up the hill to the palace grounds. They took a few steps into a courtyard and seemed to be searching for something specific. He moved in an arc, taking mock selfies while continually looking beyond his phone. His heart quickened when he saw them fixate on a section of wall. Everything in him wanted to draw his gun and rush over, confront them, and seize what they had discovered, but instead, he took a calming breath. Patience was required here. If he moved in too soon, he could lose everything. For now, he would watch and wait.

Deniz was not a good person, and he had come to terms with that a long time ago. He did what he did, not out of loyalty, but to better his position in this world. Money, position, and even power over others were his gods. Every move was calculated and weighed to make sure he came out ahead. Killing and threatening others, though pleasurable, was just his stock in trade. He had built up a small nest egg that would allow him to retire to a seaside village in a third-world country. That would never do. Besides, he was still young and enjoying the game. There was no need to germinate thoughts about getting out.

He leaned against an ancient wall. Turning his back to his subjects, he used his phone's forward camera to keep watch. The thought that there might be treasure at the end of this job was something worth waiting for, but he would only hold for so long.

Without warning, Dr. Dani Tran and then the other two vanished from his view. He spun to put his eyes downrange. Nothing. Quick walking to their last known position revealed a recently dug-out aqueduct entrance behind some tall weeds. It seemed to lead under the palace. Now, it was Deniz's turn to look around and make sure he was in the clear. He stepped past the weeds and ducked down, placing his ear to the entrance. Muffled crawling sounds and a muted voice returned. His racing heart slowed. He had not lost them. His mind bounced like a metronome. *Should I wait here or follow?* If the treasure was in this tunnel, he wanted it. The thought overwhelmed his caution, and he began crawling.

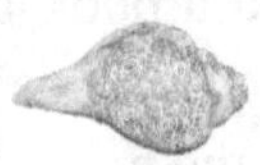

Tobias lowered his binoculars. "Two of those people were at the museum."

Nico stepped next to Tobias and borrowed the binoculars. He watched as three bodies ducked behind some bushes and disappeared. "Must have gone underground," he said, returning the binoculars. "Who do you think the third person is?"

Tobias shrugged. "They must all be connected somehow to the seashell." He watched as a short man in a maroon hat smashed out his cigarette and ran up to the base of the wall. "They've got a tail… I don't recognize him, but he looks like a local."

The short man then ducked out of sight. "He's gone underground too."

"We need to get closer," Nico said.

"I agree, but they won't be able to exit without us seeing them, and from here, they'll never see us."

Nico slowly nodded. "Makes sense."

The large, bushy shrub was the perfect camouflage. Tobias could see out from just within the branches, but nobody could see them in return. He pulled back from the brambles.

"Jason, head to the exit and let me know if you spot 'em. Jude, get up on the wall overlooking the palace and cover our rear in case they somehow squirt out the back. Call my cell if they do."

Both men left to follow their boss's orders.

Nico and Tobias casually walked up to the spot where they had last spotted their mark. They could see the half-buried aqueduct's entrance just behind the weeds. "Looks like they went in there," Nico said, staring down at the narrow entrance.

"They must come out sometime. Let's post back up and wait," Tobias said.

Dani's cell phone flashlight did a poor job of illuminating the space in front of her. It was a circular orifice made of ancient stone with a dirt floor. The farther she slithered, the more the aqueduct opened. Soon, she could crawl on her hands and knees.

"I like your style," Cable said from somewhere behind Dani, as he pushed his backpack ahead of him. She tried looking back, but his phone's flashlight was all she could see. "I think we are crawling in 2,000-year-old poop," Dani said over her shoulder.

Cable's smile suddenly closed up tight.

After a time, the tunnel ended at an open space about five feet in height. Support columns were equally spaced every ten feet. Dani's light couldn't see the other side, so she waited until Cable and Jon slithered into the room. They couldn't stand, but it was better than crawling belly down. They paused to let the dust settle.

"You take me to the nicest places," Cable said as he shined his light around in the dark, musty space. He could see the aqueduct had collapsed here, as a scattered pile of stones lay about on the dirt floor in evidence. "If I still have my bearings, the base of the alcove should be over that way." Cable pointed.

They walked hunched over till they could make out the wall ahead. Cable followed it back to the left, stopping suddenly. He reached out and started wiping his hand across a smooth section in the stone wall. It revealed an alabaster glow covered in dirt.

"The bottom of the stele," Dani whispered.

Jon stepped up and helped Cable dust off the muck-covered slab. The room quickly filled with dust, and they were forced to hold their shirts over their noses to breathe without coughing.

The white slab was mounted into the ground and rose through the ceiling, where the top, now in the museum, was once attached.

"Whatever carvings were once here have long ago faded to time," Jon said, looking at the blank stone.

"Not necessarily," Dani replied. "Hold your lights to the side."

Cable and Jon moved next to the wall and shined their lights across the stone at a harsh angle. Subtle shadows from centuries-old carvings appeared in the form of ancient Phoenician. Dani stepped up and turned off the flash on her phone's camera. She took several pictures before zooming in on the images. "There are a lot of letters missing, but we might be able to piece something together."

"What's that?" Jon asked, pointing his light up near the top of the stone. A curved, grooved line was just visible at the top of the stone. It disappeared behind a capstone in the ceiling.

Cable reached up and tried to pull the stone free. It was stuck tight.

Jon grabbed a broken stone from the floor and banged on one edge. After a few hits, the capstone dislodged and fell.

All three stepped up to the recently revealed part of the stele. It looked like a deformed upside-down bell with a line drawn around the bottom of it.

"I think that's…Africa?" Cable said, mostly to himself.

"Okay, I see that," Dani added. "This line must represent their intended journey." Her finger followed a thin outside line counterclockwise around the thicker etched outline of the bottom of the continent. It stopped at the tip of the Horn. "I guess that was all they knew about Africa at the time."

"It stops at the Horn of Africa," Jon said to no one in particular.

"That was probably part of their mission to see what lay beyond their knowledge of the continent," Dani added.

Cable snapped his fingers, and Dani almost jumped. "That's it." He pointed to the tip of the Horn of Africa. "Land's end."

"OMG, of course," Dani said.

Jon wasn't making the same connection.

Just then, the sound of a pistol racking stopped everyone in their tracks. Jon was the first to react by stepping toward the sound, but a bright light flashed in his eyes, stopping him cold.

"That's far enough," an accented voice said from behind the blinding light. "Where's the shell?"

Cable was the first to respond. "What shell?"

A sudden blast from the pistol flung him to the ground. Dani screamed and dropped to his aid.

"I have no time for games, and as you can see, I'm quite serious about my question. I will ask it only one more time. 'Where is the shell?' "

Through trembling lips, Dani said, "It's in the bag." She reached for it, and the spotlight moved from Jon to Dani's actions.

"Hold up." The light flashed back on Jon as he was just starting to creep forward. "Don't get any ideas. On your knees."

Jon slowly complied.

A low moan escaped from Cable.

"Hands behind your head and crisscross your legs." It was a position that was difficult to attack from, and until Deniz knew more about the Asian man, he would take no chances.

"Now, Dr. Dani, bring the bag next to Jon so I can watch you both."

Dani hesitated, but Jon, in a very calm voice, added, "It's okay."

She crawled over, setting the bag on the ground.

"Now, very slowly, get the shell."

She did, holding it up in the light.

Deniz almost gasped out loud. "Bring it toward me… Stop… Set it down… Now, back away next to Jon."

Dani followed the directions before kneeling back down next to Jon. She glanced at Cable, who was lying prone on the ground, bleeding. The bright light moved forward and then back.

Jon noticed the shell was no longer on the ground.

"Cable, you still breathing?" Deniz asked.

"Yeah," Cable rasped back.

"Good. Now, if you all want to make it out of here alive…tell me about the treasure."

"W-we don't know where yet," Dani stammered. She pointed behind her. "We came here for this stone, but it's missing vital information. We think it speaks of the tip of Africa, but until we investigate that, it's all just unknown."

"What is the treasure?" Deniz asked.

"Again, unknown."

The pistol fired off again, just past Dani's face.

"Don't toy with me."

"We're not," Dani said in a stronger voice. "We don't know what the treasure is or where it is, only that the next clue may or may not be at the tip of Africa. This journey and that shell are over 2,500 years old. It's a miracle we've gotten this far."

Deniz's fantasy for the treasure dropped, and he suddenly felt like shooting someone. He aimed his gun at Dani and then shifted it to Jon. He couldn't decide. Perhaps he should cut his losses. Mona was paying him a small fortune for the return of the shell. That would have to do for now.

"If I see any of you come out of that tunnel in the next five minutes, I'll shoot you." Deniz fired off another round, this time close to Jon, and just as suddenly, the bright flashlight spun and disappeared back down the aqueduct.

Jon started to follow.

"Leave it, Jon. I need help with Cable," Dani demanded.

"I'll be okay," Cable muttered. "I think it's just a graze, but it really stings."

"Let me see," Dani said as she pointed her phone's light at his torso.

Cable lifted his bloody shirt. There was a nice gash across his ribs, but the bleeding was already slowing.

"You're lucky," Dani said.

"Or that guy is an awfully good shot," Jon added.

Both Cable and Dani looked back at him.

That's when the world collapsed around them with a giant boom.

CHAPTER TEN

I T HAD ALL BEEN TOO easy, Deniz thought, as he stuffed the shell back into his messenger bag and crawled back toward daylight. He paused about twenty feet from the exit and put his pistol away. He grabbed the PE9 in his pack and attached it to the ceiling. A quick rotation of the dial and the forty-second timer began counting down.

Deniz scampered out of the aqueduct and stood dusting himself off. The smile on his face suddenly dropped when he noticed two hard-looking men holding pistols on him.

"Easy now. Where's the treasure?" Nico asked.

It took a beat for Deniz to recover. Who were these men, and how did they know about the treasure? "They have not found it yet," Deniz said, raising his hands to his sides. He slowly sidestepped away from the aqueduct entrance.

"What's in the bag?" Nico used his gun to gesture at the canvas bag hung on his shoulder.

"Tools of the trade," Deniz replied.

"What trade is that?" Tobias asked from the right.

Deniz glanced over. He was caught in the middle between the two men. "I do what must be done for my clients."

"A mercenary?"

"Of sorts… More like a fixer," Deniz replied as he took another slow sidestep away from the tunnel entrance.

"Stop moving," Nico said, holding the pistol at Deniz's gut. "Get his bag."

Tobias reached out for the messenger bag.

"We saw you following the Americans. Who do you work for?"

Tobias rummaged through the bag, producing the shell. "He's got one of these," Tobias said, holding up the 3D-printed seashell, just like the one he'd stolen from the museum.

Deniz's brow furrowed at the odd phrasing.

"Is it the original?" Nico asked.

Tobias turned it over. "No, a copy just like ours."

"Wait, what?" Deniz said.

"I won't ask again. Who do you wor—"

Just then, the PE9 transformed the aqueduct into a jumble of stone, dust, and concussive force. Nico was hit square-on with a stone chunk the size of a lunch pail, sending him flying.

Deniz and Tobias were violently thrown back, mostly unharmed.

Having expected the blast, Deniz staggered back to his feet first, covered in dust. His ears were ringing as he picked through the dust and dirt, grabbing the shell Tobias had dropped during the explosion. He pulled his pistol from its holster and turned to blast the second man, but he was gone.

Tobias rolled behind a Roman column and did a quick check to see if he had been wounded in the detonation. He lifted his gun and fired blindly back in the direction Deniz had been.

Deniz returned fire, as he ran away, bullets not finding a target from either side.

Suddenly, lead pinged all around Deniz from another direction. One shot caught him mid-stride and spun him around. He saw a mountain of a man running along the retaining wall above, firing down in his direction. Deniz emptied his mag back up that way, causing the mountain to duck. Deniz then sprinted for the exit, leaving a dust trail behind him. He put his empty gun away just as the old man from the entrance came running out of his ticket booth.

"People are shooting up there. Call the police," Deniz screamed in Tunisian as he ran past. The old man suddenly stopped, not wanting to get caught up in gunplay.

Deniz's short legs worked overtime as he dashed across the parking lot and into his car. A quick key turn and a dirt rooster tail preceded a harried exit as he fishtailed out of the parking lot. As the tires found purchase on the pavement, he glanced down at his wound. Blood was pumping out of his gut. He had been operating on pure adrenaline, but now he was starting to feel dizzy. He pulled to the side of the road and stopped. A quick glovebox search revealed a packaged battle dressing. He applied it around the bullet wound and cinched it tight before pulling back onto the street.

An eye cracked open. A black haze filled its view. Cable's side throbbed with pain, and incessant ringing filled his ears. He grunted as he sat up, reaching for his sightly buried phone, which was still providing a weak glow. A second light was pointing askew a few feet away, but the third light had stopped working. The room was somehow still intact. *Way to go, Phoenicians.* Dani was just starting to stir. "Dani. You, okay?" he said with concern.

Once she was sitting up and stretching her aching jaw, she gave him a nod for a reply.

Cable moved to check on Jon.

He had been closest to the blast and was lying on his side with a pained expression. A fit of coughing suddenly jolted him up. "I picked the wrong week to stop drinking," he croaked out in an extra-loud voice. His white teeth glowed against his dirt-covered face.

It sounded like he was speaking through pea soup to Cable.

The threesome eventually regrouped, and their hearing loss slightly improved.

Cable handed his light to Dani, who looked around the room. "We're trapped?" Dani asked.

"We're lucky this whole place didn't come down on us," Jon replied. He moved slowly through the dusty darkness to the original aqueduct exit. He shined the other phone's light around. Several support columns had given way, and the ceiling had completely collapsed by the blast site.

Dani looked at her phone's screen. "No signal down here."

"Too bad. I was hoping to call an Uber," Cable shot back with a wince of pain. He was torn between the pain from a knot on the top of his head or the graze of a bullet.

"How does it look?" Dani asked Jon, who was inspecting the collapsed exit.

"We'll need to call a serious plumber. There's no way we're getting out of that," he replied. The whole tube had collapsed.

"No one knows we're down here," Dani added flatly.

"That can happen when we go off script," Cable replied.

"Are you saying this is my fault?" Dani countered with a hint of venom.

"I'm saying…" Cable paused his direction of speech and course corrected. He knew Dani was feeling guilty about leading them down here, and destructive thoughts would only hamper their next move. "A short guy with a Tunisian accent, he's the one I blame."

"Tunisian? So that wasn't the guy from the museum?" Dani said with a touch less angst.

"No," Cable replied. "And unless he was holding his flashlight extra low, the guy was maybe five feet tall."

"Who else knows about this shell?" Dani said, her frustration clear.

"Stay there," Jon said, trying to change the subject and get them to focus on the things they could answer, like, *how do we get out of here*? He moved, hunched over, picking his way around what was left of the room. A dusty haze hung in the air like an '80s sci-fi movie, and they could just make out the glow of Jon's light as he moved farther away.

Across from the collapsed ceiling, the light stopped moving. Jon coughed a couple of times, causing the light to bounce. After a moment, they heard, "Hey, Cable, a bit of help, please."

Cable stood, bent at the waist, and picked his way toward the glow, his side and head throbbing.

Dani pointed her phone's light at the ground to help him navigate.

The original aqueduct had continued through the far wall but, at some point in time, had collapsed. Near the far wall was a small pile of rubble that seemed out of place.

"Help me move these stones."

Cable started pulling stones from the pile. Each movement brought him new pain.

Dani moved over to see what Jon had found. It didn't look promising until a black hole in the wall appeared at the top of the heap. Jon leaned up and pointed his light inside. "It's the other side of the aqueduct, and it's still intact." He looked back at Dani. "Where do you think it goes?"

"Probably to the palace's *forica*," she said.

"Latrine," Cable translated, for Jon's benefit.

"Nice," Jon said as he pulled his light back.

"Come on," Cable encouraged as he gritted his teeth and pulled another stone from the pile.

They doubled their efforts, and soon the hole had grown big enough to squeeze through.

"I'll go first," Dani said. "After all, it was me that got us into this mess."

Cable shook his head, then helped her climb over the rocks and into the void beyond. "Be careful."

"The thought had occurred to me," Dani said with a half-smile.

Cable followed next, and Jon brought up the rear with the second light.

The tube was small, and it forced them to use worm-like movements to inch forward. Dani could smell the mustiness, and every foot gained in a forward direction pushed more silt into the cramped space, making visibility and breathing a serious problem.

After about ten minutes of struggling ahead, Dani came to a plunge in the ceiling. "I can't get through. The ceiling is too low. We need to go back."

Cable leaned to the left to get a view of what she was talking about. Dani's phone illuminated through a brown fog where the blocks had slumped some centuries back, leaving only about six inches of clearance. Dani was right; they were trapped, and the only way back was to reverse slither into a cavern with no exit.

"What's the holdup?" Jon hissed from behind.

Cable explained the situation, and Jon paused for a moment to think.

"What's the ground like?" he asked.

"Sandy, I think, why?" Dani replied.

"Back when I was in the JGSDF, they taught us to dig tunnels without any support. Kinda like a… What do you call those ground animals that burrow?"

"A mole?" Dani replied before coughing.

"Yes, a mole," Jon replied. "Dani, what you need to do is use your hands to pull dirt from in front of you and push it backward along your sides as you slowly move forward."

"That is the stupidest thing I've ever heard."

"Trust me. It will work."

Dani looked at the ground around her. "Okay, but you're on the hook for my next manicure." She tried pulling the dirt away from the ground by her head and pushing it back.

Cable crawled up close and pulled the dirt farther back so Jon could continue the process. It took some time, but inch by inch, Dani moved ahead in a space just big enough for her torso to squeeze through.

After an hour of brutal effort, Dani's head popped out on the other side of the collapsed tunnel. The small tube felt like a five-lane freeway after the tight confines of the mole hole, but something was wrong with the texture of the stone. She inched forward and held still as Cable pushed through, the next into the new space.

"Don't move," she whispered.

Cable picked up on the tension in her voice and froze, half in and half out of the mole hole.

Dani moved the light across thousands of yellow-gray scorpions occupying every inch of the walls.

"Deathstalkers," Cable whispered.

"Are they lethal?" Dani asked.

"Not to a healthy adult, but their sting is extremely painful, and multiple stings… Yeah, fatal. My guess is that three or more stings would be a big problem. Certainly, the most dangerous scorpion in Africa."

"Great."

The room sounded like thousands of tiny twigs blowing and skittering across concrete.

A muffled callout from the back of the line broke the silence.

Cable carefully exited the gopher hole. His ribs still throbbed from the bullet graze, but he didn't have time to deal with pain right now.

A small light beam from their second working phone moved erratically, followed by a raspy voice. "What's taking so long? I could barely breathe in there," Jon said.

"Come out slow. We have guests," Cable replied.

Jon pulled his upper torso from the warren and shined his light along the walls, now realizing their situation. He lay there gasping and sweating, too tired to care.

"That was awful," Dani said, to no one, between heaves.

"Now I know what it feels like to survive being buried alive," Cable mumbled.

Jon pulled a lighter from his pocket and passed it forward. "Use this to clear a path."

Cable took the lighter and wriggled past Dani. He flicked a flame to life and used it to move the scorpions who were nearby away. "Keep your head down and shoulders tucked and try not to get stung."

"Says the man going first," Jon mumbled to himself. "And try not to anger anything with a stinger."

Cable inched ever so slowly through the halo of death.

"My phone's battery is almost dead," Dani said with an emotional warble as she followed right behind.

They slowly moved belly down through the pipe, trying not to rile the landlords.

Dani could feel something land in her hair and wiggle for freedom. She bit her bottom lip as she moved forward, waiting for the inevitable sting.

"Ahh!" Jon sucked it up, as his underarm took a hit.

The sound nearly sent Dani bolting.

"Are you guys purposely sending these things after me?" Jon said through clenched teeth. "The pain is surprisingly…intense."

Dani pushed a large Deathstalker that was crawling her way away with her phone. Its tail flicked at the screen, leaving a drop of venom behind. "Ahh!" Dani tried to calm down, but her heart was beating out of her chest.

"Are you hit?" Cable paused and called back.

"Don't stop," Dani called back, a bit too loud.

So, Cable pressed on, using the tiny flame to clear a path before him.

"*Tawagoto*!" Jon cried out as he felt another envenomation on his lower back. "Stop agitating the scorpions."

"I can either agitate them out of the way with this flame, or we can all crawl over several hundred on our way forward."

"Fine. Just ask them to take it easy on the last guy."

After a moment, Cable called back, "They're thinning out, and I can see light up ahead."

Dani was sure those were the sweetest words she had ever heard.

"Thank God," Jon hissed through gritted teeth.

The tube emptied into a long, narrow rectangle box with six holes situated nearly twelve feet above them. It was miraculous to finally be able to stand after nearly three hours in confined spaces and even more so to be free of the Deathstalkers.

They lay on the ground panting, as the last few minutes of their adrenaline faded.

Jon inspected his stings. They felt like someone had injected him with battery acid, but the welts were no bigger than a silver dollar.

"You okay?" Cable asked.

Jon gave him a brief nod.

Cable stretched out his spine. "I'm glad they taught you about mole-tunneling in the military, but I plan on never doing that again."

"I'll drink to that," Dani added.

"I've done worse," Jon said, with a serious grimace.

Cable and Dani shared a look.

A lone scorpion ventured from the aqueduct into the space, and Jon smashed it with his boot into oblivion. "I'm gonna come back here with a flamethrower."

"Toilets," Dani said, looking at the oval cutouts in the stone overhead with a scowl. "So, do we call for help, or will we just be inviting more trouble?"

"I think we can get out of here on our own," Jon said, as he appraised their situation. "Cable, make a wide stance. I'll get on your shoulders, and Dani should be able to use us like a ladder to climb out."

Cable followed his instructions, and soon Jon sat on top of his shoulders. Cable held his legs, and Jon reached down with one arm to help Dani get started.

"Not one comment about my weight." At five-eight, Dani had an athletic build with just the right amount of curves, but any amount of weight added to the wonky ladder would cause it to sway.

"I'm just glad you're not wearing the high heels you got in Rome," Cable said, making sure not to grunt when she put all her weight on him and started upward.

She free-climbed the human totem pole, using their body parts as jugs. When she grabbed Cable's injured ribs, he nearly dropped to the floor. Instead, he gritted his teeth, absorbing the pain. When Dani got to the top, the entire platform started to wobble.

It took all Cable had to stabilize the formation of bodies. He tried to counter any leans by shuffling his feet. The whole thing looked like a poorly conceived circus act ready to fail until Dani managed to grab hold of one of the edges of the holes above. It instantly stabilized the wobble.

Using Jon's head, she pushed off and pulled herself through the toilet hole.

Jon quickly climbed off Cable, and a moment later, Dani's head peeked down from above. "Let me see if I can find some help." With that, she scampered off, out of Cable and Jon's view.

Cable moved back to the wall and sat down. Jon turned off his phone's light and joined him.

It was quiet in the dank stone space lit by the ambient glow of six toilet holes above.

"Here." Cable handed Jon his lighter back.

Jon nodded absently in thanks, then said, "I was buried alive once."

Cable looked over, concern on his face.

"I was seven. Me and my best friend, Kōji, found an old abandoned mine while hiking in the forest outside of Kyoto, where I grew up. We turned it into a fort of sorts with candles and a few old crates as furniture. It was our escape place where we could be anyone or anything our imagination would allow."

Jon slipped the lighter into his pocket. "One summer day, we decided to dig out one side of our cave to make it larger. We hauled my dad's gardening tools up there and started chipping away. It didn't take long before one of the old support beams became unstable, and the roof gave way." Jon paused at the memory. "It buried us both."

Cable watched as Jon doodled on the ground with his finger, needing a moment.

"I was lucky. The support beam fell at an angle, leaving a small pocket of air around me. I didn't learn that tunneling technique in the military. I learned it that day in the mine, out of sheer desperation to save Kōji. I dug and pulled my way out… I just needed you both to trust that it would work."

"What happened to your friend?" Cable asked.

"He wasn't as lucky."

"I'm sorry… You might not have been able to save your friend, but I don't care where or how you learned it, you just saved three lives with that technique."

Jon nodded, his eyes misting. "It took a long time before I could do tight spaces again. At first, even a small room would make me anxious."

"How did you overcome it?" Cable asked.

"The same way I learned to like tea. I forced myself to take small sips, over and over again."

"Wait. A Japanese national who doesn't like tea?"

Jon looked over at Cable. A small smile lifted the corners of his mouth. "I know, right? My parents almost had to give me up. Still not a fan, but at least now I can do it."

"You talking about tight spaces or tea?" Cable asked.

"Both."

Cable shook his head with a grin. "I was never a fan of cauliflower, and my mom loved the stuff. After her death, I learned to love it too. I guess sometimes you just have to be in the right headspace to move your needle."

Jon nodded slightly in agreement.

Cable looked up at the dimming light coming down from above. "I think we might have a problem."

"I was just thinking the same thing. Dani should have been back by now."

Cable stood and stepped over to peer up at the toilet holes above. So close, but so out of reach. "And this is about the time scorpions make their way out of hiding."

"I'm not playing pin cushion for those guys again," Jon said as he scratched at the burning sensation on his arm.

"How's the pain?"

"About the same. How's your ribs?"

"No deep breaths for a while, but I'll live." Cable called out several times for Dani and for help in general. No reply was returned. He did a mental calculation, looking at Jon.

"What?" Jon returned.

"I think we can at least get you out with a version of what we tried earlier."

"I'd have to stand on your shoulders to reach the top. There's no way you can balance that."

"Exactly."

Cable leaned against the side wall, and Jon looked at him curiously. Recognition filled his face. Jon started to scale Cable's body with the assistance of several rough-rock seams in the wall for purchase. When he got to the top, Cable used his hands on Jon's legs to stabilize the newly formed creature.

Jon, while standing on Cable's shoulders, was now tall enough to reach the top, and holding the ceiling gave them the stability they needed.

Cable then slowly shuffled over the empty space while Jon hand-walked across the ceiling. It was a wobbly, unstable mass at best, but slowly, they moved toward the closest opening.

Once they were directly under a toilet hole, Cable stopped.

"Okay, I'm going to have to jump to grab the rim. There is a chance I will slip. As soon as I jump, you need to roll away, so I don't crash down on top of you."

"Got it," Cable replied.

Jon did a quick countdown and then sprang off Cable's shoulders.

Cable flinched in pain before rolling away the moment Jon's feet lifted off.

Jon's fingers just reached the rim, but he couldn't quite hang on, and he fell the twelve feet back to the ground, hitting hard.

He lay there for a second, grimacing.

"You're lucky," Cable said.

Jon shot him a sideways squint.

"Kyoto is one of my favorite cities, and you got to grow up there."

"You've been?"

"Spent a month there in the spring, a couple of years back."

"It has become too touristy for my tastes."

Cable suddenly tensed. "We got company."

Jon looked over to see a couple of Deathstalkers enter the space from the aqueduct. He immediately ran over and stomped them flat, then threw a bunch of dirt into the pipe, hoping to discourage the others. "Come on. Let's try again."

It took two more attempts before Jon managed to grasp the lip of the toilet hole and hang on. He slowly pulled himself up and out into the world above.

"Hang on a sec," he called down before disappearing.

Cable called up, "Any sign of Dani?" But Jon was already gone. He threw some more dirt into the aqueduct. "Hurry up." There was no reply.

The Deathstalkers were done waiting, and as if a starting gun had been fired, they began gushing into the room, all heading up and out for their nightly feed. The only good news was that they seemed to have a preset course, and the majority clung to the far wall, but several hundred still moved right for the room's sole occupant.

Cable backed up to the center of the room. There was no escape. "Jon, if you're up there, now would be a good time to do something." Cable kicked out in all directions, trying to keep the potential assassins at bay. At first, it worked, but as more and more scorpions entered, it quickly proved ineffective.

Soon, hundreds more were crossing the floor in the dying light. It looked like a small flood tide of yellow and gray rushing his way. Cable took on a new strategy. He froze in place, making himself a human statue. He hoped that if he didn't give them a reason, they wouldn't sting him. He was now just another stone to crawl on. It only took a few seconds before the first few made it onto his pants and began their ascent to the dimming light above. One managed to get inside his pants and was crawling up the back of his calf.

The first drops of sweat began sliding down Cable's face as he tried and failed not to react to his situation.

Within a few seconds, nearly fifty Deathstalkers were crawling up his pants.

"You still there?"

Cable looked up at the most beautiful thing in the world: Jon Chibi holding a Tunisian flag along with the rope that had held it high on a pole above the palace. "Yes, but you better hurry."

Jon pointed his phone's light down. "Oh, man. Quick, grab the rope."

Cable immediately lifted himself off the ground and shook his legs, dislodging several freeloaders. Almost instantly, the Deathstalker inside his pants stung his leg, sending a shockwave of pain into Cable's body. He banged his legs together, smashing the creature, and then forced himself to focus on getting out. The shot of adrenaline that came with the excruciating pain helped him scurry up the rope in record time.

Jon helped him out and over the toilet seat just seconds before more Deathstalkers flowed right behind.

"Welcome to the other side of the bathroom."

Cable quickly looked around. They were in a small stone room with a long-raised stone bench seat with six carved toilet holes on it.

A freaky and macabre scene suddenly erupted as thousands of deadly scorpions swarmed out of the holes and off into the night.

Both men backed away and ran for fresh air.

"Any sign of Dani?" Cable asked.

"No. Nothing."

"My arm is not working," Jon said, looking at his swollen appendage. "I think we need to get to a hospital."

CHAPTER ELEVEN

ENIZ CHECKED THE WRAPPED DRESSING around his mid-section. It was crimson. Blood oozed through the gauze, leaking down onto his pants and the car seat. He pulled the vehicle off the road amid an impatient driver's honking. His next destination was unclear as he couldn't go to a hospital with a bullet wound, could he? He reached for his phone. Bloody fingers slid across the screen uselessly. A quick wipe on a dry part of his shirt, and he opened the browser. There was a clinic only a couple of miles away. That, he could do. He input the address into his navigation and set the phone down.

His world began to spin, so he placed his hands on the steering wheel and held on until the sensation passed. The dwindling evening light was making it hard to see, so he reached for the overhead light. His arms felt unexpectedly heavy, and his mind struggled to focus. *Just put the car in drive and get moving*, his inner voice screamed, but the stick shift suddenly seemed impossibly far away. Maybe he just needed to rest for a moment. His head sagged down, barely focusing on the phone in his lap. He stabbed at one of his favorites and managed to hit the speaker button.

After two rings, the line connected. "What's your status?"

Deniz's words came out slurred and labored. "I may have failed you, my Sidi."

"Deniz? Where are you? What's happened?" Mona said, with urgency.

Deniz tried to lift his head for a road sign. Nothing obvious was in sight. "Listen… I don't have…much time left."

"No. You listen. I can get you help—just tell me where you are," Mona insisted.

"I have your shell. Though, I can't guarantee…the original. There's another party. Greek. Watch out. I also have…" He paused for several raspy breaths before a coughing spell ejected blood from his mouth. "There is another piece of the puzzle… Treasure."

"Treasure? What are you talking about?"

Each word was becoming more difficult to express. "Get to land's end… African…Horn…" Deniz slumped over into the passenger seat. Being horizontal felt better, as what blood he had left pumped through his brain. He suddenly lost interest in the conversation and hung up amid a tirade of questions. He pulled his phone's screen into view and accessed the photo app. With his last few breaths, Deniz scrolled through his favorites folder. These were not pictures of friends and family, or even a pet, but rather candid snaps of all his kills over the last few years.

Deniz felt a warm rush as he flicked from image to image, a proud chronicle of his greatest achievements.

As his eyes dimmed, he landed on his last masterpiece. The museum girl with her hair splayed out, floating so lifelike in her tub. A final smile faded from his lips as his eyes finally defocused. The phone fell to the floor and clicked off. It buzzed several more times to no reply.

Mona paced back and forth, slowly lowering her phone. Deniz was not picking up. Her office seemed suddenly very quiet as she processed his last few words. This was the first she had heard anything about a treasure. Not that it was important, but if he had the shell, she needed to get to him, and fast, before someone else found it. She quickly wrote down everything he had told her and then dialed a number from memory.

"Sheba," a flat, digital voice called out after three rings.

"I have a number I need you to track."

"Text it to me. What's the urgency?" Sheba asked without emotion.

"Yesterday," Mona replied.

"Okay, I'll call you back in ten."

The phone clicked off, and Mona hid her irritation as she dialed another number.

"Ahlan? Cancel all my appointments for the next two weeks." Now it was her turn to hang up on someone.

She sat down at her desk with a plop and let a plan develop. She mentally checked off a list of next steps, letting her mind focus on the words she had written down and how close she was to her final quest. After all these years, was it possible that her family's seashell might be back where it belonged, and was there more to the shell than just a legacy? She looked at the word *treasure* on the piece of paper. Her imagination wandered until she was jolted by a buzzing on her desk.

"Yes?"

"I have a location."

"That was fast," Mona said, with genuine surprise.

"Tracking phones is child's play. It's just outside Tunis."

"Tunis? Do you have anyone in the area?" Mona asked.

After a beat, the reply came. "My cousin Fawzi lives there."

"Have him get to this location and collect everything he can carry. If the man is still alive, please get him help. Have Fawzi bring me the contents here in Egypt. I will double his normal fee for expediency."

"It shall be done," Sheba said before clicking off.

Mona had used Sheba in the past but had never met anyone personally. She or he was efficient but had the personality of a rock. But she was paying for results, not a newfound friendship, and so far, the results had always been good.

Sheba was an ancient kingdom around the area of modern-day Yemen. It had a famous queen, whose name was only known as 'Queen of Sheba' but otherwise, it was anyone's guess as to the origin of the name. In truth, it didn't matter to Mona who or what Sheba was. It only mattered what they were capable of. That is what defined a person. Mona had gone from slave to one of the most powerful women in Egypt. Sheba had become the best hacker Mona had ever worked with. That's what mattered, nothing else.

Mona's phone buzzed with a request for $2,000 in Bitcoin. Now that was efficiency.

Cable walked out of the building with his shoulders visibly slumped. He had spent the last two hours dealing with the local police. Ultimately, he had gained no further information on the whereabouts of Dani. Wasted time he would never get back.

Jon picked him up in the rental, observing Cable's body language as he settled into the passenger seat. They had decided that Cable would go in alone to keep the narrative simple and direct. There was no need to complicate things with an ex-special forces Japanese national who didn't speak the language. Or their involvement in the explosion at a national historic site, for that matter. His arm had responded well to the antivenom given at the local hospital, and he could now move his fingers. Another day, and he would be as good as new. "Anything?" he asked hopefully as he drove away.

"That was a total bust," Cable replied. "The only thing I can figure is the creeper that tried to blow us up took her."

"So, he tried to kill us with a bomb, and then what? Hung around for nearly three hours while the cops combed the site? Then managed to catch Dani as she squirmed out of the royal toilet some one hundred yards away?"

"You're right. That makes no sense," Cable said.

"No," Jon agreed. "Is it possible that Dani—"

"Never," Cable interrupted. "She would not leave us over treasure. Especially when we don't even know what or where it is."

"Maybe there is another group in play here."

"That would make sense, but who?" Cable asked.

"As I see it, the only choice we have is to get to the next clue before whoever has Dani does. It is the only way we'll have any leverage to get her back."

"Trade info for Dani?" Cable asked.

"Giving up now will not guarantee her return, and if the treasure is so important to someone, let's trade her for it."

Cable let the words sink in. "How do we get in touch with them to even make a trade?"

"If we have the next clue, they'll find us."

"Okay, we need to get to the Horn of Africa, and fast."

Jon put the car in gear and left the parking lot. "I'll call Tam and update him. You figure out where exactly we're going. The Horn of Africa is some four hundred miles long, and it all belongs to Somalia. Not exactly American-friendly."

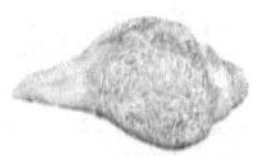

Dani sat in the middle of the backseat between two thugs who worked for the man in the passenger seat. He said his name was Nico, something or other, and based on his accent, he was Greek, or maybe Bulgarian. The sturdy Mitsubishi Pajero was driving west into the setting sun, forcing her to squint. She shifted her eyes to the side. A nice black eye was rising on the man next to her.

Dani had given as good as she'd gotten. Her elbow connected squarely with the man's eye socket as he tried to grab her. Unfortunately, two men with guns surrounded her, and she was quietly escorted to the back of the ruins and over the wall.

All of this took place while the local police and the Tunisian National Guard argued over jurisdiction in the parking lot.

She considered crying out, but somehow, the man with the pistol in her ribs anticipated that and nearly knocked the wind out of her lungs with a good jab and a warning.

They had forced her to remove her shoes and had taken her cell phone. Otherwise, there had been no questions or any kind of demands.

Kidnapping for profit was very real in this part of the world, and Dani was no stranger to the experience, but this was something else.

The man driving was familiar to her, but she couldn't place him. Had she seen him at the hotel, or maybe on the ferry crossing? She just couldn't make the connection.

They pulled into a private section of a local airport. The sign said *El Borma*, which meant nothing to Dani. She was loaded into a twin-engine prop plane and crammed into the small space behind the rear seat. A huge man named Jude, with terrible breath, sat in the bench seat right in front of her, smashing her even further into the bulkhead. The familiar man sat next to him.

A man called Jason fired up the engines and powered them down the runway. The orange sunset swallowed them as the plane reached cruising altitude.

The man who called himself Nico called back from the copilot's seat. "Dr. Dani Tran, unless you want to go skydiving without a parachute, you will tell us where we are going next."

Dani's hands shook with fear as she tried to calm herself and understand the man's words. "I'm not sure what you mean," she shot back weakly.

"We are after the same thing you are," said a man in the seat next to the big guy. He spoke much better English than his boss and held up the first 3D-printed seashell.

It all came back to her. The museum heist. "Tobias?" she mumbled.

"Good memory, Doc, but I suggest you focus on your future, not your past. Where to?"

Dani swallowed and considered her options. Apparently, there was more than one group in search of the seashell's secrets. The last person tried to bomb her out of existence, and this one was willing to toss her out of an airplane. "We found a clue that indicates the Horn of Africa."

"That is a bit vague," Tobias returned.

"West into the rising sun at land's end… So, I'm guessing the tip? It's not an exact science, especially since several millennia have passed."

Tobias turned to the pilot and called out, "We need to get to the tip of the Horn of Africa."

"That's not realistic in this airplane. I'll get us to Tripoli, and we can reassess."

Nico nodded his approval.

Dani closed her eyes and uttered a silent prayer that Cable and Jon had somehow gotten out of the pit she had left them in. They were the only people in the world who might know where she was going.

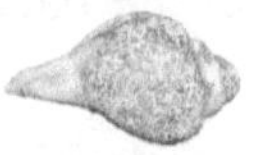

Mona stared at the map on her laptop for the hundredth time. The Horn of Africa was a desolate place with no obvious features. How was she supposed to find anything in such a location? Deniz had been onto something, something that had a direct connection to her family's heritage. Now, with him gone, was she forced to start from scratch? She went through the few clues he had given her over the phone. A Greek party of some sort was interested. That seemed very random to her. Perhaps they were aware of this potential treasure. That made the most sense, as the Greeks were always trying to line their pockets. Any past business dealings she had experienced seemed to support this. It was all so confusing. Land's end, African Horn was just as vague in her opinion.

A buzzing on her phone stopped the spiraling thoughts. "Yes?"

"There is a man here to see you. Says he was sent by Sheba? Do you know anything about that?"

"Yes. Please send him up."

Fawzi looked just like she imagined. A scruffy, middle-aged Tunisian in a traditional brown *jebba* over a collared white shirt. Both were frayed and stained by time.

"This is for you," Fawzi said as he placed a box on her desk.

"That's everything?" Mona asked.

"Everything except his clothes. I'm sorry. Your friend was dead when I got there."

"Yes. Well, he lived like he died, on the edge. This is a little extra for you. I appreciate your expediency on this matter."

The man looked confused by her words but didn't hesitate to take the envelope and look inside. "Thank you very much. May Allah bless you."

"And you as well."

Once Fawzi was gone, Mona opened the box. An unexpected gasp was quieted as her hand reflexively covered her mouth. She reached down and reverently picked up the large carved seashell. It was just as her mother had described. She slowly rotated it, marveling at the curious symbols that seemed to stare back at her. Several of the symbols she recognized from the ones on the back of the picture her mother had given her.

Could this indeed be it, a lifetime's quest realized? She sat down, her legs feeling weak. Fingers probed the texture of each carved letter as vague memories flooded back, threatening to overwhelm her. Her index finger found a rough spot on the bottom of the shell, and she turned it over to inspect it. A sudden surge coursed through her body as she slowly realized things were not all as they appeared. A quick tap on the shell confirmed it—plastic. This was not her family's shell. It was a plastic replica. She stood and placed it on the corner of her desk, then paced slowly, letting it all process. She recalled Deniz's last words to her. "I have your shell. Though I can't guarantee…the original. There's another party. Greek." If this was a replica of her shell, that meant the original was still out there. Possibly in the hands of another party, Greek.

She emptied the rest of the box's contents onto her desk.

Wallet, phone, folded paper, cigarettes, lighter, laptop.

Mona let a small smile escape as she picked up the Bic lighter. She remembered trying once to buy Deniz a proper chrome-plated Zippo, but he had refused, stating that he preferred using a cheap plastic one. He wanted people to remember his face, not anything that might draw their attention elsewhere. Because of that, he never wore jewelry or fancy clothes, only that stupid cowboy hat. He was a walking contradiction, but she would miss his efforts on her behalf.

She put down the lighter and opened the laptop. A password prompt flashed, the same for the phone.

Mona opened the folded pages and paused. There was a collection of the shell's symbols drawn across the top of the page, and below that was an English translation.

Boaz expedition around bottom of world. All dead. Treasure of a thousand kings. Rising sun to land's end. A mystical place. Followed by a *double delta* and a wide *U.*

This was a more complete translation than Deniz had given her before. Had he found more information on his quest, or had he held back the part about the treasure? She dismissed it as a waste of time before she could let herself get upset by that thought. Mona lifted the replica shell and let her eyes marvel once more. "So, you hold a secret to a treasure. A treasure that belongs to me."

She quickly dialed her phone.

"Sheba."

"I have another task for you."

The Gulf of Aden had one of the busiest shipping lanes in the world. Every vessel using the Suez Canal passed through its warm waters. Cable watched the seemingly endless parade of huge cargo ships coming and going as a warm breeze tussled his hair.

With tensions as they were in the Middle East, it seemed inevitable that this trade route would be a target. Politics and greed went hand in hand, but Cable tried to steer far from those realities. The problem was, they often didn't steer far from him.

The *Desert Rose* was an old swoop-deck fishing boat. It was making good time out of their port in Djibouti, leaving a trail of black smoke in its wake. The port city was the closest semi-American-friendly destination they would risk launching from, and it would be quite a journey to the Horn of Africa.

Somalia, or the Federal Republic of Somalia, had the longest coastline in Africa. In 2012, the federal government took control after a long civil war that ripped the country apart. In present times, Cable was aware it was considered a failed state by other nations. Had they flown to its capital, Mogadishu, their kidnapping or murder would be all but guaranteed.

The current US travel advisory stated: Do Not Travel to Somalia due to crime, terrorism, civil unrest, kidnapping, and piracy.

It was the last one that concerned Jon. Pirates ruled the coast of Somalia. And that was their entire journey and destination. The captain of the weathered thirty-six-foot wooden-hulled boat kept them close to the lineup of behemoth steel giants. These ships provided a modicum of safety. And to be honest, any pirate worth his salt would not waste his time on the old boat that looked like it missed its date with the scrapyard long ago. It had a faded, teal open bow with a small working net crane in the middle. That was followed by a white dilapidated two-level structure rising from the quarterdeck with a sagging roof. Inside was the helm, a few berths, a galley, and one head.

Since leaving the port in Djibouti, they had taken on one additional crew member, a friend of Cable's who lived nearby in Ethiopia. Kojo, with his orange beard and ever-present traditional yellow *Dorze* cap, sat on a coil of rope with a concerned smile on his face. His extremely rare blue eyes, set against sunbaked Ethiopian skin, were a genetic defect called OCA2 that occurred in less than eight percent of the population.

He had spent time working with both Cable and Dani, becoming a reliable contact and friend. Once Cable knew their next destination, he reached out for his help.

Kojo came without a second thought. That is, until he learned of their objective. "I feel like *alestes*," he said in Ethiopian-accented English.

Cable cocked his head toward his friend. "*Alestes?*"

Kojo used his hands to help describe his words. "The small fish we use to catch other fish."

"You mean, bait."

"Yes. Bait."

"We have pirates at five o'clock," Jon called out.

Kojo looked at his watch, perplexed.

Cable jumped up and squinted his eyes in the direction Jon was looking. Jon handed Cable his binoculars, and Cable soon found the threat. The small, swift wooden boats were headed for a container ship to their stern. A distant alarm on the ship sounded as the crew prepared for the fight. He could just make out the big ship starting to turn as high-pressure water jets shot out at the aggressors.

Cable slowly lowered his binoculars and handed them back.

"As long as all these huge container ships are nearby, I don't think we have to worry," Jon said.

Kojo joined them at the railing. "It's when they're not around. That's what has me worried."

The barren shoreline was just visible to the naked eye as the sun set over the dark continent. The captain had estimated it would take thirty hours to reach the tip of the Horn, and based on their current speed, that would be just before dawn the next day.

Cable found a space on the deck that seemed more comfortable than the bedbug-infested mats inside the boat and settled down. He opened the laptop they had been using, attached it to their satellite phone's data port, and clicked on the Google view of the tip of the African Horn. Just like every other time he had searched the coastline, nothing obvious popped up. It was a barren wasteland. Frustration won out, and he slammed the lid closed and gave up for the night.

Jon borrowed the phone and updated Tam on their progress. The conversation was filled with concern from both sides. The unknown whereabouts of Dani had raised the stakes, and Tam's dream of discovering the shell's secret was marred by genuine fear that he may have unwittingly caused harm to her. It took Jon several different tacks to convince him that the best course of action was to continue.

After Jon hung up, Cable spoke through closed eyes. "I noticed you skipped the part where we illegally cross into a sovereign state that would be happy to kill us on the spot."

"They have to catch us first."

"Hope you're a fast runner," Cable said.

"Not as fast as a bullet, but I can hold my own."

Cable shook his head and got comfortable for the night. The warm ocean breeze and the repetitive thump of the boat's old diesel soon had him dreaming about running for his life.

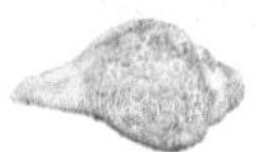

Mona stepped from her home, nerves jangling. Ever since Sheba had hacked the phone and laptop in Deniz's possession, she had a clearer understanding of what was at stake. From what she could gather, three people were on the trail of the seashell's carved message. There were pictures of each with a short bio: Dr. Dani Tran, Cable Janson, and Jon Chibi. Deniz had been earning his pay. What she didn't know was if any of the three were responsible for Deniz's death, or if they were working together or in competition. It seemed far-fetched, but she had been a party to stranger things. How did they find out about the shell, and what led them here? She had so many questions, all without answers.

She stepped into the town car waiting, her mind bouncing thoughts like an electron.

There was more to this than just her finding the answers to her family's shell. There was a race with the possibility of something more, and she intended to win it.

She gazed out the window as her beloved Cairo swept past. For all its corruption and problems, it had been good to her. Here, she had made her way, found her strength, and conquered her piece of it. Now she would add a lasting legacy to her accomplishments, and even though humans were just renters during their time on this planet, she intended to own what she could while she could, and whatever was at the end of this journey would be added to it.

The town car turned into a nearby local airport and came to a stop next to a Learjet 75 Liberty. Her newly formed team was busy loading the aircraft. The four mercenaries didn't seem to even notice her arrival, so she moved past them and boarded, taking her favorite seat.

They would be heading south to the port city of Mogadishu, the capital of Somalia. It was a place she had visited once in the past. Its mix of Arabian and African cultures gave it a unique vibe that was a nice change from her life in Egypt. As the jet left the ground, Mona was reminded of a tryst she had had in the port city several years ago. A smartly dressed businessman, Barre Nasir, had approached her at a restaurant and offered to buy her dinner. He had dark features and bright brown eyes. The kind of eyes that seemed to know what you were thinking before you did. Her first reaction was to make an excuse, but as the words started to form in her mouth, she found herself saying yes instead.

The next four days were a story for the record books, well, at least her record book. Passion was something she reserved for business, but Mona found herself lost in the moment and just enjoying the whole experience.

Her lips curled at the memories. Three days after her return to Cairo, Barre had called her. She remembered the smile that covered her face, hearing his voice. They scheduled a rendezvous at her beachside villa in Alexandria.

That was the last time she ever spoke to him. A fatal jet crash, leaving Somalian air space, killed all onboard. The dark recollection slew her smile and threatened to foul her mood. Mona pushed it down into the steel box she kept in the very back of her mind for only the most painful memories.

She looked back at the three men and one woman onboard the jet with her. They came highly recommended, and she had every confidence they would keep her safe and fulfill their duties.

Ra, a thirty-eight-year-old ex-El-Sa'ka, or Egyptian Thunderbolt Forces, was in charge. He had narrow eyes and a foul expression. His expertise was more along the lines of VIP protection, but adding a quest to the mix had not concerned him in the least.

The woman's name was Kaari from Ghana, and she had the coldest black eyes Mona had ever seen. An almond-shaped face was finished off with a subtle cleft chin.

The big one was Zo from Malawi, and he towered over everyone.

Sitting in the rear seat, a skinny, jittery South African named Arno completed the group.

They were a melting pot of African cultures thrust into a single-minded mission. They all had some sort of military background and were well acquainted with violence.

Mona, for the briefest moment, felt like Lara Croft, The Tomb Raider, on her way to claim the mysterious prize. The thought lightened her mood, and she slowly spun back around, leaning her head back and closing her eyes.

After clearing customs at Aden Adde International Airport in Mogadishu, they refueled and continued to a small landing strip east of Bosaco, the last port town on the Sea of Aden. From there, an off-road vehicle was waiting, and after loading up and checking the weapons stored inside, the team started the long, circuitous journey to the tip of the Horn of Africa. For her safety, Mona was squished between Kaari and Arno in the rear seat.

CHAPTER TWELVE

L UCKILY, THE WAVES WERE MERCIFULLY calm in the predawn light, as their raft was on the small side for three grown adults. Jon lifted the outboard as the bow kissed the sand. Kojo and Cable jumped out and pulled the craft up past the high-tide line, which was about fifty feet of smooth sand. They found some driftwood and scrub to cover the raft until they came back for it.

The captain had agreed to return at dusk to pick them up, which would give the three-man team just under eleven hours to do their search. If they came up empty, they would regroup, and what came next was anyone's guess.

The sky was slowly turning pink, giving them just enough light to see by.

Cable glanced over his shoulder as the *Desert Rose* shrank on the horizon. Waiting too close to the shore was inviting trouble for any boat, even in this godforsaken place.

Jon used his binoculars to search the coastline. An empty beach in both directions was a rare sight for the Japanese national.

Cable walked up to the hundred-foot cliff face separating the beach from the desert above. It continued along the coast as far as he could see. "Okay, Jon, you and Kojo, go right. I'll go left. Quick reminder. We are looking for any symbols or carvings or caves that might hold some type of message or—"

"Got it. Looking for anything unusual," Jon finished.

"Keep in mind, if something was put there, it was a long time ago and probably long since faded, but you never know."

"Copy that. Remember, five hours out and five hours back. That will give you a one-hour cushion," Jon said as he moved to the right. He picked up his radio and tested it. "Radio check."

Cable replied as he headed in the opposite direction, "Good copy."

Kojo had studied the symbols from the shell Cable had shown him and felt reasonably sure he would recognize one. He kept his eyes peeled on the cliff as they walked.

"So, how long have you known Cable?" Jon asked, after a time.

"He and I crossed paths a few years back at an Addis Mercato in Dire Dawa."

Jon looked at Kojo with one raised eyebrow.

"An open marketplace."

"Gotcha."

"He was slaughtering his Amharic, and I stepped in to help."

Jon nearly tripped on a mostly buried log in the dim light. "I thought he spoke like a zillion languages."

"He does, but Ethiopia speaks Amharic, along with about ninety other sub-idioms. It has ancient roots with no commonality to any other current language." Kojo squinted at a pattern on the cliff wall and then dismissed it as the work of nature. "As unique as, say, the Hawaiian language is. Anyway, he'd only been in country a week, so honestly, he was doing pretty good. I overheard him order a wrapped foot, and well, it caught my attention. So, I helped him get his order right, and we ended up sharing the meal."

"What was he trying to order?" Jon asked out of curiosity.

"Sambusas. Kinda like Indian samosas, a wrapped pastry filled with beef," Kojo replied.

"Didn't you guys discover a temple or something like that?"

"Yeah, last year we went on a hunt much like this," Kojo said. "Had an Interpol agent and a couple of warring factions to deal with."

"At least there is only one other group competing with us now."

"So far…" Kojo said, with a bit of a smirk. "Cable and Dani are good people, and I probably owe them my life."

"What do you make of that?" Jon said, changing the subject.

Both men stopped and walked up closer to a dark spot in the cliff face.

"It's a cave," Kojo replied.

"Wait till we are inside before switching on your flashlight. Don't want to advertise we're here." Jon led the way, flipping his light on once it was too dark to see anything. The natural cave started small and then opened, deadening some twenty feet into the mountainside. Except for a vein of red rock cutting across the roof, it was unremarkable. Jon and Kojo inspected every inch for anything that might not belong. Other than some stranded driftwood in the back and some empty plastic bottles, there was nothing.

As they exited, the sky had gone from pink to orange, and the first few rays of sunlight sparkled on the liquid horizon.

Jon pushed them forward, feeling the first hint of the day's heat starting to climb.

Cable jogged slowly along the beach in the other direction, taking in the sandstone cliff face to his right. The last four hours had been a mind-numbing blur of sameness. Brown, brown, and brown with the occasional shrub. Nature had a way of carving and eroding stone over time, and his hopes of finding anything that might connect to a Phoenician voyage some 2,500 years ago faded with every step. And with that came a genuine fear that Dani might be gone. He pushed the thought from his mind and pressed on.

It always amazed him how even the most remote beaches found themselves filled with modern litter. Anything that floated wound up on a beach somewhere or became part of the growing giant floating trash island in the middle of the Pacific.

He paused for a water break, wiping the sweat from his brow. The sun had come on strong, spiking the temperature into triple digits. Cable figured he had about two more hours before he would have to start back.

The sound of a helicopter began to grow, and Cable ran up a small wadi. He ducked behind a flourishing Yeheb nut bush with its distinctive yellow flowers. An old rusty gas can that had been swept up the ditch during some high-tide storm kept him company.

Within a few minutes, a dark-blue Eurocopter EC135 swept past. It was moving slowly just above the waves, taking in every detail of the coast. Cable quickly realized what was happening and grabbed his walkie-talkie. "Jon, do you copy?"

A familiar voice responded amid static, due to their distance. "Go for Jon."

"How's the search?"

"We found a couple of caves, but nothing on this end so far."

"Same here. I haven't seen even one cave. FYI, there's a civilian helicopter heading your way, and I'd be willing to bet it's our friend from the ruins with the bomb."

"Do you think Dani is onboard?"

"Certainly possible. I'm not planning on sticking my head out to see."

"Smart. We'll find some cover. Talk soon."

Cable hoped Dani was on the helicopter. It would mean she was still alive, but showing up now made the race for the next clue even more important. He waited a good two minutes after the copter passed before climbing down from his hiding spot and continuing his search.

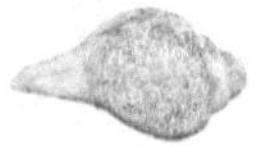

Dani stared out her window as the Eurocopter slowly flew past the cliff face along the southern coast of the tip of the Horn. Tobias sat next to her, staring over her shoulder. The pilot and Nico were up front, also looking out, but unclear as to what they were looking for. For Nico, it would require a lighted sign, *Look Here*. The pilot had to split his attention between flying and looking, so he was just as ineffective. The reality was that they were all counting on Dani, and she was doing this against her will. The real problem was the concern for her safety. It was tied directly to her ability to produce results. Something they had made very clear with the point of a gun.

The other men were several miles back at base camp, an abandoned school complex in Xandha City, a village of some three hundred people and goats. One of only two small settlements that scratched out their survival in the Horn of Africa. Dani had been surprised at the effectiveness and ingenuity Tobias had used to get them here. He had set up a working infrastructure, smoothed out visas, and added additional armed men to the task force. Money seemed to speak all languages, and being Greek seemed to be just fine with the locals.

Dani had been stripped of her shoes and handcuffed to a tent pole. Even in the shade the midday temperature was well over a hundred. She knew her socks wouldn't protect her feet should she find a way to escape. She was going nowhere for now.

The large helicopter had shuttled their supplies and equipment out from Abdullahi Yusuf Airport in Galkayo, and it was now being used to scout the coast of the Horn for possible clues.

Dani loathed everything about their operation, mostly because it was so efficient. She didn't see how Cable or Jon would ever catch up. Without them, her chance of getting out alive… She pushed the thought from her mind and tried to refocus on the cliff outside the helicopter's window. It wasn't the first time this had happened to her, but it was certainly the first time she had worked from a helicopter. At least Tobias had returned her shoes. If she got the chance, she would run.

"Possible cave," Dani called out, as a small dark area in the cliff moved past.

Tobias marked the waypoint on his portable GPS unit.

"How much farther?" Nico called back. His attention span was wearing thin.

"The tip of the Horn covers some two-hundred-fifty miles, so be patient, *afentokó*," Tobias called back.

"There are some random footprints in the sand that come and go with the wave action here," Dani called out.

"Do they lead anywhere?" Nico asked.

Tobias leaned over for a better look. "No. They seem to just be paralleling the cliff." He turned to Dani. "Keep an eye out to see if they lead to anything."

"So, watch the cliff or the footprints? Which is it?" Dani spat back.

"Watch your mouth, or it will no longer work," Tobias warned.

Dani leaned her head back against the glass and looked out. She felt helpless and considered opening the door and jumping. At least that would put her back in control of her life. But if she survived the fall and landed without breaking several bones, they would just swoop in and grab her. She needed a better plan. "Another possible cave," she called out, in a monotone.

"Excellent, that makes eight spots worth further investigation," Tobias said, with enthusiasm.

"Have Jason and Jude bring the vehicles to the first waypoint and wait for us there. We'll link up on our return," Nico said.

Tobias made it happen.

Dani started to wonder whose footprints were in the sand below.

Whatever enthusiasm Mona had for this adventure had long since faded. The never-ending bumpy road and constant view of brown had been a wet blanket to her initial fiery excitement. Sitting in the middle of the backseat between two heavily armed mercenaries was intolerable. One needed a shower about a month ago, and the other kept playing with a large knife. This was way more than she bargained for. They both had that grizzled look that came from too many violent experiences. Perhaps she should send them ahead and wait in a hotel suite for their results. She wiped the sweat from her forehead and dismissed the thoughts.

The Kenyan-made Mobius SUV's air-conditioning had sputtered and died about an hour earlier, forcing them to keep the windows down in the triple-digit environment.

Mona had no experience with armed mercenaries, searching for treasure, or even navigating out in the wilderness. She despised guns and surrounded herself back home with every modern convenience.

The people she had dealt with in the past never brought their operations to her. She was always far removed from the gritty details, but not now. Now, she had been forced to let someone more qualified run the show. Her role was nothing but financier and mid-backset passenger.

Mona's skills were more akin to corporate nuances and negotiating, not this. But this was her quest, her mission. Her promise to her mother and her family's legacy were at stake. Whatever was at the end of it, she needed to be there, not some boss pointing fingers from afar. Somewhere in this forsaken desert was a token of her destiny, and she intended to find it.

They pulled through a small fishing village named Bereeda, past the small, stacked stone mosque and L-shaped government office.

Kaari, in the backseat with an AK-74 on her lap, called out, "This *tuulada* is the last settlement on the north end of the Horn. It signals the end of the road. From here on, we will have to make our own path."

Mona frowned as they turned off the bumpy dirt road onto even rougher desert terrain. The only good news was they were still riding and not walking.

They followed a large wadi up onto a ridge that looked back down on the small tuulada, or village. "We should have access to the beach in another five miles," Kaari added.

Zo slammed the four-wheel drive into low and began creeping west.

After an hour, they found a cut in the cliff that allowed access down to the beach. Zo suddenly stopped and turned off the motor. "Do you hear that?"

Mona listened for a moment until she heard the telltale sound of a helicopter in the distance. "Is it coming our way?"

"Yeah, and I don't want to do a meet and greet out here. Find us some cover," Ra ordered.

Zo fired up the engine and slammed it into gear, rushing over the rocks and careening down into the wash that dropped them toward the beach. Just before reaching the sand, he pulled between two shaded bushes and killed the engine.

All eyes stared up as if they could see through the roof. The engine popped and clicked as the helicopter approached.

After a bit, a dark-blue Eurocopter flew past their view out the windshield.

"I don't think they saw us," Arno instinctively whispered.

The helo then popped up high above the cliffs and did a one-eighty.

"Hang on. Guns ready," Ra called out.

Everyone except Mona racked their rifles and placed hands on door handles, ready to react.

Mona tried to hide a whimper as the sudden tension in the car shot through her like a bullet.

But the helicopter just swooped back down and flew in the other direction.

"Stand down. We're clear," ordered Ra.

Faces in the vehicle shared a look as they visibly relaxed.

"It either found what it was looking for or maybe they're running out of fuel," Zo speculated.

"Let's wait a beat before following," Ra said.

Zo nodded as he fired back up the Mobius.

"How 'bout a quick pit stop?" Mona pleaded.

Ra hid his chuckle. "Sure, sounds like a great idea."

Jon heard the helicopter and picked up his pace. He had fallen a bit behind Kojo. There was no obvious place to hide, as the cliff face along this part of the beach was formidable.

"Hey, there's a crack up ahead," Kojo called out, and they both ran for the obvious narrow 'V' up the beach. Kojo climbed up into the slot that shot up on both sides nearly a hundred feet overhead. It was narrow, barely wider than two men, shoulder to shoulder. Jon followed with his head on a swivel.

The roar of the helicopter closed on them.

"Get down and take off that hat," Jon called out.

There were no bushes or rocks to hide behind, so Kojo dove to the dirt floor, pulling off his bright yellow hat and falling face down. He held perfectly still. Jon came in quickly behind him and followed suit, only he flipped around to keep an eye on what was happening behind them. Through the narrow gap, he saw the chopper taking its time, as if it was looking for something. It was flying low along the waterline, heading east toward the tip. He waited till it cleared his vision before sitting up.

"Are we clear?" Kojo asked, his face still on the dirt floor.

"Yeah, clear," Jon called back, enjoying the respite from the sun in the shady slot canyon. "Sorry about the hat thing. I forgot your orange hair has the same chance of being spotted."

Kojo smiled as he sat up and looked around. "You think that was Dani?"

"I hope so. If it was, it means we have a chance to get her back."

Kojo nodded and gazed up at the slash of blue sky above them. "We will have to start heading back soon if we don't want to be stranded here."

"I know. Maybe another half hour?"

"Whatever was once here has long ago vanis—" Kojo stopped mid-sentence. His finger slowly rose and pointed to a spot some fifteen feet above him. "Is that a double delta?"

"Where?" Jon found Kojo's finger, and his eyes followed it to the wall of the slot canyon. Sure enough, there were two overlapping deltas carved in the rock face. They were long faded but just visible from where they were sitting.

Kojo stood and slowly climbed up the cliff face to the carving. He ran his fingers in the shallow grooves. "These are manmade."

"See anything else?" Jon called up.

"Nope. Just this."

"Try looking around."

Kojo was balanced on a small ledge about two inches wide. He looked left and then right—nothing. He then carefully spun around on the narrow rock and looked at the other side of the canyon wall.

Jon watched Kojo's disappointed expression change to curiosity.

"There's a small rock outcropping jutting out a few feet from the cliff face. I think there might be something there," Kojo said, leaning out to get a better perspective. He suddenly turned back and scampered down the wall. "Hang on," he threw out, as he started climbing up the other side of the slot canyon.

Twenty feet up, he pulled himself over a ledge and disappeared from Jon's view. A few seconds later, his head popped back out, and he called down, "There's a cave here."

"Hang on." Jon picked up the radio and tried to call Cable. No reply came back, just static. "You check it out. I'm going back to the beach to see if I can get a better signal."

Kojo nodded.

"Be careful."

"You too."

Jon jogged out of the slot canyon and jumped down into the sand. The first thing he heard was the helicopter. It was heading back in his direction. He quickly tried to contact Cable and finally got a static-filled response. He filled him in on the situation and then climbed back up. A quick look around led him to an old half-buried fishing net. Jon grabbed the net and used it to cover their footprints leading into the chasm. He then tossed it and started climbing the same wall Kojo had scaled.

"I see footprints leading into a narrow canyon," Dani called out.

Tobias marked it on his GPS and looked out for himself. "Those are fresh. That might be what we're looking for." He spun back to the pilot. "Hold this course for another ten minutes, then turn around and put us down about five hundred yards from this waypoint." He showed the pilot the coordinates, and he plotted them into his nav system.

Nico looked back at the receding footprints. "Why can't we just land now?" Nico called back, his boredom suddenly vanishing.

"I don't want to spook whoever is down there. Let 'em find whatever it is and then come to us."

Nico nodded his approval. "Call Jason and have them bring the vehicles to this waypoint."

Tobias put in the call. "He says it will take them about thirty minutes to get here."

Nico nodded again, in satisfaction.

Tobias let his mind process an upcoming plan. If there was only one way out of that narrow canyon, it would be a perfect place for an ambush.

After traveling east a bit more, the helicopter swooped up and reversed its course.

Dani braced herself for the sudden change in direction and for the events that were about to unfold.

Cable put the radio back on his belt. It would take him a good two hours to get back to the hidden raft if he hustled and another two just to get to the cave's entrance. Surely, Kojo and Jon would have everything figured out and be heading back by then. It didn't bother him that he had chosen the wrong direction in this search. As long as someone found something, it would be worth it. Now, he had a long jog ahead of him, and there was no better time to start.

A noise undulated on the breeze. At first, he thought he was hearing things, but soon, the distinct sound of a motor approaching became obvious. Cable didn't hesitate, he ducked into a depression in the cliff just before he was spotted. A few minutes later, two SUVs blew past his position, moving at over sixty miles an hour.

Cable waited till they were well past before stepping out and continuing his jog east. He pulled his radio out and began to transmit. "Jon, this is Cable. Do you copy?"

Only static replied.

He repeated the call several times before he added, "Be advised, there are two vehicles moving fast in your direction."

He repeated the message two more times before giving up and stowing the radio.

Dani unbuckled her harness as the rotors started to slow. They had set down on an open patch of sand. Tobias exited first, pointing his pistol in her direction. She led the way down the beach, as Nico and Tobias followed close behind.

Arno pulled the Mobius SUV into the shade of the cliffside, and everyone exited. They could just make out the helicopter parked in the sand some five hundred yards ahead, and people close to a thousand yards ahead.

"Keep to the shade of the cliffs," Ra ordered as they stealthily approached.

Mona brought up the rear, unarmed and unprepared. Her tennis shoes quickly filled with sand, and her hijab threatened to blow off several times.

Kojo crawled on his stomach for a good ten feet before the cave opened to standing height. A sudden scratching behind him made him freeze in panic. A light suddenly flashed across his face, and he nearly jumped.

"What'd you find?"

Kojo visibly relaxed at the sound of Jon's voice. "Nothing. I just got here."

"Oh, gotcha."

They moved their lights around the space. It was a natural sandstone cavern about the size of a large living room. The ceiling was slightly domed, and the floor was covered in dirt with a few rocks. In a word, unremarkable.

Kojo's light and then Jon's landed on the far wall. A small alcove appeared carved into the smooth surface. It was empty.

Kojo stepped closer to inspect it. "This is not natural, but whatever was here is long gone."

Jon stepped next to him and then bent down. He inspected the bottom of the altar with his light. After a few seconds, he blew across the base. A cloud of dust filled the air. Kojo started sneezing.

Jon doubled his efforts and used his hands to clear the base of a lifetime of dust and dirt. Slowly, symbols appeared, carved into the sandstone.

"Incredible," Kojo whispered. He took out his phone and snapped several pictures.

"Any idea what it says?" Jon asked.

"It matches the style of the shell, so I'd say it's Phoenician, but as to what it says? We'll need an expert."

Jon slapped Kojo on the back. "We found it, Kojo. After 2,500 years, we found the next clue."

Kojo's face lit up with his impossibly white teeth. "Yes, we did, Mr. Jon. So, now what?"

"Now…we rendezvous with Cable and then figure out how to trade this information for Dani."

Tobias dropped down on the sand from the slot canyon's entrance. "There's no other way out. No footprints up there, either. Two sets of prints here on the beach. It looks pretty obvious they climbed up there, but the prints just end." He gestured to the tracks in the sand.

"Could they have covered their tracks?" Nico asked.

"Possibly, but they weren't covering their tracks here on the beach."

"Who are they, Dr. Tran?" Nico demanded, pointing his pistol.

"How would I know?" Dani replied, starting to believe the impossible. That Jon and Cable had somehow beaten Tobias and his efficiencies.

"Hold it right there."

Tobias spun to see three men with rifles drawn, staring them down.

Nico grabbed Dani and shoved her in front of him, placing his pistol to her head. "Try anything and I'll kill her," he called out.

"Go ahead, she means nothing to us," Ra said.

Tobias raised his hands in the air. "I assume you are after money, or maybe the helicopter." He casually pointed to the dark-blue Eurocopter in the distance. "Take it. It's a rental. Piracy runs in our blood as well, and we will gladly pay to be here."

"We're not pirates, and we're not here for the helicopter," Ra stated.

Dani called out, "I'm not part of this. I was kidnapped."

"Shut it, missy," Nico yelled.

The pilot, who had been biding his time inside the cockpit, was just as startled as Nico and Tobias by the unexpected guests in the distance. He could see the altercation down the beach but had been too busy playing Candy Crush on his phone to know how it developed. Slowly, he reached down and picked up the MP5 machine pistol he kept under his seat. Stepping out of the cockpit door, he moved down to the sand. The point of an AK-74 jabbed him in the ribs.

"Drop it." A woman in desert fatigues prodded him forward to join the others.

"I found a straggler," Kaari said as she approached the group with the pilot.

Mona kept to the edge of the cliff, watching everything go down.

"Anyone else you want to tell us about?" Ra asked.

"There's no one else," Tobias said, flatly.

"We didn't come here to kill anyone, but we are happy to do so. Now, lower your weapons, or we will open fire."

Nico, realizing Dani had no sway in the negotiations, lowered his weapon and tossed it into the sand.

Ra pointed his rifle at Tobias, and Tobias followed suit.

They were rounded up and forced to kneel on their palms in a shoulder-to-shoulder lineup.

"Zo, check that slot canyon up there and see if we have any outliers," Ra ordered.

The huge man from Malawi nodded and then scrambled up into the canyon.

Mona then stepped forward, eyeballing the captives. "I don't know who you are or what you're doing here, but that is someth—" She stopped mid-word when she came to Dani. "Dr. Dani Tran?"

Dani looked up at her with hatred in her eyes.

"Yes, it is you. I read your file. You have had a busy year. What are you doing with these outlaws?"

"I was taken against my will. This man"—she pointed to Tobias—"stole an artifact I was hired to authenticate and translate."

Mona looked at Tobias and then back to Dani. "Was it by chance a seashell with carving on it?"

Dani's expression softened. "Yes, with Phoenician symbols."

"Praise be to Allah. Where is the shell?"

"Back at their camp, why?"

Mona swallowed hard. "I have been searching for that shell my entire life. It belongs to me. It's my family's legacy."

"That's interesting. The man who hired me said he wanted to find the shell's history, as well. It was his father's legacy."

"How is that possible, and who is this man?"

Dani hesitated for a second and then realized withholding information was a good way to get herself killed. "He owns Suna Petroleum."

"Suna…from America?" Mona asked, confused.

"Yes, Colorado."

Mona shook her head to keep it from spinning. "How did he say he acquired it?"

"An old dying Bedouin in the Saudi Arabian Desert gave it to his father, just before he struck oil."

Mona processed the words. "Could it be? My grandfather," she mumbled before looking Dani in the eye. "Suna was my mother's name."

Dani looked shocked. "Your grandfather gave Tam McGree's father the carved seashell and the name for his company… That's either incredible or impossible."

"That shell was my birthright. He had no right to give it away."

Tobias was listening to the conversation, and an idea suddenly gave birth. "Look, ma'am. We have the shell, but we don't have any need for it. It's being held at our fortified camp. There is no need for bloodshed. We'd be happy to discuss an arrangement by which you can obtain it."

Mona shook the feelings of the past away. A negotiation, now that was something she could get behind. "First, I want to understand what's really going on here."

Cable paused to catch his breath and replace some vital fluids. The covered raft was just to his left, which meant he was now halfway to reaching Jon and Kojo. There had been no further helicopter or vehicle sightings. He was feeling relatively safe, but all his attempts to reach Jon on the radio had failed. Based on his calculations, they should be heading back his way by now, and hopefully, they would meet up in the next hour or so. He took a deep breath and then continued his jog east.

Jon was the first to hit the canyon floor, and he watched as Kojo climbed down next. Before exiting the cavern, he had taken the time to cover up the symbols on the altar. It was a weak attempt, but he needed to hide the clue from anyone who might follow. This was the information he would trade for Dani. Jon had suggested destroying the carvings, but Kojo had been against any eradication of history.

"As soon as we hit the beach, we should be able to reach Cable on the radio. I say we get back to the boat and then figure out how to play this."

Just as Kojo started to nod, Jon suddenly froze.

Kojo followed suit. "What is it?" he whispered.

Jon pointed to the beach below them. "We have company. Look at all the new footprints."

A voice behind them, with a strong African accent, called out, "Stop where you are."

Kojo and Jon turned back to see a mountain of a man in desert fatigues holding an AK-74 pointed at them. Jon could tell right away that the man knew what he was doing by the way he held his weapon and handled himself.

"Slowly. Move." Zo used the point of his rifle to add emphasis to his statement.

They slid down the sandstone to the beach and immediately noticed they were far from alone.

Dani, despite all the guns, jumped up and ran to Kojo, who did the same.

"Kojo! What are you doing here?" she called out as her tears finally flowed.

Kojo grabbed her in his strong arms and held her tight, feeling a lump form in his throat. "I'm so sorry. I came to help rescue you," were the first words to pop out of his mouth.

Dani pulled back. "This is not your fault," she whispered to him. "Where's Cable?"

"Safe. We found the next clue," he whispered back.

"Okay, enough with the reunion," Ra ordered. "Zo, escort our new guests over here."

Kojo took Dani's hand, and they all joined the lineup of kneeling captives.

Zo moved behind them, his rifle at the ready. He noticed the radio on Jon's belt and grabbed it, tossing it to Ra.

Ra looked at the radio for a second before smashing it to pieces with his rifle stock. He then gestured to Kaari. "Go bring up our vehicle."

She ran off to comply.

Mona looked over the newcomers. She had seen a picture of Jon Chibi and read a brief bio on him, but the tall man with the orange hair was a new face. "We're missing one. A Cable Janson… He wouldn't by chance be back at your camp?" she asked Nico.

"Never heard of him. Can we get back to negotiating now?" Nico groused.

"Yes, I want the carved seashell, and you can have your lives. That is my final offer. Negotiations closed."

Nico held his composure, a rare trait for him. "Fine. Like I said, the shell means nothing to me. I'll need to use the radio on the helicopter to call it in."

The Mobius pulled to a stop, and Kaari got out.

Mona looked at Ra.

"Hey, Kaari, this man needs to make a phone call. Please kill him if he tries anything foolish."

"With pleasure, boss," Kaari replied, pointing her weapon at Nico as he stood and brushed the sand off his knees.

She escorted Nico over to the helicopter and supervised as he put on a headset. Kaari stepped to the copilot's seat and donned a headset of her own. She kept a safe distance from the much larger man, making sure her weapon was ready for action. "English only," she said, not knowing a word of Greek.

It took a few moments, but eventually, someone back at camp picked up the call. "Listen, I need you to bring the seashell out to me. One man, one vehicle, understand?"

After getting a positive response, Nico disconnected the call, and Kaari escorted him back to the group.

"All good. One vehicle inbound. ETA, forty-five minutes."

Jason Asker looked over at Jude Kontos in the passenger seat of the lead white Landcruiser. They were pushing the two vehicles nearly 104 kilometers an hour across the smooth beach. Jason turned up the radio when he heard the call come in from Nico to base camp. They had listened carefully to the exchange.

"Boss is in trouble," Jason said.

"That's my take as well," Jude agreed. "How much farther?"

"We're…ten minutes out," Jason said as he pulled the white Landcruiser to a stop.

Jude jumped out and updated the team in the follow car, as he grabbed his bullpup from the back seat, racking the slide. He then stuffed several magazines in the pockets of his plate carrier before slipping it over his head.

"We'll need to wait here a bit to match the timeline," Jason said.

The driver in the follow vehicle killed the engine.

Jason grabbed an ammo satchel and stuffed it with a 9mm Glock and a bunch of old rags to give it enough bulk to approximate the seashell's girth.

Once the timing was right, he got back in the driver's seat.

Jude and another merc climbed into the rear cargo space of the lead vehicle.

After waiting for the approximate time, they drove on, leaving the other vehicle and its men standing by.

CHAPTER THIRTEEN

A SHIMMERING MIRAGE OF A WHITE Toyota Landcruiser appeared from the west, catching Mona's attention.

Ra gave a short whistle, and Zo took up the high position at the entrance to the slot canyon. Kaari moved behind the Mobius's hood and aimed her rifle down the beach. Arno dropped prone with his weapon on full auto, pointing the barrel at the hostages.

"Mona, get behind the SUV," Ra ordered, and she obeyed.

He moved to the other side of the line of kneeling captives and stood tall, waiting for the deliveryman with the shell.

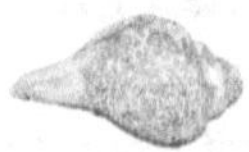

As the helicopter and another vehicle parked in the sand came into view, Jason started to slow the speeding vehicle. It took a moment before he recognized his boss kneeling in the sand along with Tobias and several others.

An armed man was clearly standing, awaiting his arrival. He angled the nose of the Toyota toward the cliff and came to an abrupt stop. Reaching forward, he hit the unlock rear hatch button on the keychain before killing the engine and stepping out.

Jude had his hand on the rear hatch, and the moment it unlocked, he pushed it open just a fraction of an inch. Then, he and his fellow mercenary waited for the right opportunity to exit.

Jason raised his hands. His left hand held the ammo satchel by its green strap. "I have what you want. Send over Nico and Tobias, and you can have it," Jason called out in heavily accented English.

"That's not how this works," Ra called back in equally broken English. "Turn around slowly. Now, lift your shirt."

Jason complied.

Once Ra was satisfied that he was not packing any obvious weapons, he approached.

A quick glance into the seating area of the vehicle revealed that no one else was inside. "Arno, bring our guests."

Arno stood and used his gun to encourage Nico and Tobias to get up. The pilot tried to do likewise.

"Not you."

The pilot sat, suddenly very concerned about his fate.

Arno herded the two men toward the Toyota.

"That's far enough," Ra ordered when Tobias and Nico were just ten feet away.

"Okay, I showed you mine. Now, show me yours."

Jason slowly opened the satchel and reached inside.

Mona leaned out from the Mobius's rear gate to get a better look at her shell.

Jude slowly cracked the rear gate and started to slip out and down.

"Nice and slow," Ra said, lifting his rifle as a warning.

Jason let his fingers wrap around the Glock inside the satchel. "We don't want any trouble, just an exchange." As he said the words, he gripped the Glock and slightly rotated the satchel up. "Here you go, *káto*." He then pulled the trigger of his pistol, sending several rounds into Ra, who twitched, danced, and died before he hit the sand.

At hearing the word *káto*, the Greek word for *down*, Tobias grabbed Nico and pulled him to the ground. Gunfire from behind the Toyota opened up on everyone on the beach.

Jon was the first to react. He shoved Kojo and Dani into the sand. The pilot stood up in a panic and was immediately gunned down. Jon used the pilot's dead body like a shield as they army-crawled toward the cliff.

Kaari opened up on Jason as he dove behind the driver's side open door. She stitched rounds through the thin metal, catching Jason just above his plate carrier and ending his fight. He slid to the sand, bleeding out in a radial pattern.

Arno screamed, sending full-auto rounds in a fan pattern, as he ran to Ra. He caught a bullet in his shoulder and stumbled to the ground while trying to reload through the pain as fast as he could.

Tobias didn't wait. He grabbed Nico and, staying low, hightailed it for the rear of the Toyota.

Zo held the elevation advantage, but the Toyota had stopped just enough back that he didn't have a direct shot. He managed to get a hit at an exposed leg before shots started pouring in his direction. He re-targeted to the driver, but he was already down. Movement caught his eye, and he shot one of the men running toward the rear of the Toyota. A returning bullet caught him in the scalp. His AK-74 clattered out of the box canyon and onto the beach.

Once out of the direct line of fire, Jon pounced on top of Dani and held her to the ground.

Mona curled up in a ball at the rear of the Mobius, closing her eyes tightly and suddenly trying to reconnect with Allah.

Kaari returned disciplined fire, keeping the shooters at the back of the Toyota pinned down.

Tobias and Nico dove behind the vehicle. "We gotta get outta here. Keep them pinned down," Tobias yelled. He quickly crawled into the rear hatch and up over into the driver's seat, diving to the floor. He reached up and started the engine. Staying low below the dash, he called back, "Get in."

Tobias jacked the car into reverse and slammed his hand down on the gas pedal. After five seconds, he spun the wheel and popped up. Putting the shifter into drive, he floored the car again, this time with his foot. Bullets followed them for a good ten seconds before the fighting stopped.

Tobias gripped the steering wheel like his life depended on it, taking their speed up to well over 130 kph.

It was Nico's hand on his shoulder that brought him back to reality. "You did good, Tobias. We can slow down. No need to die trying to escape."

Tobias pulled to a stop next to the other vehicle, and the men who had been standing by roughly four miles from the shootout.

The other mercs had heard the shooting and were jonesing to get into the fight.

Tobias looked over at his boss. "You okay?"

Nico nodded and patted Tobias on the shoulder. "Thank you."

Tobias waited for his adrenaline to pass. That's when the pain started. He looked down at an outpouring of blood from his thigh. His femoral artery was acting like an open faucet to his heart. "We need to—" Tobias slumped over, and his eyes flickered shut.

It took Nico a beat to realize what was happening. "We need a tourniquet, and now."

The mercenary in the back had taken two bullets, and his skin looked ashen. His time for helping was done.

Jude ripped into a personal med kit he carried with him and ran to the shot-up driver's door. He ripped it open and pulled Tobias from the vehicle, quickly assessing his wound. Jude then strapped on the tourniquet just above the injury and cranked it down. "I hope we're not too late," he said to himself as he worked.

The other mercenaries gathered around with concern.

Tobias's eyes half-opened for just a moment.

Nico crawled out of the SUV and dropped down next to his number two. He held Tobias's head in his arms. "Is he going to be okay?"

Jude didn't want to disappoint his boss, so he said nothing.

Tobias slowly focused on Nico. "You were the brother I never had." Then his eyes fluttered shut.

Nico pursed his lips, trying not to let the emotion get to him, but he failed. He screamed and cursed the Egyptian woman and her people.

The radiator on the Mobius hissed its final plea.

Mona stood and brushed the sand off her pants.

Kaari reloaded her AK and went to check on the others.

Jon stood, helping Dani to her feet. "You all right?"

"Yeah, thanks."

Kojo slowly stood up. "What was that? Can't people just make a simple trade without going all gangster?"

Kaari returned to Mona and reported, "Two dead, one wounded on our side, two down on theirs. What do you wanna do?"

Mona seemed at a loss. "What should we do?" was all she could come up with in her state of shock.

"We should bury the bodies and get out of here, ma'am, before anyone from the Somali army comes to investigate."

"Okay, let's do that," Mona replied.

Kaari stepped over to Jon, Dani, and Kojo. "Any of you hurt?"

"No," Jon replied.

"I could use some help with a wounded man and a burial detail."

Jon and Kojo looked over at the serious woman with her short afro and hidden curves under a desert camo.

Jon nodded. "Dani, see what you can do for him." He pointed at Arno. "Kojo, help me dig some holes."

As she walked away, Kaari turned back. "Any chance one of you knows how to fly a helicopter?"

"Under perfect conditions, yeah," Jon replied.

"Good, I don't intend to walk back," she said.

They shared a hint of a smile before she spun back to her duties.

"She is all business, but I do like a good woman with a gun," Kojo whispered to Jon.

"She's all yours, brother, but don't come crying to me when you get shot."

"Through the heart. *Fikiri*." He elongated the Amharic word for *love* before flashing his amazing smile.

"Buddha says a man who loves scorpions might get stung."

Kojo's smile slowly dropped.

Jon slapped him on the back with a laugh of his own.

Dani knelt to the injured man. "Hey, I'm Dani."

"Arno," he said as he struggled to sit up. There was a slow weep of blood coming from his left shoulder.

Jon stepped over to one of the dead and retrieved their weapon. He slung the rifle over his shoulder and walked straight to Mona. He gave her a once-over, as she did to him.

"Before I fly us out of here, I'm going to need something from you."

Mona's eyes narrowed. "What would that be?"

"I will need your personal guarantee."

"Not sure what I can do from here," Mona replied. "But I'm guessing you're tired of being shot at?"

"Something like that," Jon said as he adjusted the AK-74's shoulder strap.

"Well, me too. My interests lie elsewhere, I can assure you. Whatever has happened so far is tragic, but I'm willing to pay for what I want."

Jon took a step closer and lowered his voice. "I see a woman who is used to getting her way but has found herself in over her head." Jon watched Mona's micro-expressions for a lie. "Perhaps we could help each other."

Mona glanced down for a beat and then back up to meet Jon's eyes. "What do you have in mind?"

"We come clean about everything we know, and you help us get over the finish line. I have three civilians I'm responsible for, and all they want is answers." Jon paused to let his words sink in. "Anything we find, fifty-fifty split. As far as the shell goes, you'll have to work that out with the owner."

Mona adjusted her hijab and then slowly nodded. "Agreed. No more games."

Dani did what she could to put pressure on Arno's wound. She yanked a belt off the dead pilot and used it for a sling, immobilizing his left arm. With a little effort, she helped him stand.

Jon walked up. "How's he doing?"

"He'll be fine, as long as we get him to a hospital."

"Good. Dani, I need you to tell Mona everything we know about the shell."

"Wait. What? Everything?"

"Yes, everything. We are in this together now, and I'm tired of getting shot at." Jon walked off to help bury the dead before Dani could ask him more questions.

Kojo looked up. "Just in time. Help me lift this dude."

Mona sat on the skids of the helicopter, waiting for the burial detail to finish up.

Dani approached. "I know you must be disappointed."

Mona looked up at Dani with hard, appraising eyes. "I need to get that shell. I made a promise to my mother that I intend on keeping."

Dani nodded in understanding. "It's not real."

"What?"

"The shell they have is a 3D-printed copy of the original. Tam McGree has the original in a safe back in the States."

Mona visibly slumped. "Then, perhaps you can help me negotiate for it."

"Possibly. Tam just wants to know the origin and history of the shell. He is an old man with a final wish. The shell holds no real power for him beyond that." Dani sat down on the skid next to Mona. "Both of your family histories connect. There is something magical about that. I think you should meet."

Mona put her arms on her legs and leaned forward. "Perhaps." She looked back up at Dani. "If you know the origin of the shell and what it says, then why are you all the way out here, and what are you still searching for?"

"Well, in part, I'm out here because I was taken against my will." Dani stood. Her recent kidnapping was still emotionally fresh. "But the shell tells of a voyage that a man named Boaz took some 2,500 years ago. To a mystical place, and we are attempting to find that place." She turned back to Mona. "A series of clues have led us here, and we were hoping to find clues that will lead us to somewhere else."

"What do you mean?" Mona asked.

Jon walked up, dusting himself off. "She means that we need to get a move on if we're gonna stay ahead of the guys that tried to kill us."

Kaari followed. "Yes. It's time to get out of here."

Kojo stood in front of four sand mounds and removed his dorze cap. "Why?" He paused for a second. "It's anyone's guess. But God has the answers, and he'll sort this all out, I'm sure… Amen."

The rotors on the Eurocopter started to spin, and Kojo jogged back and climbed in.

"Where to next?" Mona called out.

Jon looked back over his shoulder. "We need to make a quick pick up."

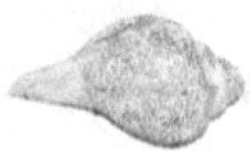

Nico smashed both hands down on the camp table, causing it to collapse. He was angry times ten. A simple negotiation for a shell he no longer needed had turned deadly, and he'd nearly been killed. The loss of the pilot was disappointing. The loss of Jason was infuriating, but the loss of Tobias had filled him with rage. He ripped off his shirt, exposing the giant gold cross he wore, and pulled on a bulletproof vest.

"Nobody kills my number two and gets away with it."

Gangster 101 called for retaliation for any death in the family, and Tobias was the closest thing he had to that.

"Get the men assembled. We're going back. I want every weapon we have," he yelled at Jude.

The big man quickly assembled a team of six in their last two SUVs and tore off down the path to the beach.

It took a good thirty minutes at speed to reach the bullet-riddled Landcruiser they had left behind and another five to the slot canyon. The shot-up Mobius and three mounds of dirt were all that was left. No helicopter, no one to shoot.

Nico let out a guttural scream of angst.

He exited the Toyota and stomped around in the sand. He looked over the scene, lingering on the three sand mounds.

The men stayed inside the vehicles, watching their boss act out.

"Should we go out there?" a man in the back asked Jude.

"No. The boss will let us know what he wants and when he wants it."

As if on cue, Nico paused his pacing and called out. "Jude, get out here."

Jude quickly exited from the driver's seat.

Nico looked up and pointed. "That slot canyon. Come on, we need to check it out."

Jude tilted his head in that direction and then started scrambling up.

"I saw them climb down from there," Nico said, following right behind. Once inside the narrow space, nothing out of the ordinary caught his eye.

"Boss," Jude said, noticing faint tracks on the ground. "Somebody climbed up and down right here."

"Give me a boost."

Jude helped push his boss up the cliff until he was able to pull himself onto a ledge, just above.

"There's a cave up here. Hold up. I'm going to check it out."

Nico disappeared from Jude's vision.

He crawled through a narrow tube, cursing as he scraped up the knees on his custom slacks. By the time he was able to stand, his handmade Italian loafers were also ruined. Nico shined his smartphone's light around the pedestrian sandstone room. Eventually, he found the small carved altar, empty. Disappointment flooded him.

"You okay, boss?" Jude called up as Nico started back down the cliff face.

"Yeah, yeah. That was a bust. There was a small altar up there, but whatever was on it, those guys took it."

"So, what now?" Jude asked.

"Luckily, our late friend Tobias was smart. Let's get back. We need to break camp. We're leaving this dump of a country."

Jon watched as his passengers jumped down to the deck of the *Desert Rose*. Arno was ambulatory enough to make the drop to the old fishing boat with just a little help. The Eurocopter had enough fuel in it to get somewhere within about two hundred miles. That meant Somalia only. Not a good proposition with the locals, the government, or Nico.

They stopped to pick up Cable, which took some doing, as they no longer had radios and he would hide every time the helicopter got close. Eventually, following fresh footprints in the sand, Kojo hopped out and coaxed him from hiding.

The group then formed a plan to track down the *Desert Rose* that was waiting for them somewhere just beyond the horizon. The problem was that by the time they found the ship, the low-fuel warning buzzer was making everyone on the helicopter very anxious.

Cable was the last to jump down, and Jon lifted the helo up and away. He set the autopilot to hover a good two hundred yards out from the boat, then dove into the sea and quickly swam away from the doomed craft. After another three minutes, the Eurocopter's engine died, and she violently spun into the sea.

Jon pulled himself onboard, and they all shared a look of relief.

Cable was so happy about Dani's return that he had a hard time letting go of her.

Dani set up a work area in the galley, and with the help of their sat phone, they soon had a workable internet connection.

The room was small, with a few faded soccer posters on stained wooden walls. A Formica table was bolted to the floor, with three mismatched chairs and a bench seat. The cooking area had an oven and cooktop, bordering a small sink, with room enough for just one person at a time.

Dani took one of the chairs, ignoring the sticky surface of the table. She sent off a quick message to Professor Beppe Lombardo and the waiting began.

Mona watched as she spread all their information out on the table. The translation pages, the second replica shell, a map of Africa, and even Kojo's smartphone with the pictures from the altar.

She took a second to organize everything to her liking and then began a recap for her expanded team.

"Okay, here's what we know. Boaz took a journey around the tip of Africa in an attempt to open new trade routes," she started. "He made it to the Horn of Africa before something happened and everyone died."

"Everyone except whoever left the message and carved the shell," Cable added.

"Correct."

"Rising sun means east and land's end turned out to be the tip of the Horn here." She pointed to the map.

"Thanks, in part, to the lost stele we found in Carthage," Cable added.

"I'm thinking the double deltas indicated the carving Kojo found in the slot canyon, and perhaps this sideways *C* must have referred to the slot canyon itself."

"That makes sense, though a slot canyon looks more like a V to me," Jon said.

"He does have a point," Kojo added.

Dani nodded thoughtfully. "According to the shell, they found some sort of treasure in a mystical place."

"Hopefully, the translation of the symbols you found will shed further light, otherwise, we are looking for a mystical place near the Horn of Africa," Cable said. "And there is nothing mystical about that place."

Dani threw her arms up. "Yeah, that's not going to get us anywhere."

Mona stepped forward and picked up the replica shell she had brought with her. "You are all quite impressive. I have every confidence in our success."

"Thank you, Mona, but hard work and good intuition can still fall short when it comes to uncovering the past," Dani said.

The captain stepped into the room and set down a bottle of waragi on the weathered table. "My last charter left this behind."

Jon started to reach for it but found himself stopping mid-reach.

"So, where to?" the captain asked with a toothless smile. He had struck a deal with Jon for four hundred euros a day to charter his boat, and as far as he was concerned, they could just keep right on going.

Cable placed his finger on the map in the ocean just off the very tip of Africa's Horn. "Let's start by heading here."

Dani sipped the Ugandan homemade gin, making a distorted face, as she looked at the computer, willing it to chime. Waiting for the professor's translation was making her stir crazy, but drinking the waragi might make her go blind. She decided to stop and pushed her glass away.

"Hey, we have dolphins chasing us, and there's a baby."

Dani looked up from the screen and smiled at Cable's news. He seemed to know just what she needed. A break.

The two exited the stuffy cabin onto the wind-swept deck. The sun was just kissing the horizon behind them, making the ocean sparkle in deep orange tones. A pod of dolphins breached and played beside the hull as the old fishing boat chugged along. Dani looked over and watched them use their powerful tailfins to push effortlessly through the water. Sure enough, there was a small one sticking close to her mother, but happy to show off her skills.

The salty air was like a reset button for Dani after the last two days. The moment seemed unreal and safe, two things she now fully embraced. She leaned on the railing next to Cable, just letting the moment linger.

"I could do this all day," Cable said, breaking the silence.

Dani nuzzled into him.

After a time, Cable spoke again. "Ever since my mom died, I have kinda locked my feelings away. For me, it was better to be alone than risk my heart being broken again. I just wanted to avoid ever feeling that kind of pain again."

Dani looked up at Cable.

He was staring out at the ocean but not seeing it. "I've managed many friendships all over the globe, and there are some that are very special to me, but love wasn't ever really on the table."

Cable paused and looked at Dani. "I met a girl a while back that challenged those thoughts, and just as I was about ready to try again, she was killed on my watch." A moment of silence passed. "That…is the kind of thing you don't typically come back from. It would take someone extraordinary to even get me thinking of trying again."

Cable's intensity and honesty pulled at Dani, and she found herself rubbing his arm soothingly, encouraging him to continue.

"Someone like you. When I thought I'd lost you, it became so consuming that nothing else mattered to me."

Dani broke eye contact and turned to the railing. "They scared me, Cable, but they also needed me. I wouldn't recommend their service to Tripadvisor, but I didn't feel in mortal danger."

Cable nodded slowly. "I just want you to understand, when I told you I love you, that was me sacrificing everything that holds me together. That's how much you mean to me."

Dani cocked her head slightly and turned back to face Cable. "Cable, you have never told me you love me." Dani watched Cable squirm for just a bit. "I told *you* back on the ferry, and you just hugged me back. Now, your actions may have been your answer, but a girl likes to hear the words now and then."

"You're kidding, right? I'm sure I said it."

"Hmm. Nope. This girl remembers that sorta thing. She marks them on her mental calendar and celebrates them every year."

"They do? I mean, she does?"

Dani nodded her head. "Are we really taking this conversation in that direction?"

"No. Of course not… So, where was I?" Cable fumbled.

Dani pulled back from the railing. "Forget it."

"Wait! Dani, I love you," he blurted out.

Dani spun back around, eyes locked on Cable.

"I really do."

She let all her fake puffery go and, in an instant, sank into his arms.

CHAPTER FOURTEEN

"WHAT IS THAT YOU ARE cooking?"

Kojo looked up from the small galley to find Kaari's dark eyes watching him.

"Beg wat with injera. It's my family's secret recipe."

"Smells amazing," she said.

"Here, try a taste." He scooped the flat injera bread into the lamb and curry stew, then placed it in her mouth.

Kaari savored the complex flavors.

"Where I come from, this is called *gursha*. Eating is a very social activity, and feeding each other by hand is an act of friendship."

"Is that so, Mr. Ethiopian Kojo?"

Kojo produced a broad smile.

"Where I come from, food is scarce, so you eat what you can, when you can," Kaari countered. "When I was younger, there were times when I would have killed someone for a meal like this."

Kojo's smile fell. "And now?" He was almost afraid to ask.

"Now, I will make sure you live. You are a good cook, Kojo, and I would like to do gursha again with you."

Kojo's frown faded, but he wasn't sure what he was feeling now.

"I will tell the others dinner is ready," Kaari said as she left the galley.

Kojo broke out into a traditional folk song.

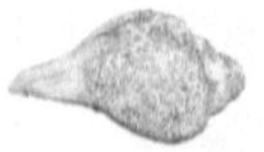

After dinner, the translation from the professor came in, but it was confusing. Dani read over it one more time.

"What do you make of it?" Mona asked.

"Three days to tiger mouth, below cloud tree." She leaned back from the screen and pushed air through her pursed lips. "It makes no sense to me."

"Could the translation be wrong?" Mona proposed.

"Sure. That is always possible with ancient languages, but in this case, we sent it to the very best there is."

Cable pulled out a piece of blank paper and a pencil. He sat down, rubbing his hands together. "Let's break it down." He wrote *three days* at the top. "If we start there…I imagine three days on foot. Fourteen hours a day hiking. That would be about 126 miles max from our cave." He placed an X right on the African map where Kojo and Jon had found the cave. He then adjusted the drafting compass he had borrowed from the bridge to represent 126 miles and began to draw a circle around the X. "That should put us somewhere here." He then stretched out the compass to a much wider setting. "If they went by boat, that would be about five knots an hour, but now they could travel twenty-four hours a day, so three days would be about 360 nautical miles, which is around 400 miles." He took the compass and drew a much larger circle around the X.

Everyone leaned in to see what he had done.

Two circles. One, much smaller than the other, marked their possible next stop.

"The larger circle touches Ethiopia, that island in the middle of nowhere, and Yemen across the Gulf of Aden," Jon summarized. "That's a lot of ground."

Cable nodded and continued his process. "We can disregard anything along the big circle that isn't over water."

"And anything on the small circle that is over water," Dani added, finally understanding.

"Of course, boats don't go on land, and feet don't walk on water," Mona said.

"Not typically," Kojo added.

"Walking gets us a lot of barren deserts," Dani pointed out. "Unless there is a hidden oasis or underground lake, I don't see that working."

"That means somewhere near Bandarbeyla or Bosaso Beach, both in Somalia." Jon pointed to the two coastal towns four hundred miles equidistant and on opposite sides of the African Horn. "Alhami on the coast of Yemen or…" He looked closer to the map to read the small type. "Socotra Island."

"Well, having been to Yemen and Socotra Island, Socotra is by far the most mystical of the two," Cable said.

"Never heard of it," Dani said.

"Me either," Mona added.

"It's the Galápagos of Africa," Cable explained.

"Let's do a deep dive into each of these possible locations. We might find something a map can't tell us," Mona suggested.

"Hang on a second," Cable said, as he tried to access a memory. "Pull up a site for Socotra. As I recall, the dragon blood tree that grows only there looks a lot like a cloud."

Dani went to work.

"Socotra Island might look small on the map, but that's a lot of ground to cover. We need to narrow it down even more," Jon added.

Dani pulled up a page about the island. "It's part of Yemen. Home to a bunch of endemic species."

Kojo looked up, confused.

"They only grow there," Cable said.

"Like this." Dani showed everyone a picture of the island's dragon blood tree.

"It does look like a cloud," Kojo said, marveling at the tree's up-turned, densely packed crown.

"Or an umbrella," Mona said.

Dani continued her download. "It's eighty-two miles long, by twenty-six miles wide, with about fifty thousand inhabitants."

"Like I said, a lot of ground to cover," Jon reminded everyone.

"Kojo, give our next location to the captain, and let's see if we can narrow down our search before we get there," Cable said.

Kojo exited the cramped galley, and Cable picked up his pencil. "Dani, can you pull up a current and prevailing wind map of this area?" He pointed to the ocean between Africa and Socotra.

It took her a few moments, but the screen eventually populated with a map filled with red and green arrows. "The green arrows represent the prevailing wind and the red arrows, the currents," she said.

Cable studied the map for a moment before drawing a line from the X to the far side of the island. He then repeated the process on the other side, adding a curve at the end that included a small portion of the backside. "This indicates the most likely landing area for a ship sailing from our X."

"That cuts our search in half," Jon said.

"Yes, but landing doesn't mean that whatever we are looking for is near the shore."

Kojo stepped back into the room. "Capitan says we have just enough fuel to make port in Qalansiyah for a refuel."

Dani pointed to the small coastal village on the northwest corner of the island. It intersected with one of Cable's lines he had drawn.

"Good place to start," Jon said.

"We just need to figure out what tiger's mouth is," Mona said, impressed with the way everyone was working together.

"I assume it is some sort of geological shape or formation, but that is pure conjecture," Dani suggested.

Cable rubbed his eyes. His brain hurt.

"Can we pick this up tomorrow? I'm sure we could all use some rest," Mona said, hiding a yawn.

"Now, that…is a good idea," Kojo agreed.

The ocean had changed dramatically overnight, and large swells tossed the *Desert Rose* like a cork as it plowed forward in the predawn light.

They were a good six hours from their refueling destination, and the first drops of rain had started to fall.

Cable stepped into the galley in his underwear. He was soaking wet, leaving a puddle where he stood. Kojo tossed him a towel, and Cable started drying off. "Ah…a good way to start the morning. I needed that rain shower. I was starting to smell."

Kojo smiled. "I'm surprised you noticed. This whole boat stinks."

Cable threw the towel back at Kojo and pulled his pants on.

"Too bad. This place finally had a nice view," Dani threw out from behind her laptop.

Cable gave her a quick pose.

"Not bad," Dani said with a flirty wink. "How's Arno doing?"

"He's stable but in a lot of pain," Cable said. "We'll get him help once we hit the island."

Kojo poured a cup of steaming coffee and passed it to Cable. "Did I ever tell you that Ethiopia was the birthplace of coffee?"

"Only about a thousand times. Thanks," Cable replied as he took the steaming cup.

"We should charge the world for our benevolence. We were once one of the richest kingdoms in the world. At just one-tenth of a penny per cup sold, we could be again." He sat at the table, sipping from his cup.

Cable set his mug down across from Dani. "I've been thinking about what you said last night."

"Whoa, hold on. No postcoital talk at the table, please," Kojo implored.

Dani blushed.

Cable ignored him. "You mentioned a possible geological formation. Socotra Island has several well-known caves. We should do a search and see if any of them look like a tiger's mouth."

"Way ahead of you. Unfortunately, Socotra is so off the beaten trail that detailed information about the island is somewhat limited. There are two famous limestone caves on the island, but from what I could gather, they don't fit the bill."

"Fit the bill?" Kojo asked.

"It means they are not what we are searching for," Cable said.

"Gotcha."

"Limestone, not volcanic?"

"Socotra is a broken-off piece of Africa," Dani said. "There's no volcanism there."

"Well," Cable said with a positive smile, "where there are two limestone caves, there will be more."

A dish crashed to the floor when the ship hit an extra-large wave, jarring everyone onboard.

"Well, that should wake everyone up," Dani said holding tight to her computer.

Cable nodded as he took another sip. "This is really good coffee, Kojo."

"See, I told you." Kojo grabbed his mug as it started to slide on the table.

The weather was getting worse.

"I did, however, find this." Dani spun her laptop around for Cable and Kojo to see.

The screen showed a middle-aged Arabian-looking man with a crooked smile. He had thick, bushy hair, sharp eyes, and a full mustache.

Cable read the name below his picture. "Mariamo Mubarak."

"He is considered the foremost expert on the island's geology and ancient history."

"Well, I can't wait to meet him," Cable said.

"That should be easy, he works for Adventure Eco-tourism Company. They take tourists all over the island."

Mona stepped into the galley, hanging on to the doorjamb as the boat rocked. She looked a little stressed. "We're not in any danger, are we?"

"Captain says it's a mild front that will blow over soon," Cable replied. "Good morning, by the way."

Mona nodded, unconvinced. She shared a polite smile with Dani and looked to the stove. "I smell coffee."

Kojo jumped to his feet. "Let me pour you a mug. It's Ethiopian coffee. Did you know tha—"

Cable interrupted. "Okay, Juan Valdez, take it back a notch."

Kojo paused for a second. "Of course. Not everyone appreciates history like I do," Kojo threw back as he poured and handed Mona a steaming mug.

Dani just shook her head. "I think Juan Valdez was Colombian," she whispered to Cable.

Kojo heard her. "Don't get me started on the Colombians. They stole our coffee plants in the late 1600s."

Mona thankfully changed the subject. "Any solutions to our riddle?"

"No solutions. Just a next step, if you will. We need to find and hire this man." Dani angled the screen for Mona so she could inspect their next hoped-for connection.

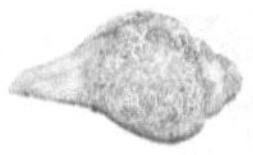

Nico let his anger fester. He had spent more money on this fiasco than just about any other venture. Tobias had been killed, and the perpetrators were in the wind. He looked around with frantic eyes. The camp was almost struck, and the remaining men were busy finalizing their exit. The real question was where to next.

The wind had picked up, and dust blew horizontally as Nico climbed into the passenger seat of the white Landcruiser.

Jude was on the driver's side, focused on his laptop.

Nico looked over Jude's shoulder as the screen showed a faint blip that flashed twice and then stopped. "What's that?" Nico asked.

"Remember when Tobias took Dr. Tran's shoes?"

Nico nodded.

"He hid a simple tracker in the heel, you know, just in case. Unfortunately, it has a limited range. We will need to get closer if we want to reacquire the signal," Jude replied.

Nico had a small flash of pride; Tobias was always two steps ahead. He would be missed. "Show me their previous positions."

Jude typed a few keystrokes, and several red dots overlayed the screen's map.

"Looks like they're heading out to sea."

Jude nodded. "That's why we lost the signal."

"What could they possibly…" Nico drew his finger across the dots, extending the line eastward on the digital map. "Zoom out a bit."

Jude widened the map.

"It looks like they are heading to one of these islands."

"Or they turned after we lost the signal," Jude said.

"Guesswork is not helpful. Extend the line farther."

Jude slid the screen over and zoomed in to get a better look at three landmasses due east of the Horn of Africa.

Two were very small islands. "The smallest one, Samhuh Island, has a small fishing village with about a hundred people. It is some kind of bird sanctuary. The other one is Abd al-Kuri Island. Looks like the government removed everyone who lived there to build a military base."

"What about the larger one?" Nico said, pointing to the island farthest east.

"Socotra Island," Jude read out loud. "It's got everything, towns, hotels, restaurants, and lots of eco-tourism."

Nico nodded, thinking. "Okay. We need to get to this Socotra Island, and fast."

Jude nodded, started up the car, and honked. He ran his hand across his shaved head as he waited for two additional team members, Sebi and Philo, to climb in the back. "Qardho has the nearest airport. That's three hours, tops." He banged the SUV into gear and spun the tires as they left the barren coast behind.

Jude knew Nico was a demanding boss. He also knew Nico was floundering. Tobias had been the brains of the operation, and he had been the muscle. Now, it seemed Nico needed him to be both. Not something he was accustomed to, but he would do what he could until things changed.

The last time Jude had been in charge, things had looked quite different.

The Hellenic Police Force in Greece had trained him and fired him. Not for failing on the job but for getting streamed and uploaded to the web while on the job.

Jude had followed police protocols, but once the footage of his chase and subsequent tackle, with his forearm thrust into the back of the suspect's head, had been edited, there was no taking it back. It looked like a brute of an officer, grinding a purse snatcher's face off on the pavement. No video was ever found of the suspect slamming an elderly woman into a brick wall before yanking her purse away.

Since Constable Jude Kontos had still been on probation, it was easier for the department to blame and fire him rather than take the media hit.

Finding himself in the employ of a black-market smuggler was the easiest path, besides guard duty at a local mall.

Now, the video of him grinding the face off some puke fed fear into the locals he typically dealt with. It had become an asset and a calling card.

As far as an international race for a treasure, that was new territory for Jude. Territory he intended to conquer.

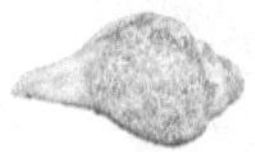

Qalansiyah was a sleepy fishing village next to a large lagoon on the northwest tip of Socotra Island. The beach was steep, and the *Desert Rose* anchored her bow in the sand. The last of the storm front had passed, leaving scattered clouds and calmer water.

The captain had come in earlier that morning to warn everyone onboard that they needed to toss all weapons overboard before getting to Socotra. They would surely be boarded and carefully inspected once they landed.

Kaari dutifully collected all their guns and tossed them over the side.

Jon was the most put off by her actions.

Kojo seemed eager to help.

Several porters were summoned to haul diesel cans down for refueling. Cable jumped off the bow and helped the others exit. Kojo and Jon carried Arno in a homebuilt stretcher onto the sand. His wound, though not life-threatening, needed immediate medical attention. He had spiked a fever in the last hour, and infection was now a genuine concern. Plus, painkillers would be welcomed with open arms.

Cable got directions for a small health clinic, and they began the hike up the beach with their patient. Before long, Arno was in good hands and expected to make a full recovery.

Mona haggled for some bottled water, fresh fruits, and vegetables for the boat. The locals seemed welcoming, with a very relaxed vibe. They were officially on island time now.

Eventually, a government official came running down the sand with a policeman in tow. He was alarmed at the presence of foreigners arriving without a visa. Mona did what she was good at and negotiated a payment to correct the problem. The policeman did a systematic inspection of the *Desert Rose* before the government official stamped their passports and welcomed them to Socotra with a gap-toothed grin.

Once Kojo and Jon returned, they all headed inland. The main road through town was a skinny strip of worn asphalt. Every other street was dirt. The buildings were stacked stone or concrete, with drab colors accenting the occasional door. A coppice of date palms led them past a dirt soccer field to the business district. Cable probed the locals for directions to the Adventure Eco-tourism Company that Dani had found in her web search. Several enterprising young entrepreneurs tried to sell him their vacation package to see the island right on the spot, but Cable kept his motives close to the vest.

It turned out that Mori, home of the Adventure Eco-tourism Company, and the only town with an airport on the island, would be their next stop. It was a good eighteen miles farther around the island.

After refueling, and those onboard indulging in some beach soccer with the local kids, the *Desert Rose* pulled back off the shoreline.

The exhaust belched black smoke, and once again, the old fishing boat chugged its way forward.

Mona stepped close to Cable as he finished stowing the anchor rode. She spoke in Arabic to keep their conversation private. "I've been watching you, Mr. Janson, and I must say I find it hard to understand your motivation in all this."

"Cable, please… What do you mean?"

"You don't strike me as the average get-rich-quick American looking for a shortcut to success."

Cable set the anchor in its box and turned to Mona. "Let's say, I prefer to live my life on my own terms. And for me, the definition of success is very different from most."

"Does that make you a religious man?"

"I wouldn't call myself religious, but spiritual, that's a word I find more comforting."

"So, what does a spiritual man with no agenda get out of a quest like this?"

Cable sat back on the railing. The warm breeze pulled at his curly brown hair. "Dani and I are starting a business together. Authenticating and determining provenance to historical objects of the past."

"Doesn't sound very lucrative."

"Oh, I'm sure it won't be. So far, we've been robbed, shot at, blown up, kidnapped, and threatened over a seashell with a few Phoenician symbols on it. What's next is anyone's guess, but I can tell you this, every time someone tries to stop us, we find a way to double down our efforts and move forward."

Mona let a rare smile slip out. "No amount of money is worth that."

"No, it isn't, but there is no better feeling in the world for us than putting the period at the end of an answered question that was once unanswerable."

"I could have saved myself a lot of pain by coming to you in the first place," Mona said.

"Yeah, well, in case you didn't pick up on it, this is our first official job."

"What was all the business I read about in Ethiopia and the lost chapel or cave?"

"Lost cave chapel… And I would call that…a trial run."

Mona came over and sat next to Cable on the railing. Her custom tan slacks and cream blouse were scraped and stained. The hijab on her head had traces of blood and dirt, and for the first time in her business life, she didn't care. Something was afoot here, and it seemed to be worming its way into her soul. Was it the prospect of finally having answers for her dead mother, or was there maybe more to life than money, power, and control?

Mona leaned back slightly and simply enjoyed the breeze.

The jet touched down with two short screeches as the speeding tires found purchase. Nico looked out at the arid valley with the tall mountain behind it. To say it looked different than Somalia would be a lie. In fact, it was possible that this place was more backwater than any other place he'd ever been.

He followed the row of passengers as they deplaned. It was quite a mix. From backpacking Eurotrash, wealthy adventurous tourists, to local chicken farmers. None of which he had time for.

Nico had barely managed to get the last four seats available on the once-a-week flight every Tuesday out of Abu Dhabi. Jude followed behind him, and they waited in the shade of the terminal for Sebi and Philo.

As they walked up, Jude passed out assignments. "Sebi, see if you can source some local weapons. Anything will do. Philo, get us a ride. I'll get the bags and meet you outside." He passed out radios from his carry-on. "These will work better than phones here, so keep it on channel three."

Once the bags showed up, Jude hauled everything out to the curb. After about a half hour, Philo pulled up in a battered orange Mitsubishi Delica, a snub-nosed van with surprisingly good four-wheel drive capability. They loaded up and drove the seven-mile trip around the point to the main city of Hadiboh. Jude arranged for four rooms at the three-and-a-half-star Taj Socotra Tourist Hotel, a two-story white rectangle with a metal roof and very firm beds.

Nico fired up the laptop and opened the tracking app. No new pings returned.

"What do you think?" asked Jude.

"She's either still out of range, or the battery is dead," Nico responded.

Jude slowly nodded. "What do we do if she doesn't show back up?"

Nico closed the screen with a huff and took his frustration out on Jude. "For your sake, you better pray she does."

Jude left the room wondering what he could do to will the signal's return.

As darkness fell, Sebi managed to find his way back to the hotel with a faded soccer duffle. Once in Nico's room, he presented his gifts. An old Beretta M1934 .380 from the fifties, a Russian Makarov with a broken plastic grip, a 9mm, and a machete.

"Sorry it took so long, but this ain't the place for guns, boss," Sebi said.

"I thought Yemen was the second most armed country in the world behind the United States?" Nico said.

"Yes, but apparently that's on the mainland. The people here are, well, just different. It's a pretty laid-back place."

"What about ammunition?" Jude asked.

"Just what's in the mags. Seven in the Beretta and eight in the Makarov," Sebi said.

Nico snatched up the Makarov and checked the mag. "Fifteen total bullets. It better be enough."

CHAPTER FIFTEEN

T HE SMALL, NEARLY EMPTY HARBOR at Mori, just east of the airport, held three boats slightly smaller than the *Desert Rose*. As they dropped anchor, the prevailing wind slowly spun the boat until its stern was facing the shore. Since their only dinghy had been left on the beach in Somalia, Cable swam to shore, hardly noticing the scab on his healing ribs. He arranged for a local, to ferry everyone else ashore.

Jon stepped onto the bridge and thanked the captain for his efforts on their behalf. He paid him for his time and fuel, including the two days it would take to get back to Djibouti.

"My friend." The captain, who spoke very little English, shook Jon's hand with vigor. His toothless grin was uncontained as he gave Jon a big hug and cheek kisses on both sides.

Jon returned the sentiment. "*Shkran lak,*" he said, slaughtering an Arabic thank you.

The captain held up his hand before Jon could leave. He reached under a bench into a secret compartment and pulled out a dirty folded towel, which he handed to Jon. Jon hesitated but didn't want to seem ungrateful, so he took the towel. It was heavier than expected, so he lifted the corner to reveal an old five-shot Webley revolver .45 wrapped inside. "No, I couldn't," Jon said, handing it back to the captain.

But the captain wasn't having it, and Jon realized, in truth, the gun might really come in handy, should they have a second run-in with the Greek mobsters. He switched gears and thanked the captain, grateful.

Once everyone and their gear were ashore, the group waved good-bye as the *Desert Rose* weighed anchor and headed for the open ocean.

A local with a battered highlander offered to take them around the point to the main city of Hadiboh. With a population of just over eight thousand, the largest city on Socotra was home to most of the island's amenities and the main government building.

The driver dropped them off just past the hospital on the east side, then sped away with a toot of his horn.

Jon led them into town to the Homestay Hotel, a two-story solar-powered complex by the water. It was surrounded by a stone wall and several date palms. Jon stepped inside and arranged for everyone's ac-commodations. He then took the time to unpack and properly hide his revolver in his rucksack.

Once he was settled, Cable took a stroll through town to the Adventure Eco-tourism Company.

Next to an empty lot with a pile of rubble sat a small building with a dusty glass front. The sign above the door was in Arabic and English, confirming Cable's destination. He stepped inside and walked up to the counter. The space was small, with several ill-matched chairs lining the walls and a collection of framed pictures of foreign tourists exploring various parts of the island. The only light was from the dirty windows, giving the space a milky glow. It smelled musty, with overtones of carda-mon. A struggling air conditioner dripped rusty water in the corner. There was no one in sight, so Cable reached for the bell on the countertop.

After a minute, a young woman appeared through a worn red cur-tain. She looked at Cable with dark, judging eyes and immediately spoke broken English. "I help you?"

Cable returned with flawless Arabic, and she visibly relaxed.

It took a bit of back-and-forth, but eventually, they came to an agree-ment, and Cable left with an awkward wave.

A small dirt courtyard at the back of the hotel had two weathered tables with chairs. Everyone ordered tea and took a seat, enjoying the ocean breeze and being back on land. Cable broke the silence. "We meet our guide tomorrow at eight. He will pick us up here at the hotel and take us wherever we want to go."

"Did you ask about the tiger's mouth or the blood tree?" Mona asked.

"No, I thought we should keep that information to ourselves for now. Let's see what our expert thinks when we meet him tomorrow."

Mona nodded. It seemed like the right approach.

"Any sign of the Greeks?" Dani asked.

Cable shook his head.

After tea and small talk, they broke up and returned to their rooms.

A faded red Nissan X-Trail with a dented hood pulled into the gravel courtyard the next morning. Cable came out to greet their guide, a frown growing on his face.

The driver opened his door and popped out with a huge smile. He wore sandals, blue board shorts, and a white T-shirt. His hair was shaggy, and his beard was nicely trimmed. He was young, maybe twenty-three. This was not Mariamo Mubarak.

Everyone else watched from the hotel entrance as Cable walked up to the young man.

"I am Faisal, your guide today."

"I ordered two vehicles," Cable said to the driver. "And where is Mariamo Mubarak? He's supposed to be our guide."

"Yes, most unfortunate… His car, not go."

Cable switched to Arabic, trying not to let his impatience show.

After some renegotiating and a couple of phone calls, another vehicle was on its way with Mariamo.

By nine o'clock, the second vehicle arrived, and an older gentleman, much older than his picture, stepped out. He had a dark brown Kufi hat, a scruffy gray beard, and tired brown eyes. His baggy tan pants were held up by a piece of rope, and his collared green shirt was well-faded.

He reached out a hand to Cable. "I am Mariamo Mubarak. It is a pleasure to make your acquaintance."

Cable introduced the rest of the group and decided now was as good a time as any to show his cards. "Mariamo, thank you for coming. We are looking for a place that is mentioned in an ancient text," Cable started. "It is described as a tiger's mouth. We think it is a descriptive name for a geological place or formation. The text also mentions it is below a cloud tree, which we believe to be a dragon's blood tree."

"Makes sense. Okay… How old is the text?" Mariamo asked.

"Around 2,500 years," Dani replied.

"Wow… Any tree would be long gone by now. Hmm, let me think." Mariamo looked up for just a beat. "There is a fairly prominent point called *ras alhisan*."

"Horsehead," Cable translated.

Mona was anxious to get started, and another history lesson was too much for her. So, she opened the passenger door to the second vehicle and sat.

"And we have several famous caves that might look like a mouth. They are all named after the people who found them. However…the one exception is Alayeh cave."

"*On him* cave?" Cable translated, with a scrunched forehead.

"Nobody knows how it got its name… 2,500 years, huh? That can change a lot of things."

"Any chance there are carvings or markings in these caves?" Dani asked.

"I am aware of nothing that dates back that far, and frankly, I would be the guy who knows," Mariamo said with a slight chuckle.

"I think the best course of action is checking the caves one by one," Cable proposed.

"Yes, agreed," Mariamo said. "I know just where to start."

They all loaded up and headed east on the main road, RR 01.

Cable took the passenger seat next to Mariamo, who drove the lead Nissan, with Dani and Kojo in the backseat. Faisal followed behind, with Mona, Kaari, and Jon.

Mariamo swerved around a pothole. "Socotra has been known by many names through the centuries. It was an important sea trade stop for several ancient peoples, including the Greeks, Sultans, and tribes from both Africa and India. Alexandria traded here. Even China has a connection to the island."

Mariamo pulled close to the road's edge as a larger truck moving toward them passed.

"But 2,500 years ago…this island was uninhabited and unknown."

Nico was busy dressing. Since checking the computer this morning, the tracker has been pinging a weak but constant signal. After a small amount of research, he had Dani pinpointed, less than a mile away, at the Homestay Hotel on the other side of town.

He hustled down to the lobby and joined Jude and Philo. Sebi appeared a few moments later, carrying hot cups and wrapped food. He passed everything out, and they loaded up in the orange van. As they left the parking lot, Nico took a sip from his steaming cup. "Augh. What is this, piss water? Where's my coffee?" He tossed the cup out the window.

"Sorry, boss, they only have tea at the hotel," Sebi explained.

They rode in silence for a time.

"Anyone get any sleep last night?" Jude inquired. "That bed was really small and hard as lead." He turned left and dodged two older women on their way to the market.

"Yeah, I don't think I can move my neck to the left," Nico said while trying to do just that.

"I could really go for some Greek food right now," Philo complained as he ate his mystery-meat breakfast wrapped in flatbread.

The pings on the computer screen led them to a street with a derelict retaining wall. Jude pulled to a stop just as the Homestay Hotel came into view. He killed the engine and lit a cigarette, letting the smoke billow on the outside breeze.

"Our tracker's battery is dying," Jude said, looking at the laptop.

"Then we best not lose her," Nico warned.

Shortly after nine o'clock, two Nissans pulled from the courtyard and turned left, heading out of town.

Jude started the engine and waited for the SUVs to put some distance between them before pulling out onto the road.

They followed for twenty minutes before the fading pings on the screen changed course, heading off the highway and up into the mountains. Within a few minutes, the signal on the screen died.

"No more cell signal," Nico said to no one in particular.

"Where does that road lead?" Jude asked.

"It looks like more of a trail than a road, and it goes to a place called Alayeh."

Jude looked over at Nico for more information.

Nico just shrugged.

Jude turned onto the off-road trail that led up into the mountains.

After about thirty minutes, he pulled to the side and stopped the car. "Look." He pointed.

Nico could see a group of people hiking up to a small dark spot on the mountainside. He reached back to Philo. "Hand me the binoculars." After getting a better view, he said, "That's them. It looks like they're heading into a cave, and that Egyptian woman and one guard are with them."

"Should we take 'em?" Jude asked.

"No. Let's follow Tobias's lead, God rest his soul, and let them bring the treasure to us."

Nico raised the binoculars back up and watched as the group disappeared into the black maw.

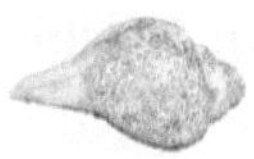

After a few minutes, they pulled from the narrow-paved road onto a trail.

Mona held on as they bumped their way up into the mountains.

After about a half hour, they came to the end of the trail and parked.

Mariamo pointed up through the windshield. "Alayeh Cave."

An unremarkable gap in the mountainside was all Dani could make out. She exited the vehicle and squinted against the rising sun without much improvement.

"Faisal will take you. I am too old for this cave," Mariamo announced as he lit a cigarette.

Mona soon understood why. The trail up was very steep and narrow. Thorns reached out all along the way, and loose rocks made footing a challenge.

As they closed on their objective, the small black hole grew slightly in size. It was thirty feet wide by five feet high, with rugged rocks protecting the entrance.

Mona decided to wait outside and see if anything was found before venturing down into the hole.

Faisal scrambled up and over the jagged rocks and down into the limestone cavern.

The rest followed.

Kaari stepped next to Mona. "I will stay here with you. I don't trust the remoteness of our situation."

Monas nodded her agreement. "Thank you, Kaari."

"You coming?" Kojo asked, looking back at Kaari.

She shook her head, and Kojo did a quick nod before scrambling over the rocks and out of sight.

The cave started shallow, with low headroom for about fifty feet, and then opened to the right, where a long, tall chamber extended for about fifty yards.

"It curves to right up that way and dead ends," Faisal announced. "There are ancient paintings over here." He pointed left.

"Okay, split up. We need to check every inch of this place for anything that might look Phoenician. Dani, you take the cave paintings and see what you can make of them." Cable switched to Arabic and asked Faisal to show Dani the paintings.

There were signs of flowstones and a few small stalagmites reaching for their mirrored twin, stalactites. Evidence of a small collapse was near the rear dogleg.

Each person took a flashlight and moved along the cave, searching in their own way.

Dani followed Faisal to a large, flat surface of limestone that reached the ceiling. About five feet up was a grouping of faded black symbols painted on the rock. Time had claimed a few, but there were many symbols still visible. She studied them very carefully and took several pictures from different angles. Referring to her phone's screen and then back to the original, she studied the curious markings. "Has anyone ever tried to translate these?"

Faisal shook his head. "Not that I know… They look Arabic, but it is not familiar to me."

After a good hour of scouring every inch of the cave, daylight was a welcome friend.

Cable looked to Dani. "We got nothing. How about you?"

Mona stepped over to listen to the results.

"The drawings on the cave look to be Quranic, or classic Arabic, which dates to about the seventh century."

"Too new?" Jon asked.

"Yeah, by about a thousand years. There was, however, this geometric shape, which is unknown to me." She showed everyone a picture on her phone of a bulbous vertical line with three horizontal lines crossing it. "But, based on the look and style, I'd say it was all painted at the same time."

"So, none of it is old enough," Cable summarized.

"Exactly," Dani said.

They turned and headed down the trail.

As they approached the parked vehicles, Cable called out to Mariamo. "Okay, next stop."

"Very good, my friend. Hoq Cave is the closest, and it is quite magnificent, but we will need to stop and eat first. I know just the place."

They all loaded up and started back down the mountain.

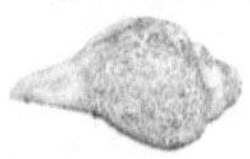

Nico lowered his binoculars. "I don't see them carrying anything."

"Unless it was another clue," Jude offered.

"Possibly… Let's get back down the mountain before we're spotted."

They all jumped back into the Mitsubishi Delica and fired up the diesel motor.

"Boss, what do you suppose this treasure is?" Jude asked.

"Treasure of a thousand kings." Nico looked over at Jude. "That says gold and jewels to me, but if it's here on this island, it might still be in raw form, which means we'd have to figure out how to get it out of the ground."

"Without being noticed," Sebi said from the backseat.

"Right. Tobias died for this treasure, which means we deserve it, not anyone else."

They came to the narrow-paved road, and Jude paused the van.

"Go left about three hundred meters and pull to the side. We can wait there and follow once they hit the main road."

After about ten minutes, the two Nissans pulled back onto the main road and continued east farther around the island.

Nico popped the laptop open and waited for it to boot. The pinging tracker was no longer working.

"They're back in cell service, but I got no signal. Battery's dead," Jude said.

"Give 'em another two minutes," Nico said, looking over his shoulder.

Jude waited and then spun the van around and headed after their target.

The coastal road moved inland at Delisha Beach and then back to the coast once they crossed a small bridge accessing a lagoon. They stayed a good mile behind the two vehicles they were following. Every once in a while, they would catch a glimpse of them in the distance.

Nico let the anger inside him continue to percolate. He had lost time, money, and a dear friend. Someone was going to pay.

After an hour, Mariamo pulled off the pavement and down a one-lane strip of dirt. He parked next to a small stone-stacked hut with several goats and chickens wandering about. A lone woman tended a campfire out front.

The dust from the vehicles swirled and blew slowly inland as Mona exited and stretched her aching back.

Faisal ran from the follow vehicle to give the woman, who was wearing a traditional black abaya and hijab, two cheek kisses. He then introduced everyone once they caught up. "This is my sister, Badia. She makes the best beef mandi and a few other things." He gave a proud smile.

"You're in for a treat," Cable said. "Mandi is one of my favorite dishes."

Mona watched, slightly taken aback, as the group all sat on the ground around a small campfire with several steel pots. She joined them on the dirt as Badia served them lunch.

The beef mandi stew, with long-grain saffron rice, red lentils, and dates, was excellent, and they washed it all down with some Adeni tea.

It took another forty minutes to get back onto the main road before they turned into a small wadi and headed inland. At one point, the dry wash they had been following ended, with several large, jagged rocks blocking the way.

"We walk from here," Mariamo said, as he killed the engine.

Cable stepped out. It was dry and hot with no breeze and no shade. He looked over to Dani, who seemed less than enthused. Were they wasting their time here, or had they missed something? Archaeology was not an exact science, and ancient clues rarely connected to modern times. Even something as well known in ancient times as the Hanging Gardens of Babylon was still disputed as to where and if they ever existed. The chance they were going to find an answer to something as obscure as Boaz's journey was incredibly low, and that feeling was starting to take hold of the entire group.

Cable could read her mind. "We're here… Might as well." He tilted his head, and Dani nodded in agreement.

"Faisal, show them the way. I will watch the vehicles," Mariamo called out as he hunched his shoulders and lit another cigarette.

Faisal nodded eagerly and started toward the rocks blocking the wash.

Mariamo stepped over to Dani and Cable. "Hoq Cave is very large, three kilometers, and there are no known cave paintings or carvings, but I wish you luck on your quest."

Cable shook Mariamo's hand, before turning and following Faisal up the boulders.

Mona was tempted to go, but the ruggedness made her pause.

"Come, miss. I help. Flat on other side," Faisal called back.

Mona replied in Arabic, and Faisal realized his error. He tried again, as he headed back, reaching out with a hand and a smile to help her.

It took another half hour of hiking over rocks and dirt along a narrow path. The geological isolation of Socotra Island made it unlike anywhere else. With unique and varied fauna and flora, it was a feast for the eyes. Strange butterflies of every color flittered about. They passed a few small dragon's blood trees and desert rose trees and even saw a Socotra bunting singing from a branch.

A Julodis beetle flew past, catching the attention of the group with its purple and orange coloration, and several cucumber trees with their bottle-shaped trunks grew next to the trail.

The oddity of it all wasn't lost on the visitors. Jon, in particular, seemed to be consumed by it all.

It was a foreign planet, here on Earth.

"So, you are a working mercenary?" Kojo asked Kaari, making small talk as they climbed.

"I prefer the term 'hired killer,' " Kaari shot back, giving Kojo a follow-up stare-down.

Kojo almost stopped walking. He looked back at her stern eyes and suddenly needed to make a pit stop.

Then, slowly and very subtly, Kaari cracked a smile.

Kojo realized she was messing with him, and he nervously smiled back.

"I was one of two women to make it through airborne, from the Ghanaian sixty-fourth infantry regiment. The training is solid, but the pay…ridiculous. So, once my contract was up, I found work elsewhere. I usually do HV protection."

Kojo looked unsure.

"High Value, like politicians or VIPs."

Kojo nodded. "Now, you're on a treasure hunt."

"Looks like…maybe we can all retire after this."

"Retire? Where's the fun in that?"

Kaari looked back at Kojo. He was not what she expected. The Ethiopian was so much more.

By the time they reached Hoq Cave, everyone was dripping with sweat. The view back down was stunning and included a large slice of azure sea.

The entrance was like a large domed cathedral carved into a precipice of reddish rock. Several stalactites hung down, giving it a mouth-like appearance, which wasn't lost on the hopeful group—tiger's mouth.

Cable looked up optimistically, but there were no dragon's blood trees above the entrance. Dani noticed the same thing.

A quick question to Faisal, and they had their answer. None of the cloud-shaped trees grew up by the cave, at least not in modern times.

The first thing Cable noticed as they climbed into the cooler interior was the humidity. There were signs of water and moisture everywhere. The rock looked like God had taken a giant blow torch and melted his way into the cliff. Flowstones, giant stalagmites, and stalactites were everywhere, all frozen in time. Some were jagged like dripping-wet sandcastles, others smooth and shiny. There were soda straws, popcorn, draperies, and helictites. Every limestone cave formation was represented. Some were as small as a pinky, others enormous, reaching hundreds of feet upward.

Because the entrance was so large, daylight filled the cave for nearly three hundred yards.

The group walked down the slope into the belly of the orifice. Heads rotated in every direction at the splendor of it all. A small creek flowed down the middle of the floor. Cable stepped over it and looked back at the group. "Okay, let's spread out and see what we can find." He flicked on his flashlight and headed deeper into the cave.

The group dispersed, trying to cover every inch of the massive space.

As they left daylight behind, slow, methodical drops fell from the roof. Round crystal-clear pools of water, with natural calcite dams, dotted the floor. Nature was showing off in a grandiose style.

A good hour later, the group exited the cave, muddy and wet. The sun was lower on the horizon, but there was still plenty of heat in the arid air. It had been another bust, and more cracks of frustrated morale were starting to show.

Mona had a slight smile on her face as she climbed up, still panting. "That cave was unlike anything I have ever seen."

"Yes, it is magnificent," Dani added, enjoying the woman's simple enthusiasm.

Even Jon, who had been all business, had to agree.

It's funny how one little thing can change so much, Cable thought, as he patted Kojo on the back. They all started down the mountain.

Nico was swearing with every step. They had parked the car in a small village and tried to find where their target had gone. The tracker had completely stopped transmitting, but they had a general idea of where the group had gone, just nothing specific. The local terrain was rocky and uneven, and the heat had long since won the battle, soaking his clothes. He was miserable, and with that came a dangerous temper.

He grabbed the binoculars from Jude and scanned the horizon. "This is stupid," Nico said, stopping suddenly and shoving the binoculars back into Jude's hands. "We're not going to find the treasure chasing after them like this. We need to get ahead of this thing."

Jude took a look for himself. There was no sign of Dani or anyone. He paused, waiting to see what his boss was going to do next.

"We need a new plan. I'm done watching and waiting." He turned and started back to the van.

Jude spun on his heels and clambered after him, with Sebi and Philo right behind.

"I think we should raise the stakes, boss," Jude said, carefully.

"You're reading my mind, Jude."

"We'll need a place to operate from," Jude said, more boldly.

"I saw an abandoned warehouse along the beach, not too far from our hotel," Sebi said.

Nico was still sweating, but now his mood had focus and a plan. It would quench his anger for now.

CHAPTER SIXTEEN

DINNER BACK IN HADIBOH WAS subdued. The magic of the island was the main topic, with little talk about the quest.

They had selected a small seafood restaurant called Seafood Restaurant. The place was wall-to-ceiling patterned tile, none of it matching—brown tones, oranges, pinks, purples, and reds. It was a kaleidoscope to the eyes.

Cable focused on the fresh fish and flatbread in front of him, trying to keep his eyes away from the garish walls.

Mariamo would be back in the morning to pick them up at eight. They would then travel to the other side of the island to visit the only other two known caves.

Cable knew that if they didn't find anything the next day, this journey would be at its end. In fact, they all knew it.

It was a bittersweet thought as he sipped some mango nectar. The last time Cable had been to Socotra Island, he had been working on a fishing vessel out of Oman. They had experienced some bad weather and needed to stop for repairs. Cable stayed behind on the island for another week, exploring, before heading for his next migratory job. He was going to be a translator for an international dig site on Failaka Island, off the coast of Kuwait. There, he had made many new friends and lost one that was very dear to him.

He shook the thoughts from his mind and refocused on the conversation, realizing they were talking about him.

"That's when he went looking for a video camera," Kojo said, animatedly.

"What, he just left you there?" Dani asked.

"To be fair, he wasn't going anywhere," Cable replied.

"I was tied up. Army ants were heading my way," Kojo exclaimed with increasing volume.

"Those things can bite and sting, real nasty," Kaari added.

"Remind me not to count on you in an emergency," Jon said, with a smirk to Cable.

Cable raised his hands. "First of all, in my defense, he did look pretty funny strung out like a lamb for the slaughter on the ground. Secondly, and most important,"—Cable gestured to Kojo with a thumb—"I give you Kojo the Magnificent, alive and doing very well."

"No thanks to you," Kojo mumbled.

"*All* thanks to me," Cable countered. "We both got bit and stung, and we both did the ant-dance to get any stragglers off us as we ran for our lives. That's what I call commitment. Look, I still have a scar." He lifted his pant leg, but the scar was so small nobody could see it.

Kojo lifted his tea. "To Cable and his alleged scar and last-minute heroics." He cocked his head, pausing. "And very good friendship."

Cable did likewise. "Love you, brother."

Kaari raised her cup. "Now, if we could just find some alcohol on this island. I'd even take a warm beer at this point."

Mona raised her tea as well. "I might actually join you for that, my dear."

"A dry country is working just fine for me," Jon said, no longer afraid to talk about his past struggles.

They all shared a smile and a laugh.

Mona tried knocking again with the same result. Kaari was not answering. She convinced the hotel owner to open the door.

The group stepped inside.

"Her bed is made, and her clothes are still here," Jon said as he looked around. "No sign of a struggle. She either left us abruptly, or perhaps there is foul play at work here."

"Kojo, weren't you the last person to see her?" Cable asked.

Kojo looked a bit defensive. "Ah…yes. We went for a walk on the beach. You might not realize it, but there is a soft side to Kaari."

"Just tell us where you last saw her," Jon said, a bit forcefully.

"Sorry. She left me sitting in the sand, looking at the stars. I'd say around eleven. Said she needed to get some rest. I saw her walking back toward the hotel. That was it."

"Okay, so, somewhere between eleven and now," Jon summarized.

"We need to go look for her," Kojo said.

"Where?" Mona asked.

"We should call the police," Dani said.

"And tell them what, exactly?" Jon asked.

"Our friend is missing," she replied.

"Correct, missing, but with no signs of foul play," Jon said. "And not even for twenty-four hours. She's an adult. There is nothing they will do."

No one had any other ideas.

"I'll check with the hotel staff and see if anyone saw anything," Jon said.

"Good idea," Cable agreed.

"But from now on, no one leaves the hotel alone. We need to be very careful," Jon said as he looked at everyone. "Got it?"

Heads nodded.

Mariamo and Faisal pulled up at ten minutes past eight in the two Nissans. They were ready for another long day.

The hotel staff was no help. Kaari had simply disappeared.

It left a jittery feeling in the group as they shuffled outside and loaded up.

Jon checked his pack for the third time to make sure he had quick access to his pistol. This was the kind of thing that had his spidey senses tingling. Something was very wrong.

Jude wiped the blood off his hands with a rag. His knuckles ached from the beating they were taking, but that was nothing compared to the person's face they had been hitting. It was all puffy and deformed. Two broken orbital bones, a flattened nose, and a jaw that just hung loose. Blood oozed and dripped from a once-perfect cleft chin.

They were not going to get any more information out of this one.

"She knows less than we do," Nico spat.

Jude and Philo had taken the young female last night by surprise as she strolled along the beach, whistling. Using their two guns, it had been easy to persuade her to join them.

After subduing and transporting her back to an abandoned warehouse, they had methodically chained her up, arms outstretched, between two steel beams. That's when Jude had gone to work. Initially, he worked her torso, but after several broken ribs, he moved to her face.

Nico had asked the questions, and frankly, they had gotten many answers.

Her name was Kaari. She was from Ghana. Hired to be protection for a wealthy Egyptian named Mona Helal. The Egyptian woman they had encountered at the beach in Somalia. The group was looking for clues to an ancient treasure that was connected to a voyage a Phoenician ship's captain named Boaz took some 2,500 years ago.

That was hardly new to Nico, and it frustrated him how long it took to get that information out of the woman. She was one stubborn lady.

The one piece of new news that he did obtain was the fruitlessness of their search on the island so far.

That was helpful, but what a waste of time and a human. He stepped closer. Her black eyes still burned with hatred. She tried to spit at him, but with a broken jaw, it just spewed out over her lip.

"Too bad," Nico said, without emotion.

She was strong and defiant. Under any other circumstance, she would be a good asset to add to his team. Today, however, it was time to talk or die, and it looked like she was choosing the second.

"Get rid of her," Nico said as he turned and left the warehouse.

Jude stepped forward and raised his Beretta.

Kaari let out a guttural cry before the pistol bucked twice, silencing her mid-scream.

Jude watched, as her angry eyes glazed over, and then her chin dropped to her chest. He pulled the magazine out and inspected it. He was down to five bullets. "Dump her," he said to Philo and Sebi, as he slammed the mag back into the gun. He would have to be more prudent with his ammunition.

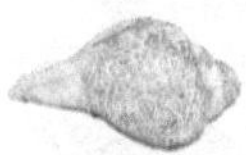

The long drive to the other side of the island had been filled with silence. Cable felt like he could cut the tension in his car with a knife. Everyone was worried about Kaari and what else might be waiting for them.

Dani stared out the window, her head on the hot glass. There had been no sign of the Greeks, but with Kaari missing, she couldn't help thinking about them. Were they responsible? She knew if that was the case, they could be coming for her. It was a troublesome thought.

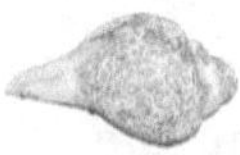

Two more caves later with no results, Cable conceded the fact that they had reached the end of their journey.

Mariamo had no other ideas or known caves for them to investigate.

The group slowly loaded back into the vehicles and headed home.

Home. It sounded good to Dani. She was accustomed to finding dead ends in archeology. The past and its secrets were never guaranteed to be uncovered. They had gone far on this quest and almost reached the end. It was nothing to be ashamed of. Perhaps someday in the future, someone would find the next clue, if it was still out there.

Mariamo pulled her from her thoughts. "I have seen many people over the years come to my island looking for more than just its natural beauty. Every one of them went home disappointed. Those who come here to connect with our unique spirit are the ones whose lives are changed by the magic." Mariamo looked in the rearview mirror at Jon and Dani, then over to Cable. They were covered in dried dirt, and each wore an expression of disappointment.

Dani forced a small smile for him.

Mariamo gave his head a brief shake and drove on. This group had missed what was right in front of them.

The sun was dipping behind the mountain as they pulled into the gravel driveway of the hotel. Slowly, everyone exited the vehicles and thanked their guides for their help.

Cable tried one last time before they officially gave up. "You are sure there is nothing more you can think of?" he asked Mariamo.

He shook his head before speaking. "We have been to all the known caves. Faisal, have you heard of any other caves?"

Faisal shook his head.

"And there are no *tiger-mouth* geologic formations or similar names that I am aware of," Mariamo said thoughtfully. "I can try asking around to some of my older friends. Here, take my card. If I can be of any further assistance, please call."

"That would be appreciated," Dani replied. "Thank you again for your efforts."

Jon accepted Mariamo's business card and stuffed it in his pocket. He made sure the bill was all taken care of for the Adventure Eco-tourism Company, including a generous tip for Faisal and Mariamo.

They all said their goodbyes and started for the hotel, exhausted, but mostly disappointed.

After cleaning up and a quick dinner, Jon headed for his room. He was coming to the end of his contract with Tam McGree, and it was time to update his employer and arrange for their trip back to the States.

Tam had been nothing but supportive and encouraging as they had skipped across the globe on this wild goose chase, all on his dime.

Jon wished he had more clients like him. He let his mind drift to what came next. Going back to Taipei to off himself in a shanty of a hotel room was no longer on the table. He would have some money. Maybe enough to go back to Japan and try again. The thought of it made his stomach turn, and for the first time in a week, he needed a drink.

Jon forced the thoughts from his mind as he opened his door and stepped into his room. A violent shot of pain exploded on the back of his head, and he watched as his world went sideways and then black.

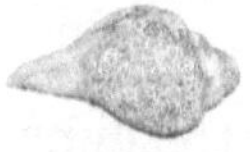

Pain. His head throbbed, and it forced him to open his eyes. Everything was blurry at first, but slowly, things came into view. It was night. The next thing he noticed was the smell. Musty with a hint of copper—blood.

Jon looked down to see a significant pool of recently dried blood at his feet in the dim light. That's when he realized he was standing…no, hanging by his arms. He slowly straightened, taking some of the pressure off his shoulders.

He was chained between two rusty steel beams with his arms fully extended. His feet were tied together with another chain that was bolted to the ground, giving him very little ability to move.

The room was expansive and looked like an old warehouse space. Piles of junk were strewn about, just visible in the soft moonlight, coming through a tall row of windows.

As his senses continued to return, the sound of muffled waves could be heard just outside, which was followed by voices.

Someone was coming. Jon flexed and tried to pull free, but it only aggravated the pounding in his head.

A light blasted his eyes, forcing Jon to look away.

"He's awake," came from the left.

A large silhouette of a man appeared to his left and several others to the right. There were four of them.

Jon squinted through the blinding light. "I know you…from the beach," he rasped.

"Looks like we finally caught ourselves a smart one," Nico replied.

Jude stepped up and blasted Jon with a powerful fist to the side of his head.

Jon almost lost consciousness. His head spun in circles, threatening to make him puke.

"Hang on. What is it you want?"

"Answers," Nico replied.

"That's easy. This is not some sort of secret spy mission. We're just following up on a quest for a client. What do you want to know?"

"Tell me what you found," Nico demanded.

"Nothing," Jon answered.

Another blast came flying. This time to his ribs.

Jon could feel the air leave his body and dry sucked several times before he caught his breath. "I'm not lying." He gasped for air several more times. "We found a clue in a cave back at the beach where we met. That clue sent us here."

"I saw that cave. There was nothing in it but an empty altar. What did you take from it?" Nico asked.

"Nothing. I swear. The cave wa—"

Another punch flew, this time an uppercut to Jon's chin.

He felt his teeth crack and saw a flash of white. After a second, he continued. "Look, if you're just going to beat me every time I speak, I'm done. Bring it."

Nico used his head to signal Jude to back off.

Jon moved his jaw back and forth before continuing. "The altar was empty when we got there, but we uncovered some writing. That was the clue that led us here. Three days to tiger's mouth, below cloud tree."

"I didn't see any writing."

"I covered it back up before we left the cavern."

"How did that lead you to Socotra?" Nico asked.

"Long story short…" Jon paused to get his breath back. "We have some really smart people in our group."

"Yes, I was quite impressed with Dr. Dani Tran," Nico said.

"The problem is, once we got here, the trail went cold."

"Cold? What do you mean?" Nico demanded.

"Cold. Dead end. Bupkis. We found nothing. I was just about to arrange travel back to the States when your guys paid me a visit."

"So, you were leaving…giving up?" Jude asked in broken English.

Jon nodded.

Nico paced back and forth for a moment. Had he been through all this for nothing? No. That would not do. He needed to get to one of the really smart people.

"We need to get the girl back. Kill him, and dispose of the body," Nico said as he turned to leave.

Jude didn't hesitate. He pulled his Barretta, but at that moment, he remembered he had already wasted two of his seven bullets on the girl. He aimed his pistol dead center.

Jon looked him square in the eyes and threw himself forward against the chains. "You son of a—"

Jude fired into Jon's chest, knocking him back. He stepped forward, inspecting his kill. "Toss him in the ocean."

Sebi and Philo pulled the body down and dragged it out the back door. They trudged through the sand and into the water, releasing the corpse into the outgoing tide, just like they had done with Kaari.

Cable woke with a hangover. How that was possible was anyone's guess. He hadn't imbibed one drop. But every part of his body felt like he had really tied one on last night. He lifted his feet to the floor and squinted his eyes. Then, as if every movement counted against an impending tally, he slowly got dressed.

Dani knocked on the door, and he opened it.

"Forgot to grab the key," she said as she pushed inside carrying two glasses of peach nectar.

"I didn't hear you get up."

"You were out cold… Wow, you look…"

"I know. I feel like I slept in a dryer," Cable said.

"That bad?"

"Even my teeth hurt."

"Got it… Teeth. Let's get some breakfast and then see what Jon has planned for our exit strategy. I'm pretty sure there is only one flight a week," Dani proposed, with an upbeat edge.

"You seem awfully chipper."

Dani looked at Cable as he headed for the door.

They started down the hallway. "I have concluded that we did everything in our power to find an answer to an ancient mystery that is no longer solvable. Hey, it happens."

Cable shuffled around the corner into the lobby with Dani.

"Failure was always on the table, and honestly, we got pretty far on this one."

"I'll pat myself on the back later," he said.

"I would have never taken you for a poor loser," Dani said, with a dose of sarcasm.

"Give me one person who likes losing…"

Dani's attempts at cheering him up were not working. "Okay, stay moody. I'm going to the beach."

Cable raised one eyebrow and looked Dani over.

She hesitated, then tried, "*We're* going to the beach?"

"That's better," Cable said, with the first hint of a grin.

The front door to the hotel burst open, and Faisal hurried inside.

He rattled off several Arabic words in overzealous excitement before Cable could get him to slow down to an understandable pace.

"Try that again," he said.

Faisal quickly swallowed and started over. "There is one more place you must look."

"You know of another cave?" Cable asked.

"Not a cave, a…" He tried to explain it, but Cable wasn't following. "A friend, this morning…he reminded me of a place…a Littoral," Faisal said. "A place like a cave but made from waves." He used his hands to help convey the waves, the actual term eluding him.

After several attempts, Cable's eyes widened in understanding. "Yes, of course…*kahf albahr*," he said in Arabic. Then repeated in English, "a sea cave," for Dani.

"Yes, a cave in the sea," Faisal exclaimed. "There is one by the Detwah Lagoon. I talked to Mariamo, and he agrees it is worth looking into."

For the first time in many hours, Cable sensed they might be back on the trail. "Can you take us there?"

"Course. It is why I am here," Faisal said proudly.

"Dani, get the others. We've got one more place to look," Cable said, as he dashed back to his room and grabbed his gear, suddenly feeling better.

As he stepped back into the hallway, Kojo and Dani were approaching with a worried look. "What is it?"

"Jon is missing," Dani announced.

"Just like Kaari. His bed is untouched," Kojo added.

Cable thought for a second. "I'll go to the police. You stay here. The cave can wait."

Both Kojo and Dani nodded.

"Call me if there is any change."

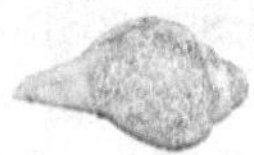

The rising sun was just starting to sparkle on the water. Jon half-swam and half-drowned as he fought to keep his head above water. The bullet had done damage, but surprisingly, he was still somewhat ambulatory.

When he was first tossed into the water, he had covertly gulped air, allowing himself to float face down for a time. It seemed to do the trick, as the thugs who tossed him out like yesterday's trash quickly lost interest. He then slowly rolled face-up and did everything in his power to keep his head above the water.

The tide had swept him out at first, sapping most of his energy. He leaked blood into the sea like a chum bucket. Luckily, there had been no sharks yet.

Keeping one hand pressed firmly on the wound, Jon pulled and kicked his way back to land. It had taken two hours, and the current had moved him far from any civilization.

As Jon dragged himself onto the sand, he passed out, with his feet still in the water.

The tide continued to recede gradually from the beach, eventually leaving Jon on dry land.

Eyes fluttered open. A strange, sand-colored crab with white claws scuttled past.

Jon didn't know how long he had been there, but the sun was higher in the sky, and his face felt like it was on fire. He tried to sit up and was immediately rewarded with a shot of pain to his torso and renewed bleeding. He rolled on his side and assessed the bullet hole.

It was a through and through, which meant the bullet had passed clean through his body. That was a small blessing. The front hole was just to the left of the center, below his last rib. Another small blessing. Nothing too vital was there, save it be his stomach, spleen, or the bottom of a lung. He tried taking a large breath. Again, the pain nearly doubled him over, but no rasp or fluid sound emanated with the exhale. That meant his lungs were okay. A third small blessing. They were adding up.

Jon took his shirt off and ripped it into one long strip, then tightly wrapped his torso. He managed a knot to hold it all together. After a time, he struggled to stand, using every bit of energy and gritting his teeth through the pain.

One foot in front of the other, he wobbled up the beach in search of anything or anyone that might help him.

An invisible force of will seemed to push him forward, against all odds. One step, then another. He heard a car pass in the distance. He was getting closer. He paused to lower his head as a dizzy spell briefly consumed him. Then he was back at it, one foot followed by the second. He saw the paved strip appear before him and reached out to wave the next car down, but he lost balance and collapsed by the side of the road, no longer moving.

CHAPTER SEVENTEEN

THE DRIVE WEST ALONG THE shoreline was filled with a mix of emotions. Cable had convinced the police to be on the lookout for both Kaari and Jon. He prayed they were okay and even hoped for a brief moment that they were off somewhere having a tryst, but the odds of that were zero.

Dani put her hand on Cable's shoulder. "We'll find 'em," she said, lamely.

Cable nodded in return.

"She is a very capable woman. I'm sure she is okay," Kojo added with unrealistic hope.

Faisal had taken Cable to the police station and assisted with the report. He was known on this part of the island, and it proved helpful. The police took the report serious and were actively looking for the two missing members of the team.

After they had done everything they could with the police, Cable and Faisel left the station and drove back to the hotel.

The remaining group decided to press on. It was the only thing they could do, besides wait, and that held no sway for them.

Faisal pulled out of the parking lot with his four passengers, Dani, Cable, Kojo, and Mona. It took about two hours of driving before he pulled off the narrow, paved road onto virgin dirt.

They bumped along until the Nissan X-Trail came up over a rise, revealing a huge, teal-colored lagoon stretching out before them.

Faisal stopped the car. "Detwah Lagoon," he announced.

Mona, Dani, and Kojo squeezed out of the rear seat.

"You can't see it from here. We must climb down to the water." Faisal led them along a narrow path, down the rise, and around toward the lagoon. "Some locals call it Fath Alfam."

"Open mouth," Cable translated. Dani and Kojo both shot him a look. *Could this be tiger's mouth?* They marched on with renewed hope.

Cable took up the rear, looking back over his shoulder every few minutes. He was expecting to see John or Kaari hurrying to catch up, but there was no one. The safety and security for everyone was now on his shoulders.

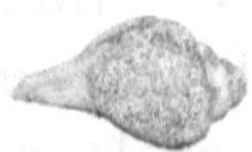

Nico was surprised when he got the call.

"They're on the move," Sebi said over the radio.

Jude looked over his shoulder. "I thought they were heading home?"

"There is only one flight a week here, so wanting to leave and being able to leave are two different things," Nico replied.

"Where do you suppose they are going?"

"Well, either Jon lied to us, and they are not done searching," Nico said, "or they have decided on an impromptu vacation."

"They're heading west and will be passing your way in about five minutes," Sebi transmitted over the radio.

"What do you want to do?"

"Sebi get over here and pick us up." Nico turned to Jude. "Get Philo. I want to put an end to this cat and mouse, once and for all."

A few minutes later Sebi screeched to a stop in the parking lot in the orange Mitsubishi. Everyone loaded up, and they quickly headed west along the narrow, paved road. Jude was pushing the van's limits. He wanted to catch up and put the red Nissan X-Trail within sight, just in case they went off to a remote part of the island again.

After about forty minutes, he spied the Nissan about a quarter mile ahead. He slowed down and kept pace with them.

Nico used his binoculars to get a closer look. A small dust cloud popped up in the distance. "They've gone off-road again."

Jude floored the van.

"Yes, moving right, toward the ocean," Nico added.

The orange van nearly went airborne off a rise in the road, and Jude was nothing but a passenger for a brief second. They bounced back down hard, and he immediately started to apply the brakes. The van fishtailed slightly before Jude got it back under control.

"Try not to kill us before we get there," Nico said while white-knuckling the chicken bar in front of him.

A dust trail just off to the right caught Jude's attention, so he pulled to the edge of the road and stopped the vehicle.

They watched until the dust disappeared before Jude spun the wheel right and followed the recent tracks into the dirt.

"Lost 'em," Nico announced, squinting through his binoculars at an empty horizon.

"Don't worry, boss. I got 'em," Jude said. "They left us two nice sets of tire tracks to follow."

Nico nodded. A slow smile that looked painful grew on his face.

After several minutes, they came around a corner to see the red SUV parked on a rise just up ahead. Jude smashed the brakes reflexively but soon realized no one was in sight. He pulled closer, and they all got out.

Sebi and Philo started quarreling over who would carry the machete.

"Would you two stop it… Sebi, it's Philo's turn to carry the machete," Jude hissed.

"That's easy for a man with a gun to say," Sebi griped.

"How would you like to carry my Beretta in your dead hand?" Jude countered.

It seemed to do the trick, as Sebi became quiet as he handed the machete to Philo. "Choke on it."

Philo countered, "Try me. I'll slit you tongue to nuts."

Nico knew they were all on edge. The last few days had been rough and nonstop, but this was what it had all come down to. One final clash for a treasure of imaginable wealth. Well, that's what he told himself, but in truth, he had been doing a lot of imagining lately.

"Shut it," Nico called out. "We are all a bit fatigued here, but we are at the end. We will find what we came here for or exact our revenge."

This seemed to appease the two gangsters.

"I got several tracks going this way," Jude called out after a brief scout of the area.

"Looks like they're heading down to that lagoon," Nico said.

Eyes cracked open. Everything was white… Heaven? Jon started to move, and a shot of dull pain gripped him. No… Hell. He had been given something, and it was starting to wear off. A few devices around him seemed familiar, a hospital room. He looked down to see his wound tightly wrapped with gauze. This was a good sign. To his left was a chair with his pants and shoes. He pushed himself up on his pillow and waited for the throbbing to die down.

A friendly face attached to a body in scrubs entered the room. "I see you are awake."

"Not sure how I'm still here, but I'll take a guess and thank you for that."

"You are a lucky man, Mister…?"

"Jon, call me Jon."

"Mister Jon, you were found on the road and brought here. I was most concerned. You have been shot, but the entry and exit wounds are surprisingly clean. We had to stitch a part of your spleen back together and, of course, the bullet holes, but I feel you will make a full recovery in no time."

"Shot?" Jon acted confused by the concept.

"The police are on their way. Perhaps you can help them find who did this to you."

Jon nodded his head. "Thanks, Doc."

"Of course, please, the best thing for you right now is rest."

"Oh, Doc, you wouldn't happen to have a phone on you? I'd like to call my friends at the hotel and let 'em know I'm okay."

"Absolutely." The doctor handed his cell phone to Jon. "I will be back in a few minutes with some pain medicine."

Jon called the hotel, but no one from his group was there. It seemed they'd left with Faisal an hour earlier. As he hung up, Jon pondered his next steps. Then, he remembered the business card in his pants. He climbed out of the bed and grimaced while he slipped his pants on, one leg and then another. It took some doing, but he finally managed.

The doctor may have seemed optimistic, but the pain was intense.

Next came the shoes. He skipped the socks and fought through the pain to get his laces tied. After a few minutes to recuperate, he reached into his pocket and pulled out a soggy business card. The ink had mostly run, but somehow the phone number was just readable. Jon pulled the IV from his arm and dialed, letting a plan slowly form. He needed to warn the others, and then it would be payback time.

The lagoon was filled with sea life. A narrow sand spit circled the ocean side of the calm water, separating the lagoon from the open sea. Cliffs reached up a good hundred feet on the opposite side, casting a shadow on the crystal-clear water. From the shoreline, Cable could just make out the open hole in the center of the cliff face. And from where he was standing, it looked very much like a half-open mouth. Two jagged protrusions of rock from the ceiling resembled incisors, and the configuration of the rock face had an eerie resemblance to a big cat.

"This has got to be what we've been looking for," Dani said to Cable.

Kojo reached out his hand and pointed. "If that's not tiger's mouth, I don't know what to call it."

"You think this is it?" Faisal asked with excitement.

"No blood trees," Mona said, pointing out the obvious.

In fact, the vegetation in the area was extremely sparse.

"I mean, 2,500 years is a long time. Climates change," Cable said.

"Everything changes," Dani added.

"I think the fastest way in is through the water." Cable decided to keep his shoes on, not knowing what the sea cave floor might be like. They skirted around the lagoon, close to the cliff's edge in the shallow water. A couple of times, the water got past their waist, but for the most part, it was calf high.

As Cable approached the black opening, set against the tan rock face, he could see water inside the cave. An obvious high-tide mark was represented by a salty white line just above his shoulders.

They would have to be careful. The sea around them moved with life. Fish of every color, snails, urchins, starfish, and even an octopus shot past.

"This area is protected. That's why the sea life is so plentiful," Faisal said.

"They don't seem too afraid of humans," Dani added.

Cable stepped inside. Immediately, he noticed this was a very different-looking cave. Gone were the flowstones and formations. In their place was a common, rugged, and jagged rock. Light shimmered off the water, rippling the walls. It was a massive tidepool, tinging the damp air with salt, and teeming with life. Every step required careful negotiations between foot and resident.

Cable flicked on his flashlight and began looking around the space. Soon, everyone was following his lead.

Several sections were too deep and required swimming. It was a good two hundred yards to the rear of the cave.

Cable's light bounced off a small, white sandy beach in the very back. He took his time inspecting the walls and ceiling as he progressed. Nothing looked unnatural or out of place.

"I don't see any carvings or paintings," Dani said as she walked up onto the small beach at the rear of the cave.

"Me either," Cable replied. "A sea cave is under constant erosion. Anything carved into one of these walls would be long gone."

"Surely, the person who left the clues would have known that," Mona said, trying to be helpful, as she walked from the water on shaky legs. The deeper water had pushed her limits, bringing back bad drowning memories from her childhood. She forced herself forward, focusing on the strip of sand ahead. As her feet touched the shore, the fear of having to go back was threatening to take hold. She closed her eyes and pushed the destructive thoughts aside.

Faisal noticed her expression. "Are you all right?"

Mona nodded a reply.

Cable looked back to the sea cave's entrance. A beam of sunlight on the water made it glow a bright green. It was magical. Dani turned to see what had captured his attention. She grabbed his hand, and they let the moment linger.

Kojo was the last to join them on the little beach. "I tripped over so many sea snails getting here. There must be like a million down there."

"I had a fish nibbling on my leg," Dani added.

Mona cringed, happy that neither of those things had happened to her.

Cable turned away from the entrance and did a more thorough examination of the rocks in the back of the cave. "Look for possible caverns that might branch off."

Everyone joined him.

"I got something," Kojo called out after a few minutes.

Sure enough, there was a small crack that opened into a space beyond.

Cable and Kojo dropped to their knees and started pulling sand from the fissure to widen access. After a bit of work, Cable wriggled his way inside.

Kojo and Dani soon followed.

Faisal hesitated but did not want to be left behind. He started, then stopped and gestured for Mona to go first.

"Not a chance. I'll be waiting here," she said.

It was the excuse he needed to stay behind.

Cable stood, once he had crawled through the narrow passage and into a small cavern. Kojo and Dani followed suit.

"Not much wave action ever gets in here," Dani said as she panned her light around the space. It was the size of a New York studio apartment, with a sand floor. Uneven rocks made up the ceiling. The beam of her light caught an unnatural pattern, and she stepped forward.

Cable and Kojo followed.

On the right wall, about five feet up, was a carving. A closer look revealed an obvious design they were all familiar with, a Phoenician ship.

"Just like the one in Tunis," Dani whispered.

Cable moved his light around the nearby rock. "I don't see anything else."

Kojo stepped up and inspected the rock face with his fingers, looking for anything out of place. "No hidden levers or seams here," he said, with objective confidence.

Cable dropped down and started digging in the sand below the symbol. "The sand is like two inches deep. Looks like solid rock below that." He stood back up slowly, frustrated.

"That's it? Just this symbol?" Dani mumbled.

"Whatever was here has been taken," Kojo said.

"Probably a long, long time ago," Cable added.

"This symbol proves the Phoenicians were here. Long before this island was inhabited. That's a piece of history we have added to Socotra," Dani said with slight enthusiasm.

Cable and Kojo lingered, taking in the disappointment and the completion of their quest.

After a moment, Cable broke the silence. "Come on, let's get back and tell the others."

Dani took a few pictures of the carving with her smartphone and then followed them out.

"That's far enough." The familiar voice froze Dani as she exited the fissure.

Nico and Jude had guns and flashlights pointing their way. Mona and Faisal were on their knees in the sand, with two men standing behind them. One held a machete.

"Where's the treasure?" Jude demanded.

"Long gone," Cable replied. "See for yourself." He gestured to the crack in the rock behind him.

"Over here on your knees," Nico said before gesturing for Sebi to check it out.

They watched as he shimmied into the fissure.

After a couple of long minutes, Sebi crawled back out. He shook his head as he stood. "There's nothing in there, boss."

Nico looked over his captives. "I'm getting tired of those lyrics." He saw Cable and Dani share a look of concern, and a crooked smile crossed his face. "Jude, if you will."

Jude stepped up behind Cable and grabbed him by his hair. He placed the pistol at the base of Cable's neck and jerked him to his feet.

Dani screamed, "No! We've told you the truth."

Cable started to squirm, but Jude jabbed his pistol harder into his neck. "I can just as easily kill you right now and then go to work on your girlfriend."

Cable stopped fighting.

"That's what I thought," Jude hissed as he pulled Cable into waist-deep water and slammed him under.

It happened so fast that Cable had no time to gulp a breath.

He could hear Dani's muted voice crying and pleading as he struggled to find a way to get his head back above the water. The man holding him down was immensely strong, and no matter what he tried, it didn't work.

Jude held tight to the squirming man, countering any move with his massive strength. He knew it was just a matter of moments before the fight would be over.

Cable's strength was fading as he used up the last of his oxygen. He had an overwhelming urge to breathe, and he was about to give in to it when suddenly, he was yanked back out of the water. Coughing and choking, he gulped for air.

"We can do this all day. Now. Where is the treasure?" Nico called from the shore.

Cable looked up at Dani. He tried to give her a reassuring gaze before shifting his eyes to Nico. "The treasure is gone."

As the last syllable escaped his mouth, Cable was plunged back into the water. This time, he didn't fight against his captor. Cable opened his eyes and tried to enjoy his last moments on Earth. He could hear Nico drilling the others for answers. Answers he knew would never come. This was it. If they were going to kill him, there was nothing he could do about it. He had fought with everything he had the first time, and now he was already feeling lightheaded. His strength was sapped, and the urge to inhale was growing insurmountable.

Cable let the moment sear into his brain. The last week had been incredible, and he let it replay in his mind. Holding hands with Dani. Professing his love. The sex. The only thing that mattered now was her. She was his rock, the person who had conquered his personal and emotional wall. She would be missed most of all.

As his thoughts faded, he gulped in a mouthful of seawater. It was violent at first, causing his body to jolt and spasm. Then, peace seemed to invade as his eyes battled to stay focused. The sea floor was covered with life, unaware and uncaring of his approaching death. Perhaps even waiting their turn at an easy meal. As the last of his consciousness dimmed, he had a sudden, clear, and resolute thought. He knew where the treasure was… Then everything turned off.

Jude released Cable's still body and stepped to the shore.

Dani sobbed uncontrollably, no longer caring what happened to her. She had pleaded and begged for Cable's life. Even the truth had failed to save him.

"That's for Tobias." Nico looked over the four remaining hostages. "Okay, who's next?"

Faisal shook with fear. Mona stayed stock-still, glaring at the Greek Mafia boss. Kojo put his arm around Dani, trying in his own way to protect her. Dani's head had dropped to his chest, as her bereavement consumed her.

Nico nodded to Jude, then used his gun to point out Kojo.

"Stand up, nice and slow," Jude said as he approached the Ethiopian.

Kojo released Dani. "I'll be okay." He whispered the words, both knowing they were a lie, as he stood. His plan was simple. He would go down swinging before he would let the beast drown him. He moved subtly to the balls of his feet and slightly bent his knees.

Jude seemed to anticipate this and backed off a couple of feet, keeping the gun aimed at Kojo's midsection.

Kojo had no choice, two feet away or four feet away, it was now or never. He started to spring when a shot rang out, echoing off the cavern walls.

Jude was the first to react and turned to see what was happening.

Nico's mouth gaped as he looked down at this chest. A small bloom of blood seeped through his shirt. He instinctively ducked just as another bullet whizzed by his head.

Jude lifted his gun to return fire but was still unclear as to the source.

Kojo sprang, hitting Jude in his midsection and managing to knock the pistol free. They both went down in a heap of swinging arms and kicking legs.

Philo raised his machete to dispatch Mona and the others. A bullet tore through his left eye, flinging him to the ground.

Nico dove to the sand and spun back on a knee just in time to see the Asian man they had killed holding a smoking pistol. He was wading through the tide pool, keeping low in the water. How he was still alive was a mystery for another time. Right now, he had to be stopped. Nico twisted his Makarov over to line up a shot, and a sudden impact from behind tumbled him into the water.

Mona used the distraction to jump up and launch her body forward. She threw herself into the back of the mob boss, unconcerned with her safety.

Dani followed Mona's lead, only she ran for the water. There was only one thing on her mind.

Jon stumbled over several large sea snails. His gun wavered for just a moment as he tried to regain his footing.

He had called Mariamo from the hospital and found out where Faisal was taking his friends.

After picking Jon up at the hospital, Mariamo drove him to his hotel, where he retrieved the Webley. They zoomed west along the island highway, passing the odd vehicle, while Mariamo negotiated with the police for support on his cell phone. Every bump and pothole jarred Jon's injury, leaving him grimacing in pain.

By the time they pulled up next to the orange van, Jon knew he had to hurry. His wound was starting to bleed again, and there was no telling the danger his friends might be in.

Mariamo had tried to convince Jon to wait for the police, but he was having none of it.

He ran down the trail, both arms held tight against his injury, and waded through the lagoon to the cave's entrance. As he rounded the corner, he heard Dani sobbing. Something was seriously wrong.

Jon shot the man who had ordered his death. He then fired again to finish him off, but the man had ducked just as the bullet meant for his head passed.

He had no time to react. A thug in the back was raising a machete at Mona. Jon aimed and fired again, dropping him. He retrained his pistol on Nico, but Mona slammed into him, eliminating a clear-sight picture.

Sebi spotted Jude's Beretta in the sand and raced over to grab it.

Jon noticed the movement and dispatched Sebi as he lifted Jude's fallen pistol to fire at Kojo.

Faisal curled into a ball and chanted out loud with fear.

Kojo quickly realized he was outmatched. Jude weighed nearly twice as much, and although Kojo was slightly taller, his slender frame was no match for the brute's bulging muscles. The fight would soon be over. Kojo had absorbed several powerful hits to the face, and his vision was blurred as he swung a fist, hoping for a stroke of luck.

Jon stumbled from the water and dropped to his knees. The repaired bullet wound was bleeding through his shirt, and he felt lightheaded. He tried to shake off dizziness and focus—*not now*.

Mona and Nico thrashed in the shallow water. Mona gave the injured gangster all he could handle.

Jon turned and tried to line up a shot to help her out. The image of the two fighters doubled for a second, and he was afraid to pull the trigger.

Dani hauled Cable from the water and immediately started CPR. She had once trained in college and was trying to remember the steps. *Was it fifteen or thirty compressions before one or two rescue breaths?* She settled on twenty, then two, and went to work.

Jon had one bullet left. He couldn't decide if he should help out Kojo or Mona. In the end, the decision was made for him, and he passed out from loss of blood.

Jude head-butted Kojo in the face, breaking his nose. A gush of blood covered Kojo's face, and his legs went weak. A final uppercut ended the fight, with a short circuit to Kojo's consciousness.

Jude stood on wobbly legs. The tall man had been surprisingly difficult to best.

He leaned over and pried the gun out of Sebi's dead hand.

Jon was face down in the sand.

Faisal was a quivering ball.

Kojo was down for the count, and Dani seemed helplessly engaged in a futile attempt to bring back the dead.

So, Jude turned his attention to his boss.

Nico and an enraged Mona sparred in the water. Mona was surprisingly quick, and Nico had a bullet in him that was slowly robbing his strength. They were wrestling for dominance in three feet of water. Jude hurried to the shore and took careful aim to not hit his boss. *Click.* He reracked the slide, putting a fresh shell in the chamber. Then, he reacquired his target and squeezed. A sudden blow to the back of Jude's head sent the shot wide, and he collapsed face down in the water.

Faisal stood behind him with a large chunk of rock gripped tightly in his shaking hands. He heaved with anxious stress and dropped to his knees to puke. His last-minute action had saved Mona.

Mona renewed her vigor and, using her full body weight, managed to get enough water down Nico's throat that he stopped fighting back. She let loose, and he crawled to the shore, hacking and wheezing.

Mona picked up Jude's fallen pistol and took charge. "Faisal, thank you. Please check on Jon."

Faisal ran over to Jon and rolled him over. Jon looked pale, but his eyes were half open, and his face was filled with agony. Faisal gave him a huge smile. "He is still with us."

Mona stepped next to Dani, keeping an eye on Nico and Jude. Nico was sitting up, but the fight he once had was gone.

Jude had gone into the water face first and had taken a deep breath of seawater down his lungs, which he was now trying to hack back up.

Dani was silently weeping as she followed the CPR steps over and over.

"Any luck?" Mona whispered.

Dani shook her head but didn't stop. She would do this for the next two days if she had to.

Faisal stood and went over to help wake up Kojo. He knelt and gave him a few slaps to the face. "Kojo, come back."

After a few seconds, Kojo's eyes wavered open. "Faisal?" His face was a bloody mess with a flattened nose. He sat up slowly, as pain racked his body. He had at least a couple of broken ribs to match his broken nose.

Faisal noticed a missing front tooth. "You're missing…" He pointed to his mouth.

Kojo used his injured tongue to inspect the damage, but he was too battered to care.

"He's okay, Ms. Mona," Faisal called out with glee.

Just then, five policemen with guns drawn, led by Mariamo, came wading into the cavern.

Kojo slowly stood, and he and Faisal stepped over to watch Dani. Twenty compressions and two rescue breaths. Like a metronome, she repeated her actions.

The police took Nico and Jude into custody. Then, they organized transportation for the dead and wounded.

Sobs accompanied Dani's actions as she deliberately counted each compression on Cable's chest. "Sixteen, seventeen, eighteen."

A sudden jerk came from Cable, and he started hacking and coughing. He then turned his head and threw up.

They were the sweetest sounds Dani had ever heard. She grabbed Cable and hugged him so tight he had trouble coughing. Tears continued to flow from Dani, but now, they were tears of joy.

After a time, Cable spoke croakily. "I thought I'd lost you."

Dani hugged him again. "Never. Not in this life or the next."

They both held on to each other with a newborn fervor. This was not the end but the start of a new beginning.

EPILOGUE

THE DRY SUMMER AIR REMINDED Mona of home, but the majestic Rocky Mountains in the distance with their snow-capped peaks were like nothing in Egypt.

Denver traffic was surprisingly light, and her driver soon pulled to the curb of the Rioja Restaurant. The flight from Cairo had been tedious, but she had managed to get some sleep in her first-class pod.

The restaurant was a fusion of Mediterranean and local seasonal influences. Its exhibition kitchen, with a copper-topped bar and simple decor, allowed its menu to shine.

Mona stepped from the car and purposefully slowed her pace. Her heart was pounding, and she needed to take it back a notch.

Following the maître d, she walked past the aged brick wall displaying its considerable wine collection.

He pulled a chair back at a linen-covered table in the corner and patiently waited for her to sit.

Mona appraised the older man sitting across from her. He immediately stood and offered a brief greeting, allowing Mona to sit before he returned to his chair.

Tam McGree was dressed in a bespoke navy-blue suit with a robin's-egg-blue custom-tailored shirt and a royal-blue patterned silk tie. His hair was still thick, though completely gray, and he wore black-framed glasses that perfectly accentuated his face.

"I must admit, I have been nervous to meet you," he said as she sat.

"Oh, why is that?" Mona asked.

"Well, I have long had a mystery in my family. One that has perplexed both my father and me. I could have never predicted this outcome."

"Yes, we are joined, it seems, in the same story," Mona said.

"And, what a story it is."

They spent the next twenty minutes sharing their histories and filling in details that the other was missing.

Mona started with her mother's journey to slavery and her desperate attempt to break that chain for her daughter. It was touching and heartfelt. With nothing more known about her mother since the day she had literally run to freedom.

Tam shared his father's exploits in the Arabian Desert and the final details of Mona's grandparents, as he knew them.

The report Dani and Cable supplied was surprisingly detailed with everything, including their final findings. It had been extremely satisfying for Tam and eye-opening for Mona.

They ordered appetizers and then a meal.

Tam went with the charred apple salad and seared venison.

Mona ordered the goat cheese tart and artichoke tortellini.

The conversation continued long after the food was consumed.

Two halves of a single story, divided by time and distance. It was remarkable and cathartic for both parties.

After a time, Tam set a leather box on the table. He unlatched it and slid it over to Mona.

Mona's hand shook as she lifted the lid and removed the seashell her family had discovered and died over. It was exactly like the replica she had in her possession now, but everything about it was different. The hardness of the shell, the weight in her hand, and even the aged symbols had a consciousness to them. This was her family's legacy, but it was Tam's, as well. "Incredible," was all she could say.

"Yes, a truly unique artifact," Tam said.

She let her fingers roam across the myriad carved symbols before carefully placing the artifact back in the box. Tears moistened her eyes as she looked up at Tam. "Thank you," she managed.

Tam gave her a kind smile. "These last two months have been filled with something I thought had vanished from my life," he said. "I've had a virtual adventure, renewed knowledge, answers to life-long questions. It's all very novel." He took a sip from his wineglass. "The quest for knowledge is never done, I guess." He looked at the box as if weighing a huge decision.

"Mona… I want you to have it."

Mona was taken aback.

"Your grandfather found it, and it belongs to your family. I'll be happy with a plastic replica."

Mona swallowed hard. "You have done me a great kindness, Tam. I'm not sure I can ever repay you. Perhaps you would come to Cairo. I have a spectacular beachside villa in Alexandria. We could…trade more stories?"

The thought quickly grew on Tam, and he cocked his head with the slightest smile. "That sounds like a date."

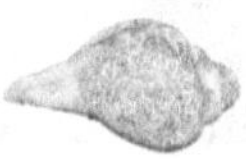

The last empty box was hauled from the office, and Cable set about organizing his desk.

Dani had her own space just to the left of him.

Cable had converted his father's office and a downstairs bedroom into a modern open space with gleaming white walls and natural wood tones. It had plenty of natural light and would be their base of operations for the newly formed Transon Limited. It was a portmanteau using parts of their last names. Tam McGree had suggested it. He had been excited and financially helpful in getting Cable and Dani up and running.

Dani took a phone call and, after a minute, hung up. "I just turned down an authenticating job for my old company, Peak Insurance."

"Oh yeah?" Cable said.

"That means I am no longer employed anywhere. So, we need to get a client if we are gonna make this thing work."

"I thought we worked just fine?" Cable said.

"We work amazingly, but I'm talking about work-work."

"Never fear—" A ding on Cable's laptop pulled his attention. He opened a file to see an image of Kojo with his big, perfect smile. "You might want to open your email. Someone's got a new tooth."

Dani opened her screen as a knock on the front door interrupted her focus.

Cable popped up and left the office. A moment later, he returned with Jon Chibi in tow. "Look what showed up."

Dani shot to her feet and ran to hug him.

A sudden grimace filled Jon's face.

"Sorry, did I squeeze too hard?" Dani asked, backing away.

"Almost," Jon said. "It is so good to see you both."

"You look great. When did they let you out? What are you doing in Denver? Can we take you out for dinner?" Cable rapid-fired.

"Well, I got out of the hospital yesterday. I wanted to surprise you both…and I also needed to finalize things with Mr. McGree before I head back." Jon tried to remember all of Cable's sudden questions. "Oh, and I'd love to go to dinner."

"Japan?" Dani asked.

Jon ignored the question. "But, most of all, when you two visited me in the hospital, you mentioned you had figured out what the treasure was and then left without telling me."

"I'm surprised you remember that. You were very drugged up," Dani said.

"Oh, I remember," Jon countered.

"I told you he'd be back. Best medicine in the world is to leave 'em wanting more," Cable said.

"Yes, you did, and apparently, it worked like magic," Dani replied.

Jon looked from Cable to Dani. He was feeling manipulated, not one of his favorite things, but with these two, it seemed okay.

"Please, have a seat," Dani offered.

They all sat down at a small seating area to the right of their desks. Jon took the brown leather loveseat, and Dani and Cable took the cream oversized upholstered swivel chairs. Cable poured drinks and distributed them. A seltzer water for Jon.

Cable took a moment, gaining some liquid courage. "Bear with me, because this memory has baggage." He took a calming breath. "When

I was drowning in the lagoon. Right before I lost consciousness, I had a moment of clarity. I was able to…think like a Phoenician, for just the briefest moment." Cable paused and took another sip from his glass. "And, as I glared at the bottom of the lagoon, with my last synapses firing, it all became clear."

Jon leaned forward. "What became clear?"

"Sea snails. The place was crawling with them, and they were huge. Boaz had found a new supply of sea snails for his people's trade in purple. Thousands upon thousands of snails. A completely new source."

"We did a little research when we got back, and the snails on Socotra are a giant version of the Murex snails coveted by the Phoenicians for their Tyrian purple," Dani said. "Worth a hundred times its weight in gold."

"Boaz must have recognized that," Cable added.

Jon narrowed his eyes for a beat. "You mean the treasure of a thousand kings was just another supply of sea snails?"

"By 400 BCE, the Phoenician empire was already running low," Dani said. "Their current Murex source was nearly extinct."

"And…Boaz found a new supply?" Jon said to no one in particular.

Cable nodded. "A new supply that was worth—"

"—the treasure of a thousand kings," Jon finished. He leaned back. "So…he, or someone, carved the shell, made it back to the mainland, and while trying to return to Egypt, what…?" His mind continued to process. "Died in the desert. Lost to the sands of time?"

"Then, Mona's grandfather dug it up," Dani finished.

"All those wasted lives, for snails," Jon said to himself.

"People see what they want to see, and Nico had treasure eyes," Cable finished.

Jon nodded slowly as he took a drink. He placed the glass down on the coffee table. "What do you two know about ancient jade carvings?"

Cable shared a glance with Dani. "Well, it takes something like sixty million years to create jade," he said.

"And it's very difficult to date carvings that have no provenance. You must inspect the tool marks and style," Dani added.

Jon just smiled and shook his head. "I have an old client that reached out to me. He is looking for someone to prove the authenticity of a piece he has acquired. Know anyone that might fit the bill?"

Cable and Dani just smiled at each other.

Jon added, "It might be dangerous."

"Do you know anyone who can handle security and logistics?" Dani asked.

"He's gonna need his own desk," Jon said, looking around.

"I guess we have our next job," Dani announced. "With an interloper."

"An interloper you're taking to dinner," Jon said.

Cable stood up with his hands outstretched. "Hang on a sec. Let's not get ahead of ourselves. Dinner first, because I'm starving."

"We're in, Jon," Dani answered. "I mean, what's the worst that can happen?"

Cable looked at her like she was crazy. "Are you friggin' kidding me?"

IF YOU LIKED THIS BOOK

I would appreciate it if you would leave a review. An honest review helps me write better stories. Positive reviews help others find the book, fueling my ability to add more books to the series.

It only takes a moment, but it means everything.

Thanks in advance,

Brent Ladd

AUTHOR'S NOTE

This is a work of fiction. Any resemblance to persons, living or dead, or actual events is either coincidental or is used for fictive and storytelling purposes. Many elements of this story are inspired by true historical events. All aspects of the story are imaginative events inspired by conjecture.

Grain of Sand was a true labor of love. Like life, the writing process is a journey, one meant to be savored, and to me, it's more about the pilgrimage itself than the destination. I learned a ton while writing this book, and I hope it's reflected in the story and prose. Only you, the reader, can be the judge of the results. Drop me a line if you have feedback or just want to say hi.

Brent Ladd

BrentLaddBooks.com

ACKNOWLEDGMENTS

With deep appreciation to all those who encouraged me to write, and especially those who did not. I wanted to thank the following contributors for their efforts in doling out their opinions and helping to keep my punctuation honest: Jeff Klem, Hilary Glaholt, David Ihrig, Steven White, and Christy Monge. A host of family and friends who suffered through early drafts and were kind enough to share their thoughts. Extra thanks goes to my lovely wife, Leesa, who is my first reader and best critic. And my editor, Debra Hartmann.

A special thanks to my publisher, American Real Publishing, who helped make this possible, as writing is only half the total equation.

As many concepts as possible are based on actual or historical details. Special thanks to the original action hero, my dad, Dr. Paul Loefke.

Lastly, writers live and die by their reviews, so if you liked my book, *please* review it!

More Cable Janson coming soon! – BrentLaddBooks.com

ABOUT THE AUTHOR

Writer-director Brent Ladd has been a part of the Hollywood scene for almost three decades. His work has garnered awards and accolades all over the globe. Brent has been involved in the creation and completion of hundreds of commercials for clients large and small. He is an avid beach volleyball player and an adventurer at heart. He currently resides in Irvine, California, with his wife and children.

Brent found his way into novel writing when his son Brady showed little interest in reading. He wrote his first book—*The Adventures of Brady Ladd*—making Brady the main character. Enjoying that experience, Brent went on to concept and complete his first novel, *Terminal Pulse, A Codi Sanders Thriller*—the first in a series—and followed it up with *Blind Target, Cold Quarry, Time 2 Die*, and *Fatal Measure*, which takes our characters down another rabbit hole. *HU 2.0* is a near-future sci-fi thriller that is often too close to the truth of where we are heading. *Grain of Sand* is a fun romp through history with some favorite characters and the second in an adventure series.

Brent is a fan of a plot-driven stories with strong, intelligent characters. So, if you're looking for a fast-paced escape, check out the Codi Sanders series, Jericho's journey in *HU 2.0*, or Cable Janson's search for missing treasure in *The Eye of Faith, Grain of Sand*, and the upcoming *The Bell Tolls*. You can also find out more about his next book and when it will be available by visiting his website, BrentLaddBooks.com.

Connect with the author on Facebook:
https://www.facebook.com/brentladdauthor